ROAD RAGE

To my family, I couldn't be who I am without you.

ROAD RAGE

by

John Stewart

Gotham Books

30 N Gould St.
Ste. 20820, Sheridan, WY 82801
https://gothambooksinc.com/

Phone: 1 (307) 464-7800

© 2025 *John Stewart*. All rights reserved.

No part of this book may be reproduced, stored in a retrieval system, or transmitted by any means without the written permission of the author.

Published by Gotham Books (May 24, 2025)

ISBN: 979-8-3493-3506-8 (P)
ISBN: 979-8-3493-3507-5 (E)

Because of the dynamic nature of the Internet, any web addresses or links contained in this book may have changed since publication and may no longer be valid.

The views expressed in this work are solely those of the author and do not necessarily reflect the views of the publisher, and the publisher hereby disclaims any responsibility for them.

CONTENTS

CHAPTER 1: Life at Home 1
CHAPTER 2: A change of plans 20
CHAPTER 3: The Mission 35
CHAPTER 4: Mexico 52
CHAPTER 5: Losing the Tail 66
CHAPTER 6: "A New Plan" 86
CHAPTER 7: Getting the Upper hand 90
CHAPTER 8: The FBI 105
CHAPTER 9: A New Game 121
CHAPTER 10: The Release 134
CHAPTER 11: In America Again 158
CHAPTER 12: Not the Plan 179
CHAPTER 13: A Hard Right 193
CHAPTER 14: Family Reunited 210
CHAPTER 15: Recovery Time 226
CHAPTER 16: Catching the Drugs 244
CHAPTER 17: The Bait 263
CHAPTER 18: Change of Plans 279
CHAPTER 19: Moving Forward 292
CHAPTER 20: Restoring Hope 306
CHAPTER 21: Fight to the End 319
CHAPTER 22: Reunited 326
POST SCRIPT 337

CHAPTER 1

Life at Home

Steve walked into the kitchen and pulled the lid off the pot took a deep breath. In through his nose and back out. He sighed with smile as he breathed in the gumbo. He turned and called his son Max for dinner. His wife Heather had made her famous gumbo again, and the whole house smelled delicious. She would cook all day long, by six o'clock the boys would be so hungry, they would be foaming at the mouth.

Max ran into the kitchen bouncing off the cabinets. "A big bowl for me!"

Steve smiled at Heather. "Me too!"

Heather laughed as she shooed them out of the kitchen with one hand and stirred the pot with the other. "Did you both wash your hands?"

Steve looked at Max and down at his hands with grease under his nails, quickly putting them behind his back. "Yep!"

Heather brought two bowls to the table, almost overflowing. "It's hot! Let me see your hands."

Max held up his hands. Steve kept his under the table. "You too!"

Steve frowned. "C'mon Max let's go wash our hands again for mom."

The two of them got up looking wounded. Being so close to that gumbo without even a taste was torture. Steve squirted GOJO on his hands and picked up the scrub brush beside the sink. Max squeezed in between his dad and the sink and stuck his hands under the water.

"Hey kid that's breaking in line."

Max looked up with puppy dog eye's. "I'm hungry Daddy, and you take too long."

Steve backed up enough for him to get in. His hands were working back and forth under the water. "Use soap you little brat."

He sighed looking up at his dad. "Okay."

Max was done and gone while Steve scrubbed. Heather hated grease under his nails, she always had. She was proud of how hard he worked. Through all the troubles New Orleans had seen, Steve had kept working. Where they lived, the water from Katrina never made an impact. A little wind damage but no flooding. They were lucky this time.

Katrina was a bad hurricane, but really good for Steve's work. A lot of cars got water damaged and wouldn't run, the shop was full all the time. Steve was a mechanic and learned the trade in the Army. Once he got out he took the job at a local mechanic shop and never looked back. He worked hard and was a damn good mechanic. Most days he was gone by seven and didn't get home until after six.

Steve looked in the mirror as he rinsed his hands. He turned his head side to side noticing the gray hairs creeping into his temples. He held up his chin, noticing the slight bulge of a second chin starting. He had on a white T-shirt that covered up his chest but as he turned off the water, he flexed his arms and chest.

"Not bad for 38." He said to himself.

A laugh came from his left as Heather stood in the doorway. "What's the matter baby?"

Steve turned red and shook his head. "Oh man! How long have you been standing there?"

Heather stepped up next to Steve and put both arms around him. "Long enough. Are you feeling old?"

Steve raised both arms up and flexed his biceps again. "I look pretty good for thirty-eight, don't you think? Still fit, strong. Maybe not as strong as I was in the Army but I ain't bad."

She reached up and touched the gray on his temple. "Yeah baby, I think you're damn sexy! When we go to bed, I'll show you how sexy I think you are."

Her hand slid down his chest then to his crotch where she grabbed a handful and squeezed with a slight giggle. "Damn sexy!" She said again with a devilish grin.

He smiled and kissed her shutting the bathroom door. "Why wait for bed! This is good."

She kissed him back and pulled away. "Max is ten feet away, maybe later though! I kind of like the thought of hanging onto that sink while you have your way with me."

Steve watched her as she turned and opened the bathroom door. Smiling at him as she walked out, throwing him a wink, with the flip of her hair. The smell of gumbo rushed in and Steve heard his stomach growl.

"Later!" He said smiling at himself in the mirror.

Steve had a rugged good look about him, blue eyes and a strong jaw. Light brown wavy hair made him a good-looking guy compared to most. He had been popular in high school, but was always just one of the regular football jocks. Not quite good enough for a scholarship, but good enough to be a starting player and get the girls.

After high school he was working part time but never could find anything that really fit him. He ended up joining the Army as the war in Iraq got going. He felt like it was his duty to serve. Once in, he found himself in Sniper school and quickly got the honor of top shot. As a sniper, he saw his first active duty as the war really heated up. He was calm and collected under pressure. He naturally knew how to wait for the shot that counted and that made him deadly. Every shot counted with Steve. He got the reputation quickly as the guy that got it done. "One shot" quickly became his nick name around the base.

After his second tour in Iraq, Steve headed to the states to start Green Beret school and a career in Special Forces. His commanding officer had recommended it saying he had the inner strength needed to be a trained killer! Steve wasn't sure what that meant when he said it, but thanked the man as he got on the C130 transport plane leaving the desert.

Two months later all that ended, as he hit the ground sideways parachuting at night into a heavily wooded area during training. The compound fracture and surgery later on his ankle ended that part of his career. He decided at that point, the military would not be his career and he went to mechanic school to learn something he could use when he got out.

When he met Heather, Steve had just started at the garage. It wasn't going to be a long-term job but then they had Max and the bills just kept coming. They bought the small house just before Katrina hit. Steve always wanted better for his family, but he wasn't doing bad. He wanted to one day move to the Garden District of New Orleans, but the houses were expensive and for now that was just a dream that he would keep dreaming. In his spare time, he and Heather would look at foreclosures here and there thinking if they could pick up one that needed work, they might be able to make the jump. So far, he had not found one that he could afford.

So, like most young families, Steve and Heather worked and loved through every day. They both were very happy with their life. Heather was a great mom and Steve always made time for both of them even when he was busy at work.

Finally, Steve came out of the bathroom holding up clean hands like a surgeon. Max was half way done with his bowl and Heather was waiting for him. He sat beside her and she kissed him on the cheek.

Whispering in his ear. "I love you baby."

He smiled and winked. "I love you too."

After dinner, the three of them sat around watching TV until bedtime. Max drug his feet having to go get a shower. Heather fussed and Max kept dragging. Finally, Steve looked at Max and said, "Enough!" Max pouted and went into the bathroom.

Heather came in and sat on the couch next to Steve. "Why is it like that? Why do I tell him ten times and he argues, but you say it once and he goes?"

Steve laughed. "Because he's afraid of me. I might get up and knock the shit out of him and he knows you won't."

Heather sat back looking angrily at Steve. "That's not true. I've spanked him before."

Steve pulled her close and kissed her. "I love you babe. You're a great mom; you're a nurturer and a kind spirit and that's great. Little boys need that, but they start taking advantage of that at a young age. I'll talk to him about it, okay."

Heather got serious and crossed her arms, holding her teeth closed as she spoke. "Okay nothing! I will knock the crap out of him the next time he smarts off to me. Nurturer my ass, he'll be nurturing a fat lip when I'm done with him!"

Max came back into the room after his shower. Wet combed hair and smelling like soap. He hugged both and sat on the couch looking at the TV. Steve grinned at Heather and nodded at Max. She looked puzzled. Steve pointed at his watch and pointed at the bedroom.

Heather grinned. "Max it's time for bed."

Max scoffed loudly. "Do I have too. It's only like eight o'clock."

Steve made a fist that only Heather could see and pointed at Max.

Heather cleared her throat. "Now young man."

Max turned in shocked and looked at his mom. "Right now!"

Max got up. "Why are you yelling at me?"

Heather was almost in tears. She grabbed Max and hugged him. "I'm not buddy. Mommy was just acting tough."

Steve smiled, knowing she would never be hard on that child ever. Max was the love of her life.

She took him to bed and tucked him in. Twenty minutes later she was back. "That precious thing. Did you see his face?"

Steve laughed. "It was even funnier watching yours."

Heather smiled too as she pulled him up from the couch towards the bedroom. Steve turned the TV off and began smiling thinking about the scene in the bathroom earlier. Heather never turned the light on as they went into the bedroom. The faint blue glow from Steve's alarm clock lit the room slightly and as Steve's eyes adjusted, he could see heather's shirt clearing her head as she took it off.

As he reached her, his hands touched bare skin and he felt her bra brush past and then Heathers arms around his neck. Her lips touched his as they slowly eased onto the bed. Steve's hands caressed her bare breast and stomach. Heather's breath caught with the touch of her nipple by Steve's tongue. A gasp escaped her mouth. Steve's eyes were adjusting to the blue glow of light now and his eyes met hers as he hovered over her. Heather smiled as she unbuttoned his pants. Steve pulled his t-shirt off and threw it towards the bathroom. Heather's feet began to pull his jeans down and off onto the floor. Steve rolled Heather over on top and with one hand pulled the sweats she had worn off, throwing them also randomly towards the bathroom.

Giggles and cries of passion filled the room as the two made love. Steve had never known this kind of love for anyone in his life and he could not imagine life without it. Heather lay on Steve's chest now, panting trying to catch her breath for several minutes after they had made love. Sweat covering both of them. Exhausted from the exhilaration, neither of them moved for a while, just enjoying each other's bodies and the way they fit together. Steve slowly began to stroke Heather's hair. Heather smiled at that as she buried her head further into the crux of Steve's neck. This was home for her, where she belonged. This is who she belonged too. She was his forever and she was glad. So many of her girlfriends had been married and divorced by now. She felt blessed to have such a great guy.

The alarm went off at six on that Thursday morning just like it did six out of seven days a week. Steve rolled over and hit snooze and felt Heather roll up next to him. He wrapped his arms around her and she buried her head into his chest and neck again. He closed his eyes, wishing it was Sunday.

Sunday's for the two of them were spent sleeping in and lying around the house. By far, Sunday was Steve's favorite day. At the shop he worked all week and usually at least a half day on Saturday. Counting Steve, there were two mechanics at the shop and the guy that owned the place. Steve had been to school after the Army to learn even more about Diesel mechanics and new cars.

The owner of the shop was in his 60's now and didn't work on much anymore, but a beer gut. Steve ran the shop for the most part and Tyrone, the other mechanic worked on whatever he said. Tyrone was young, only twenty-four, but a great mechanic. He had gotten into a little trouble in his teens stealing cars and stripping them but a short stay in Juvi had straightened him right out.

Steve hired Tyrone for some shop help a few years back, but quickly found he was more than just street smart. The kid could fix anything. Steve had started giving him small repair jobs shortly after he started and now, they just divided the work as it came in. Steve was glad that he could count on him when times get busy.

As the alarm went off again Steve rolled Heather over and sat up in bed. He silenced the alarm and swung his feet to the floor. It was spring time, but the floor was hanging onto winter. As his feet hit the hardwood floor, he felt the sting of the cold and goose bumps ran up his legs. He looked back at Heather, all warm under the covers and wondered just for a second what would happen if he just crawled back in and skipped work today. A small snore came from under the covers.

He laughed and stood up. Heather stirred slightly as he left the bed but never woke. She always got up around seven and took Max to school at around eight, on her way to work. Steve stood in the shower, letting the warm water flow across his back. He thought about getting older and what Heather had said last night in the bathroom. He thought about her touching his temple as she said it. As he stood in front of the mirror, he looked at the gray hair and wondered about maybe dying it.

He laughed out loud at that. "I would never hear the end of it from Tyrone."

As Steve got dressed, he looked at the clock on the bathroom counter. 6:28, he needed to leave by 6:30 to be on time.

"Where is the adventure in life he thought?" He kissed Heather's barely exposed head as he left. It was a far cry from being a sniper in Iraq. It was definitely not near as exciting as jumping out of a C130 in paratrooper school. He laughed again. That was the very thing that ended his Special Forces career in the Army. One wrong landing and he was done. Once he healed up it was off to mechanic school for him.

Their neighborhood was big like most in New Orleans, but he knew the people that lived around him. He certainly knew their cars. Over the years he had worked on just about everyone's on his block at one time or another. This morning as he got into his truck, he noticed a van in Ben's driveway. Ben was the neighbor right across the street from Steve. Cool guy in his forties, divorced and dating. Maybe this was a new girlfriends van but it didn't look like something a girl would drive. Missing a hubcap on the front and tinted windows, just not a chick's van. Steve laughed thinking maybe he had hooked up with a biker chic. He would have to ask for the story later over a beer.

Steve dismissed it and headed to work. Maybe later he would walk over with Max and see if Ben had picked it up for a good deal. Steve often had thought about getting a van as well to set up a mobile mechanic business. Maybe Ben would sell it cheap if he got a deal.

He got to work right at seven as usual and Tyrone was sitting on some tires waiting. As Steve pulled in, he thought he needed to get Tyrone a key so he could get coffee started. Tyrone waved as Steve parked.

Steve got out and stretched in the morning air. "Morning Tyrone! Do you live like right behind the shop or something? You're always here waiting on me."

"Na boss. I take the bus from the ninth ward area over here. I get here at 6:45 every mornin."

Steve nodded. "That's good Tyrone. You're very dependable. I appreciate that. I'll get you a key so you can come in when you get here and get the coffee going for us."

Tyrone smiled and stood. "I would appreciate that. I can get things going inside too. Turn on the compressor and everything. Have it ready to go by the time you get here Mr. Steve."

Steve looked sideways at Tyrone. "What did I tell you about that Mr. Steve crap. It's Steve. I'm not that much older than you."

Tyrone looked at Steve. "Naw, you a lot older than me man."

"Forget it. I'm not getting you a key after that comment. You can just sit out here in the dark."

"Oh man! Don't be like that. You ain't as old as Mr. Jack. He way old!"

Steve laughed. Jack was the owner. "Jack's Garage" was the name of the shop. Steve unlocked the door and hit the lights.

"Don't make me whip your ass little boy. I might be older, but I got some guns still." Steve flexed but the sweat jacket concealed any muscle.

Tyrone laughed. "You better keep that jacket on. You might get embarrassed if I show you my arms."

"Let's see what you got punk."

Tyrone pulled his jacket off as he came through the door. Tossing it on the table and striking a pose like a body builder. "Welcome to the gun show!"

Steve turned looking at Tyrone. He started to speak but through the still open door he could see a white van parked across the street in the bakery parking lot. Steve squinted and walked past Tyrone. Tyrone slowly dropped his arms. Steve walked outside staring across the street at the van.

"What's up Steve?"

Steve looked back at Tyrone. "Do you know that van across the street?"

Tyrone walked outside. "Nope, you think you know em?"

"I think it was at my neighbor's house this morning."

"Really, you sure?"

Steve starred at the van. "I don't know, but it looks like it, it's missing a hubcap just like the one this morning."

The van began to pull away. Steve watched it leave but couldn't get the tag. He couldn't remember exactly what the one at Ben's house looked like but he was pretty sure it was the same one.

Tyrone laughed. "You got the FBI looking at you boss."

Steve looked back at Tyrone. "Yeah, I'm really a drug lord. That old truck of mine is just a cover up. The Bentley is in the garage at the house."

Tyrone laughed. "Mr. Steve, you don't look nuttin like no drug lord. I know some of them guys from back in the day. They bad. Kill you for nuttin man. Nuttin at all."

"What are you saying Tyrone? I ain't bad enough to be a drug lord."

"I don't think so, them boys is mean. They killers man; you ain't no killer Steve."

Steve grinned. "I'm gonna kill you if you don't get that Ford fixed today. That guy has been waiting for two days."

"You been workin on that Honda longer than I been on this Ford. You the slow one."

"We both need to finish before the weekend gets here. Jack promised two or three more customers we would have them in here by Monday. Are you working Saturday?"

"Yeah, I'll be here. I need the money. I'm tryin to buy me a car. This guy I know has an old Chevy that ain't runnin so good. I thank I can get it for five hundred bucks. Maybe less. It just needs a new carburetor. I told that old fool before that's what was wrong. He don't listen."

"That would be good Tyrone. You're really doing good here, I'll talk to Jack and see if I can get you a little raise. It's been almost a year. You deserve it!"

Tyrone turned to face Steve. "Man, that means a lot to me Steve, I really appreciate that. I want to do good for you. You gave me a chance when no one else would. I appreciate ya."

Steve picked up the coffee and poured a cup. Looking out the small window, searching for the van.

"Is it still out there?"

"No, it's gone, but I swear that was the same van I saw this morning. It was right across the street in my neighbor's driveway. It kind of gives me the creeps. Makes me think someone is watching my house.

"That ain't cool. That's what they do you know. They watch them houses and when people go to work they come in and take everything. You seen that on TV aint you?"

"Great Tyrone, you're making me feel so much better. I don't have time to run home. Shit!"

"What about your wife? She still home?"

13

Steve looked at his watch. "Maybe."

Steve called home and there was no answer. He looked at his watch again. 7:30. Heather should still be home. He thought.

Steve looked at Tyrone and then at his watch again. "Dammit! Tyrone, I'm running back home. She isn't answering."

Tyrone wiped his hands. "You want me to come and watch your back?"

Steve smiled. "No, just get the Ford done. I'll be back in a little while. If Jack gets here, tell him I had a problem at home and will be back in an hour."

Tyrone nodded. "You know how to sneak up on somebody, right."

"Yeah, what do you mean?"

"I mean you don't need to fly up in your driveway and let them know you there. You need to sneak up and mess they shit up! You follow me?"

Steve nodded as he put his coat back on. Steve picked up a twenty-ounce ball peen hammer as he walked by the tool box. "I know what you mean. I'll be back."

Tyrone laughed. "Who you, the terminator. I'll be back!"

Steve smiled and walked out the door. Nervous and scared that Heather didn't pick up the phone. He had tried the house and her cell now and he got nothing on either. Steve drove faster as he made his way back home. twenty minutes away and it seemed like forever. At five till eight, Steve turned into his neighborhood. He thought about what Tyrone had said. He needed to sneak up on the house. What if the van had come back to break in and Heather and Max were still home.

Steve could feel the anger inside him start to rise. His hands gripped the steering wheel harder. Steve pulled over four houses away from his own. He could see Ben's driveway, no van. Steve got out of the truck, hammer in hand. Two steps, four, eight, finally he could see Heather's explorer in the driveway. Why hadn't she answered?

Steve cut through the neighbor's driveway and into the back yards. He was running now, staying low and out of sight. He got to the house and eased up to the kitchen window. Steve looked in but couldn't see anything. "Damn it!" Steve said. He moved down the house and up onto the porch really slowly. From there he could see into the living room. If they were there, Max would be watching cartoons waiting on his mom to get ready.

Why hadn't they left by now? Max had to be at school by eight and it was now 8:03. Something was wrong. Steve was suddenly wishing that the hammer in his hand was really a 9mm!

Steve eased up to the sliding glass door. Just barely looking inside to see what was going on. As he scanned the room he caught movement out of the corner of his eye. Steve ducked back out of sight. His heart was pounding inside his chest. He slowly looked again but there was nothing.

Steve's cell phone rang in his pocket scaring him half to death. He dropped the hammer with a loud bang on the deck board and almost fell down the stairs he was perched on trying to see in.

Fumbling to retreat and answering the phone. "Hello!"

"Steve, where are you? Your truck is on the side of the road in the neighborhood."

Hearing Heather's voice calmed him down immediately. "I'm at the house. Where are you?"

"I'm in the middle of the road, looking at your truck. Why are you home?"

Steve paused. "It's a long story. Are you okay?"

"Yeah. I'm late. My alarm didn't go off and Max woke me up at 7:45. Why are you home? I have to go. Where are you?"

Steve was walking around the house as Heather backed into the driveway. She looked at Steve holding the cell phone in one hand and the hammer in the other.

"Wow! Now that's a scary sight. Why do you have a hammer?"

Steve closed his cell phone as he walked up to her window. Heather sat staring at him. Steve motioned again.

Heather cracked the window an inch. "Drop the hammer!"

Steve held it up looking at it with a laugh. "I guess that looks a little strange huh? I thought I might have to beat up some bad guys."

Heather's window rolled down. "Bad guys? What the hell are you talking about?"

"It's a long story and you're late. I'll tell you tonight. Kiss me."

Steve leaned down and kissed Heather. "I love you babe."

Heather looked puzzled. "Are you okay?"

Steve smiled. "Yeah, I'm fine, I just got weirded out by a van I saw in Ben's driveway and then again at the shop. Who knows, maybe Ben has a new girlfriend or something. Whatever, go, you're late. I love you guys."

Heather smiled and touched Steve's hand. "You came home to protect me. Why didn't you call?"

"I did a bunch of times. You didn't answer."

"Oh, my cell was charging in the car and the ringer is off in the bedroom. I guess I was in the shower. I'm sorry."

Steve looked over at Max. "Why didn't you answer the phone when it rang?"

Max shrugged. "I don't know. Wasn't for me."

Steve stood up. "Love ya! See ya later."

Heather waved and took off. Steve looked back at the house and headed for his truck. The whole way back to work, he couldn't help but think about the van in Ben's driveway and how it compared to the one at the bakery. Steve concentrated on the images of both vans. Same model, same wheels and tires, same van he thought. Who would be watching him?

Steve got back to the garage and Tyrone was hard at it. Jack still wasn't there so he didn't have to spend an hour explaining.

Tyrone looked up from the steering pump he was mounting in the Ford. "Well, what you see?"

"Nothing. Heather was there, just running late. Her cell phone was in the car and she was in the shower when I called. Max like a dork didn't answer the phone. Said it wasn't for him."

"You see the van at your neighbor's house?"

"No. I'm telling you, Tyrone, that van was the same one that was across the street this morning. Something's not right."

Tyrone nodded. "You better figure it out. I'm telling you, you gonna come home to nothing in your house. They stakein you man."

"What, would you speak plain English."

"They watchin yo house man. They see what time you leave for work and your girl. If they followed you here, they tryin to figure out how long it takes you to get to work before they go in. I'm tellin you man, you gonna come home to a broken in, empty-ass house."

Steve threw the hammer into the tool box. "Well what am I supposed to do about it? I can't stay home all day."

"You probably scared them off today, bro. Just make sure yo place ain't too easy to get into. Call the police and tell them you think someone is watching yo place. You white, they might ride by for you!"

"What the hell does that have to do with anything?"

Tyrone smiled and looked back into the engine of the Ford. "Shit, ain't no cop in New Orleans ridden by no brothers house cause he said someone was watchin it. We lucky if they ride by when someone is shooten a gun off."

Steve pulled his jacket back off. "Whatever man. I aint got nothing to steal anyway. My neighborhood ain't full of big houses. It's average."

Tyrone never looked up. "That don't matter to a crack head!"

Steve raised the hood to the Honda. "I guess I'll lock the place down tonight and hide the wife's jewelry."

Tyrone laughed. "Yo wife can stay with me. She fine! I keep her safe Mr. Steve."

"HaHa Tyrone. I'll bet you would."

They both got to work and the day went on as usual after that. Heather had called Steve twice during the day to find out what was going on. He told her what he saw and how weird it was. She dismissed it to coincidence and told Steve not to be so paranoid. Steve laughed and told her he would be home around six.

CHAPTER 2

A change of plans

At five o'clock Steve called Heather. "Hey baby. Everything okay at home?"

"Yeah. Max is doing homework and I just started dinner. You still gonna be home by six?"

Steve looked at the Honda, still not running. "Yeah. I'll leave in just a few minutes. I didn't get done with this Honda today but I am worried about that van. I want to talk to Ben across the street and see if he knows anything."

"The house is fine baby. If you need to work, then do what you have too."

"I haven't been able to concentrate all day. I'll leave in just a few and head home."

Heather sighed. "Okay babe. I'm sorry you're stressing on this. I'm sure it was nothing. I'll see you when you get home."

"What's for dinner?"

"Meatloaf and mash potatoes."

"Um. I love me some meatloaf."

"I know. I love you. See you soon."

"Alright, love you too."

Steve hung up and looked over at Tyrone. The ford was running and he was grinning. Steve really had not gotten anything accomplished today. He threw down his wrench and went over to the sink. Tyrone laughed as he backed the ford out of the garage. Jack came out of the office and looked at the Honda.

"Do I need to have Tyrone take over?"

Steve looked up at Jack. "Maybe! Changing a timing belt on these Honda's, is a pain in the ass. You wanna do it?"

Jack smiled. "Nope! That's what I pay you for. My days of twisting wrenches are over, boy! I'm too old for that crap now. Go home and make sure your wife and kid are good. Tomorrow I need this Honda done."

"Yeah, yeah. I know. She called today wanting an update. I told her we were waiting on a part but would have it completed by tomorrow."

"Lying to the customers now, are we?"

"I just couldn't focus today Jack. I'm worried about that van. I know it was the same one. Why would someone be watching me?"

Jack put his hand on his chin. "You don't owe anybody money, do you?"

Steve laughed. "You mean like a loan shark? Hell no!"

Jack laughed. "Just thought I would ask. I didn't want them shooting up the place trying to get at you."

"No, I don't owe anyone and I ain't in trouble with the law either. I can't figure it out. I'll tell you this though. I see that van again and I'll find out."

"Be careful. Lot of crazy people in this world."

Tyrone walked up to the sink. "You want me to finish that Honda?"

Steve laughed. "No! I'll finish it in the morning. You guys are on my last nerve."

Steve walked outside and looked at every parking lot. No white vans. Tyrone stood beside him looking as well.

"Crazy! I'm going home. See you in the morning Tyrone."

"Okay Mr. Steve. See you in the morning."

Steve looked at Tyrone as he pulled his keys out. "Tyrone hang on." Steve pulled the shop key of his key ring. "Here, you've earned it."

Tyrone took the key. "Man, I sho do appreciate that Mr. Steve."

Steve shook his head. "What did I tell you about the Mr. Steve crap."

"You right. I appreciate it Steve. You alright. I'll have coffee ready for you when you get here. You can count me man."

Steve smiled. "I know I can. See you in the morning."

Steve pulled out of the garage and headed home. He called Heather, but she didn't answer. Steve thought she was probably peeling potatoes or something. He had just talked to her ten minutes ago anyway. He turned up the radio and rolled his window down. It was a nice afternoon and he needed to relax about the van.

Four cars back the black BMW slipped into traffic. Following Steve was easy, he had done this many times. He knew where Steve was going. If he lost sight, it was no problem. Easy to stay out of sight when you know where your target is going.

Steve hit 10 West and was rocking out to "Highway to hell." He still couldn't get the van out of his head. What would someone want with him, he was nobody. Steve looked up to see brake lights. The traffic on 10 was always bad at five o'clock.

Carlos, the driver of the black BMW pulled up beside Steve. The tinted windows prevented Steve from seeing anything and Carlos laughed noticing Steve looking at the front of the BMW. He had no idea that he would be seeing this car again soon.

At home Heather was peeling potatoes and preheating the oven for the meatloaf. Her phone was on vibrate in her purse and she missed Steve's call. The van had parked two streets over and the two men were in the back getting ready for Carlos's call. Both wore black and were heavily armed. They each looked like something from a swat team.

Steve had moved to the point he could see around the curve of the expressway and saw nothing but tail lights. He looked down at the radio and began to hit stations looking for a traffic report. After hearing a random selection of song tidbits, he got to one talking traffic. The announcer reported a three-car pileup, four miles ahead of where Steve was.

"Shit!" Steve exclaimed. "This is why I work until seven."

Steve began to get over to hit the surface streets. He grew up in this town and he knew just about every short cut there was. There was an exit in a half mile and he could hit one of the main drags from there. Carlos watched as Steve changed lanes. His lane wasn't moving so he watched as Steve made his way to the shoulder and drove away.

Carlos picked up the cell phone and called his men in the van. "We hit traffic. He got off and I'm stuck in it. Get out and I will tell you when to come back."

"No problem. Do you want us to go ahead and grab the lady and the kid?"

Carlos paused at the thought of trying it when they were all home. It might be messy. "Take them. Keep it quiet and stay close. We need to get him as soon as he gets home. You have about fifteen minutes."

"You got it boss. We only need five!"

The two men finished preparing and headed for the house. They backed into the driveway. The garage door was open anticipating Steve's arrival. They both put on face mask and exited the back doors leaving them open. As they came through the door to the house the first man yelled police!

Heather jumped at the door flying open. As the man yelled police, she put her hands up seeing the guns being drawn and pointed. In a matter of seconds, her and Max were on the floor and their hands were zip tied behind them.

"What the hell is going on?" She yelled out as the man pushed her to the floor.

"Be quiet and do as you're told. You're under arrest! Do what you're told and no one will get hurt."

Heather winced as the zip tie cut into her skin. "That hurts. What am I under arrest for?"

The man shoved her head down against the floor. "Be quiet I said."

Max was thrown down next to his mom and zip tied as well. Max was crying and Heather told him it would be okay. There had been a mistake and Daddy would get everything straight. As Heather spoke, the other man came behind her and put a black bag over her face. Heather began to panic.

"Why are you bagging my head? This is bullshit. Answer me. Max are you okay?"

She felt the man's hand grab the back of her head. She was being pulled off the ground by her hair. Heather began to scream. As she did the heel of the 9mm struck her in the forehead and she went limp. The man picked her up and went out the door with her.

Max cried out. "Mom! Mom, where are you?"

The other man bent down next to Max. "Max, you need to be quiet as a mouse. Do what you're told and your mommy will be fine. If you don't, I will hurt her more. Do you understand?"

Max shook his head yes. The man picked Max up by the arm and walked him towards the door. In the van, Heather was still out and they put Max down beside her. Max leaned over so that he was touching her. He started to cry again. They pulled out of the driveway. The house remained just like they found it. Garage open and dinner cooking. In three minutes, they were in and out.

Rico called Carlos. "It's done. They're in the van and we're gone. The house looks the same."

Carlos smiled. "Good job. Any trouble?"

"No. We yelled police as we came in and they threw their hands up. I love doing that. She started to get mouthy a little."

"Did you hit her?"

"Yeah. Gun butt to the forehead. Knocked her out. She'll be okay."

"Rico, so violent. You better make sure she's okay. I don't need her dead yet!"

"I didn't hit her that hard. I'll check on her and make sure she's okay. It'll be convincing for the husband."

"Yeah, but I need him to go along, too much violence and they always want to fight. It's not time for that. Be back in ten minutes. Wait for my call before you get back in sight."

"Yes sir. We'll stay close."

Carlos got over and got off at the same exit. Steve was not in sight, but he knew he was headed home. Carlos headed there as well. Steve would spend five minutes trying to figure out where Heather and Max were so he would be confused as they came in. The plan always worked.

Steve pulled into the driveway comforted by everything looking normal. Heather's car was in the garage and the lights were on. He got out of the truck and headed inside. He took his boots off at the door as usual and went in.

As he did, the house smelled like food burning. Steve looked towards the kitchen, but Heather wasn't there. Smoke was coming from the oven and the potatoes on the stove top were boiling over. Steve, confused, ran to the oven, turning burners off, and grabbing for pot holders inside the drawer.

"Heather! Max! Are you guy's home?"

Steve fanned the smoke as he pulled the burning meatloaf from the oven. Throwing the food into the sink turning on the water to put it out.

Carlos pulled into the neighborhood and made the call to Rico. "Now. I am two minutes away."

Rico put the van in drive and gunned it. Steve was managing the burning food while looking around the room. Max's books and homework were on the table. Undisturbed. Heather's purse was there too, no signs of a struggle.

Steve waved his arms as the smoke covered his face. "Good grief!"

Outside the van backed into the driveway again. Carlos's BMW pulled in beside the van. Carlos and Rico got out and headed towards the garage. Pedro stayed behind to watch Heather and Max.

As the door to the garage opened Steve spun, thinking he would see Heather and Max. What he saw was the end of two weapons pointed at him and men dressed in black. Steve turned putting his hands up.

"Police!" Carlos yelled out. "On your knees."

Steve hesitated looking at the uniforms and the hoods on the men. "Police my ass. Show me a badge."

Carlos hit Steve in the face with the butt of his gun, knocking him against the cabinet. "On the ground asshole!"

Steve closed his eyes in pain as the sting of the blow pulsed through him. The taste of blood filling his mouth. Being forced to the ground by the other man, Steve put his hands behind his head. Not fighting realizing that Heather and Max must have already been taken. He felt the tip of the gun touch his head. "Cooperate and don't be stupid."

Steve didn't speak as his hands were pulled behind him and zip tied together. His head was bagged and he was pulled to his feet.

Carlos stepped in front of Steve. "Good, you are listening. Your wife and child are fine. You will be with them shortly. Do what you are told and no one will get hurt. Do you understand me Steve?"

Steve nodded yes.

"Good. We are taking you to the van. Do as you are told."

"A white van?"

Carlos smiled. "Yes. The one you saw at work. You are very observant Steve."

"What do you want?"

"We'll get to that soon. Where do you keep your passport?"

"My passport? Why? What do you want? I don't have any money. You obviously know I'm a mechanic, certainly not rich. Are you stealing my identity or something? What do you need my passport for?"

Carlos laughed. "You're going on a trip and you'll need it. Now answer the questions please or I will have to remind you again who is in charge here."

Steve still had a mouth full of blood from his busted lip. "It's in the desk against the wall. Just Heather and I have one. Max doesn't."

"Heather and Max are staying with me Steve. We just need yours."

"What the hell do want?"

Carlos went to the desk and pulled the passport out. "Got it! Take him to the van. Get him secure and take off."

Steve resisted. "Wait! Where's my wife and kid?"

"They're in the van. Now cooperate and my associate will take you to them."

Rico headed out the door with Steve and Carlos walked back to Steve's bedroom. Opening several drawers, looking around at the tidy home, noticing several pictures along the dresser. Finally getting to the closet. Carlos turned on the light. Heather's side full of dresses, scrubs, Jeans and sweaters. Shoes all along the floor. Up top, an overnight bag. Carlos grabbed it. Stuffing two pairs of Steve's jeans in it. Tennis shoes, belt and three shirts. Back in the room to the drawers, some under wear and socks. As he finished, he took one picture of the three of them at the zoo. Such a nice-looking family. Carlos smashed the picture on the corner of the dresser sending glass and frame to the floor. He bent over and picked the picture from the mess. Stuffing it into the bag as well.

Carlos turned off the lights and headed back to the kitchen. Checking the stove to make sure it was off. Turning out the lights and locking up. He opened the door to the garage and shut the garage door. He then headed out the front door locking it behind him. As Carlos got in the BMW he looked around for witnesses. No one was out. He was clean. Carlos headed out of the driveway to meet up with Rico.

As Carlos pulled away, he dialed Rico. "Bueno."

"Pronombre todo?"(Everything Okay?)

"Yeah boss. Just fine. They're huddled together. She is waking up now. We're almost there. You have any problems?"

"No. No problem. Nobody pays attention to what goes on in the neighborhood anymore. You could rob a house in the middle of the day and no one would see a thing. I will be there in ten. Get everything set up."

"You got it."

Carlos hit Hwy 10 east heading back into the city.

In the van Steve talked to Max. "You okay buddy? What happen to Mom?"

Max was crying. "They hit her in the head. Is she dead? I'm scared Dad."

Pedro turned around. "She's not dead kid, just unconscious. She'll be fine."

Steve leaned against Max. "See, she's okay. I'll figure out something. It's gonna be okay, I promise. Be tough for me now, okay."

Max, trying to stop crying. "Okay, I'll try. What do the police want us for?"

Steve shook his head. "These aren't cops buddy. I'll find out what they want, don't worry."

Heather started to wake up and began to scream. "What the hell is going on?"

Steve leaned over Max putting his head against hers. "Baby it's me. It's okay. We're all together."

Heather started to sit up but felt the pain surge through her head from the blow. "Why are the police treating us like this?"

"These ain't cops' baby. I don't know what's happening yet. I think we'll find out soon."

"Who are they then?"

Pedro turned around. "Enough talking."

Steve wanted the hood off, so he could try and see where they were going. He began to try and pull it off against Max. Pedro slapped Steve on the top of the head. "Leave the hood alone!"

Steve sat back and tried to listen to every sound he could hear. New Orleans was an unusual city full of unusual sounds. If he could just hear any of those he would know where he was. The whistle of the paddle boat at the river. The draw bridge raising. The ocean. Any sound that would tell him where they were.

As he listened, he could hear traffic, but nothing that was defining. After about twenty minutes or so, he felt the van stop and heard a large garage door open. The van pulled in and he heard the door shut. The van stopped and the men got out. He could feel his heart rate quicken. Whatever this was, he would know soon.

Steve leaned back over to Max and Heather. "Okay, we're here. Stay calm. I don't want you guys hurt, whatever this is. Just do what they say and I'll figure it out."

Heather sat up. Looking in the direction that Steve's voice was coming from. "Do you know these guys? Are you in some kind of trouble?"

Steve sighed. "No, I'm not in trouble. Damn Heather, how could you say that?"

"Well shit Steve, two men came into my house and tied Max and I up. I was knocked unconscious and put in a van. Something's up, don't ya think?"

"Well yeah, but it ain't me. Maybe they want you for something."

Carlos opened the back door. "Hey love birds. Let's hold it down. There's a child present. Mommy and Daddy shouldn't fight in front of the child. What's wrong with you? Come on now, slide down to the back of the van. Come towards my voice."

Steve slid first and felt someone grab his arm, standing him up. He immediately could smell the musty smell of mold and mildew. The hood was snatched off his head. Steve looked around at four men, armed and all wearing ski mask. Heather and Max were being helped out of the van next to him. Their hoods were removed too.

Steve looked at Heather and felt tears well up in his eyes as the bloody black and blue gash went across most of her forehead. Steve turned back to the man who had spoken.

"What do you want?"

Carlos smiled. "So full of anger, Steve. If you don't want her hurt anymore, I suggest you do exactly what I say, all of you. Do what I tell you and you will all be fine. Everyone understand?"

They all three nodded their heads yes. Steve spoke again. "Who are you?"

"I will call myself Sam! Let's go in the office and get more comfortable. Then we can talk about the business we need to do together."

Carlos pointed, and they began to walk. As they got to the office Rico and Pedro pulled Heather and Max away leading them into a separate office. Steve could still see them but couldn't hear them at all.

"Why are you separating us?"

Carlos smiled. "Steve, please come in and have a seat. Our business is with you. Your wife and child are just here to make sure you do what we want. Now take a seat."

Edgar closed the door and Carlos sat down behind the desk.

"What is it you want me to do? You need your car fixed, because beyond that I'm not gonna be much help."

"Oh, I don't know about that. You seem like a guy who can get things done when you need too."

"What do you want me to do?"

"I want you to go get something for me Steve. While you do, I will hang on to your wife and child to make sure you do what I say. You remember that while you're gone. You fuck this up and I will kill them both, understand me so far."

Steve began to understand now. He nodded yes and he felt his gut begin to churn.

CHAPTER 3

The Mission

Steve turned and looked at Heather. She was sitting on the other side of a glass wall with Max standing beside her. Tears were rolling down her face.

Steve looked back at Carlos. "Fine, I'll do whatever you want but let them go. You don't need them. I give you my word."

"Are you a man of your word Steve?"

"Yes. Just let them go and I will do what you want."

"You don't even know what I want Steve. How can you say that? What if I want you to kill someone? Would you still do it?"

Steve looked at Carlos. "Why would you want me for that? You are surrounded by men that look like they would have no problem killing someone."

Carlos smiled. "You're right about that. You remember that, okay Steve."

"So, what do you want?"

Carlos looked at Edgar. "I like this guy, eager! That's good Steve. That attitude will save your wife and kid. You remember that too."

"Yeah Sam, I get it! What do you want from me?"

Carlos lost his smile. "You have a license to drive a tractor trailer, right?"

Steve looked confused. "Yeah, I have to for work. You want me to drive a truck for you?"

"Do you know what a mule is in the drug world, Steve?"

He sat back in the chair. "Oh shit. You want me to drive a truck full of drugs somewhere? Based on the passport question from the house, I would assume Mexico."

Carlos smiled. "You are one smart guy Steve. See, I told you he was our guy."

Edgar nodded. "You were right boss."

"You know I will never get over the border with a truck full of drugs. They have dogs and all kinds of stuff looking for that shit."

"We have dogs too. Getting over the border is tricky but you can do it if you are motivated!" Pointing at Heather and Max.

Steve followed his finger to the two. "I will kill you and everyone you know if you hurt them."

Carlos laughed. "So strong. Look around you Steve. You don't know where you are or what any of us look like. You will do nothing but what I say and when I say do it. If you don't my friend, your wife and kid will die."

Carlos waved his hand at Rico and he started to take Heather and Max back to the van.

"Wait! Please let me at least say goodbye to them. I'll do what you want. Please."

Carlos motioned at Edgar. "We can do that for you Steve. I told you, I am a reasonable man. Make it quick."

Steve stood and walked over to Heather. She was crying harder now. Steve put his face against hers. "Just hang in their baby. I'll get you away from these people, I promise."

Heather sobbed as Steve pressed against her. "I love you."

As she said the words Steve thought about how this would end. Even if he did what the man asked, she would probably die. Steve had no idea how he would change that, but he would. Somehow, he needed to make sure she was safe and that she and Max would stay that way.

Steve leaned in close to her ear. "I love you too butterfly!"

Edgar pulled Steve away as he whispered. Heather had never heard Steve call her that and was puzzled by the nickname. Edgar snatched Steve hard. "Let's go!"

"Wait I need to say goodbye to my son as well."

Edgar looked at Carlos who waved a let's go hand in the air. Edgar pulled harder and Steve pulled back. "Just a second."

Edgar stuck the gun to Steve's head.

Steve bent down next to Max. "I love you buddy. Take care of Mommy for me okay."

Max pushed against Steve. "I will Dad. I'm scared though."

"It'll be okay bud, I promise."

Edgar put the gun to Steve's head again. "Now!"

They stood and walked back to Carlos's office. Edgar pushed him back in the chair. Steve sat and watched as they were hooded again and loaded into the van. The door opened and the van backed out. The door closed, and Steve looked back at Carlos.

"Please don't hurt them. I'll drive the truck wherever you want. Please don't hurt my wife and kid."

Carlos sat up putting his hands on the desk. "You have my word. You do what I ask and I will give them back to you. Do we have a deal?"

"Yes!"

Carlos nodded at Edgar as Rico came back in the room. "Cut him loose."

Rico walked over and cut the zip tie off Steve's wrist. Putting the tip of his gun to Steve's head.

"Now just so we understand each other. You try and escape, they die. You try and be a hero, they die. You go to the cops, they die. You get the picture?"

Rubbing his wrist. "Yeah I get the picture. Tell me what I have to do so I can get on with it!"

Edgar pulled off his ski mask. Steve turned away, shielding his eyes. "Dude, I don't want to see your face. I will do what you ask, just tell me where and I will go."

"This is Edgar. He will be your shadow for this whole trip. You're going to the airport in about an hour. There you will get on a plane going to Mexico City. He will take you to where you are picking up the truck. He will give you a map to the best border crossing and money for the trip. You get in the truck and drive. You get gas when you need it and you sleep when you need to. Don't be stupid. Stop at all the weigh stations and inspection points. If you stay cool they won't see the drugs. You act stupid and they will catch you. You will go to jail forever. Your wife and kid will die."

"Did you pay off the border guards or something?"

"No. That's very hard to do, especially on the American side. The truck is made to hide the drugs. You stay cool and everything will be fine. If something happens, you do what you have too, to get away. You understand so far?"

"Yeah I understand."

"If Edgar doesn't check in with me or tell me that everything is going fine, I will kill the wife and kid."

"If it's that easy, why don't you just have Edgar go get his license and drive the truck back yourself. Why risk kidnapping someone and killing someone?"

"That's true. But you see, if Edgar does it, they look at him closer than a white American guy driving. If he gets caught they make him tell where I am and where the warehouse is. You don't know anything. If Edgar gets scared, he may run away and my drugs get confiscated. If you go, you have a lot to lose. You are motivated to get back here with my drugs. If you get caught I lose the drugs, but no one comes looking for me. Your wife and kid turn up in the river and we do it again with someone else."

"How many times have you done this?"

"Don't worry about it my friend, enough to be good at it."

"How do I know you won't just kill them as soon as I leave here?"

"I gave you my word Steve. Is that not good enough for you? I thought we were going to be friends."

"Well, forgive me if I don't believe you, but you're a killer and a drug dealer. Not to mention a kidnapper. I want some guarantees."

"Steve, I guarantee you that I will kill your wife and kid if you fuck with me in any way. You go down there, follow the plan and get back here with my drugs. When you get back here I will let you and your family go. As a bonus I will let you keep whatever money you have left over as pay. You can make a few thousand bucks if you're smart."

"No thanks. What if I go to the cops?"

Carlos stopped and looked at Steve. "Then I will kill you and your wife in front of your kid. Then I will kill him too Steve. Because you're right about one thing, I am a killer and I'm surrounded by men that will kill for me too. But you're not that stupid now are you. I know where you work and live. Do the job! Make a little cash for Christmas and go home. It's simple. Just go along and there will be no problems.

"I want to talk to my wife while I'm driving."

"No."

"You'll kill them if I don't. I will get back here with the drugs no matter what it takes but you've got to give me something."

"I don't have to give you shit. I expect you back here with my drugs in three days. You do that and you and your family go free. You do anything other than drive straight here with my drugs and I will kill your wife and son. Do you hear me Steve?"

"I hear you, but come on. I need something, please. You say you are a man of your word so what's the problem?"

"Edgar will fill you in on everything you need to know. He has the money, the maps, that's all you need."

"I am just trying to keep them alive. You aren't giving me any hope here Sam. I'm risking everything for you. All I want is to talk to my wife during the ride back. If you're a man of your word, what's the problem?"

Carlos stood angry. "Get the fuck out! You get my drugs and get back here or they die. That's your hope. Who the hell do you think you are? I will kill you and them now and get someone else. Are you trying to get your wife and kid killed?"

Steve didn't say anything else. He started walking for the door. "I'm not trying to question you or cause a problem. Will you please let me talk to her at least once?"

Carlos still stood at the desk. He looked at Edgar. "Can you believe the balls on this guy? I tell you what, Edgar will call me when you are in Mexico. I will let you talk to her then. Fair enough?"

Steve smiled. "Thank you Sam. That's all I'm asking. Thank you."

Edgar pointed to a green Chevy parked in the warehouse. "Get in the front passenger seat and don't touch anything. I will be right there."

Steve looked at the BMW as he walked to the car. He made a mental note of everything he could see. The tires, wheels, tinted windows. He looked around the warehouse for anything he could see that might lead him back here later.

Steve needed to get control of this situation. He had to stay calm. He had to find a way to protect Heather and Max. Right now there was no reason for Sam to keep them alive after he talked to them. He suspected that Edgar's orders were to shoot him once they got back to New Orleans as well. He had to get control of this, he had to get control of the drugs. That was his only chance. All of his training as a sniper and what little he had in Special Forces taught him to stay calm. Outsmart your opponent. Get control of the situation.

This was out of his control for sure. He had no idea where Heather and Max had been taken. He was out numbered and unarmed. He needed a break and he needed it now. Steve knew that Sam was the key. If he was going to get away from this he would have to kill Sam. Steve had no problem with that. He would enjoy it if he got the chance.

Edgar got back in the car with Steve's bag. "Sam packed for you. He thought you might need a few things for the trip. Whatever you don't have, buy it with the money I give you. Your passport is in the bag."

Edgar started the car. Steve starred at him. "How the hell can you do this to people? Do you not have a soul at all?"

Edgar put the car in reverse and backed out of the garage. "Look Steve. You do what you're supposed to and don't be stupid. You try and turn this thing around, he'll kill you."

"Well Edgar, the only face I know is yours so what does that say about what he thinks of you. Either the plan is to kill me or to kill both of us. So why don't you just tell me the truth."

"No problem, I live in Mexico man. I get twenty large for babysitting and then I go away. You'll never see me again my man. I'll tell you this though. You fuck with Sam, everyone you know will die. He will kill those dudes at the garage and burn it to the ground just to be mean. Don't be stupid. Just do this and go home amigo!"

"I'm not your friend Edgar. I want my wife and kid back. I want my life back."

"Then be cool fool. Drive the truck and don't be stupid."

Steve looked in the bag. "He packed a bag for me? What about my tooth brush? My hair stuff. Go by my house so I can get the rest of my shit."

"No. We have to go now to the airport. Our plane leaves in two hours. We gotta go! Besides, I don't follow the plan it's my ass in trouble with Sam. That's not gonna happen."

"Well that's just great. Stop at the store then so I can buy a hat and some tooth paste."

"Stop trying to change the plan. No stops. If I don't call at the times set at the places I'm supposed to be I don't get paid. I was waiting tables before this for about .50 an hour in Mexico. This is a good deal for me. Just do what you're told or your family dies. Don't you get it?"

Steve sat back in the seat. "Yeah, I get it. You're a victim too and you don't even know it, Edgar. Sam will probably kill you too when this done. You're nobody, just like me."

"Whatever man, all I have to do, is follow you back to New Orleans and get on a plane. No big deal. No more talking either. You talk too much."

Steve stared out the window looking at where he was. He knew exactly where this was. He was down by the old airport, in the buildings that were flooded during Katrina. They had been empty for years. It would do him no good though. All this stuff was in foreclosure. Sam probably just broke in and used the building when he wanted to. Nobody ever came down here. Steve looked over at the steering column of the car they were in, it was busted and hanging loose, stolen as well. So far, Edgar was his only lead and he was nothing. He probably didn't know much more than he did. Some kid they offered more money to than he could ever make and he took it. He would disappear and when the money ran out, he would be back waiting tables somewhere.

He thought about Heather and how scared she must be. He wondered what kind of awful crap she would have to deal with over the next three days. He thought about Sam killing her as soon as they talked. He had to come up with something that would keep her alive.

Steve looked over at Edgar. "You know I'll kill you if they hurt my wife, right?"

Edgar smiled at Steve. "You think you can get this under control, but you can't. They've done it too many times. They're good at it. They're crazy too. Not the kind of guys you want to mess with."

"They're gonna kill her and my kid aren't they?"

"Look man, just get the truck and get home. Sam will give them back. No problem."

"Oh it's a problem."

They pulled into the airport and parked in one-hour parking. Edgar threw the parking ticket on the floor.

"Won't you need that for later?"

"Nope. We stole this car from your street this morning. I just need to wipe my fingerprints off it. How about you touch the wheel for me."

"No thanks. I don't want to be connected to this thing anymore than I have too."

"See, now you're thinking. Just do this and go home. That's all you have to do."

Steve got out and walked around to the driver side. Edgar was wiping off the door handle when Steve grabbed him by the shirt. Slamming Edgar into the car. Edgar tried to push back but Steve had already pulled Edgar's arm around behind him and pushed his face hard against the glass. He grabbed his other hand, turning it palm out. Steve pushed it against the glass window leaving a sweaty hand print. Steve spun Edgar, jamming his hand hard against his throat. Edgar gasped for air.

"What are you doing? Carlos.... Sam will kill you if you don't get on that plane. You don't even know where your family is."

Steve leaned in close. "You do. If you take me there right now, I will let you go. Carlos will never know what hit him."

"I don't know. He will kill me for telling you his real name. They don't tell me anything. I just got here yesterday. I'm telling you the truth."

Steve looked hard at the man and loosened his grip. Edgar you try and man handle me ever again and I will kill you. If I thought you really knew where they were, I promise I would make you talk. You better help me out anyway you can. That might be the only thing that saves your life later."

As Steve let go, Edgar grabbed his throat. "Are you trying to get your wife and kid killed? If I tell Carlos what you just did, they die. What's wrong with you?"

"Nothing, I just wanted you know who you were dealing with. You take me there and set up the deal. Stay out of my way, but listen to me Edgar. If anything happens to my wife or kid, you die. I will hunt you down and kill everyone you know. I am far worse than Carlos."

Snatching Edgar away from the car, not giving him a chance to wipe the hand print away from the window, Steve turned and picked up his bag from the concrete.

They got the tickets and headed for security. Edgar didn't say a word. He hung back from Steve so that the two didn't appear together. Edgar had given Steve the five grand as they walked to the terminal.

They got to security and Steve looked around at all the police and TSA officers. He couldn't do a thing to get help. Edgar was ten people back and had a cell phone. Even if he could get away who would he call? He still had no idea where Heather and Max were. At least he had learned Sam's real name. Edgar's slip would help him later.

There were no body cavity searches and Steve went right through. Edgar got stopped and Steve made his way to the gate. He would at least warn Tyrone to be on the lookout. He was a smart kid and knew the streets.

As Steve disappeared down the escalator he could see Edgar spreading his arms and legs for a nice pat down by TSA. God bless them he thought. Steve looked around for a phone as he hit the concourse. Surprisingly there were none. Cell phones had pretty much killed the pay phone business. Two people passed by talking on their phones. He would have to borrow one.

ROAD RAGE

Steve walked up to a lady getting a drink from the snack bar. "Hi. Can you help me?"

The lady looked at Steve very suspiciously. "I doubt it. I certainly will not carry anything on the plane for you!"

She started to walk away. "No" Steve said. "I didn't bring my cell phone on this trip and just needed to make a real quick call to work. Could I borrow your phone for just a second?"

The lady walked away shaking her head. Steve tried again with the guy standing behind the counter. "Seriously I just need to call my work for two minutes. I will give you my wallet and stand right here. Can I borrow your phone, please?"

The guy stared at Steve for a second and pulled out his phone. "It's local right?"

Steve smiled. "Yeah, just down the road. You can dial the number."

The man laughed. "It don't matter. I get unlimited everything. Make your call and hurry up. You gotta buy somthin though."

Steve dialed Tyrone's number and handed the guy a twenty. "Keep it. You're saving lives."

The guy laughed and stuck the twenty in his pocket.

Tyrone answered on the third ring. "Yo what's up? Who is this?"

"Tyrone its Steve. I only have a second so listen close."

"What? What the hell are you sayin?"

"Look that white van was kidnappers and they have Heather and Max."

"What the…"

"Shhh. I am going to Mexico to get drugs for these guys and drive them back in an eighteen wheeler. Tell Jack what's happening and why I'm not there. You guys need to stay away from the shop for a few days. If this shit goes bad they may come there. You understand?"

"Holly shit! You want me to call the cops?"

"No, just answer your phone no matter what number it is. Lay low for a few days and watch your back. Get to my house and get Heathers car. There's a key under the plant to the right of the front door. I don't know how but I have to get control of this thing. Be waiting on my call. Can I count on you?"

"Sure you can. I got you."

Steve closed the phone and handed it back to the guy. Smiling, "Just my boss. I like messing with him when I go on vacation. I was just kidding."

The guy didn't say a word as Steve walked away. He put his phone back in his pocket and sat back in his chair. Edgar walked by just as he did. Steve strolled down through the gates like nothing had happened.

Edgar called out as he got close. "Steve!"

Steve turned to look at him. "They find any drugs on you Edgar?"

"That's real funny. Did you do that?"

"No. I don't want anything to happen to my wife and kid, remember. I am going along. It was pretty funny though. If they knew who you really were, you would be in handcuffs right now."

"Just go to the gate. Stay where I can see you. I need to call Sam."

"You mean Carlos don't you?"

"No, I mean Sam. You better keep your mouth shut if you know what's good for you."

"Hey dip shit. Carlos is probably not his real name either. Why would he tell you? You're just a babysitter."

Steve took a seat at gate number twenty-three. The monitor read, New Orleans to Mexico City, flight leaving on time. Edgar took out his phone and hit redial. He turned his back and started to walk away. Steve looked down at his bag. He opened it to see just what Carlos had packed. Right on top he found the picture of the three of them at the zoo. Instantly memories of that day flooded his head. Thoughts of what Heather must be going through right now. How scared her and Max must be. As he gripped the picture he thought about killing everyone involved. Heather and Max would surely die as soon as Carlos didn't need the leverage any more. Steve looked up at Edgar who was still talking.

Steve raised the picture and kissed Heather and then Kissed Max. "I will keep you safe, somehow."

Steve put the picture back in the bag as Edgar walked back towards him. "What was that?"

Steve looked up at Edgar standing over him. "That was none of your damn business! What did your boyfriend say?

Edgar looked at Steve as he sat down. "He said if you gave me any trouble at all, to just call him. He said your wife was very pretty and he would enjoy fucking her if he needed to."

Steve turned and looked at Edgar. "When this is over, you better pray to whatever God you believe in, that doesn't happen. I will not only kill you but I will kill everyone that knows you too. You think Carlos is bad? You ain't seen nothin until you've seen me mad."

Edgar's smile faded. I didn't tell him about what you did in the parking lot. So you don't say anything about the Carlos deal. Fair enough."

Steve nodded thinking of nothing but Heather possibly being raped by this man. He could feel himself beginning to shake. His hands trembled. He could visualize punching Carlos over and over in the face. He wanted to kill him now. He wanted to kill him slow and make it hurt. If he raped Heather, he would not sleep until the man was dead. That's all there was to it.

Steve nodded and sat back in the seat. "We have about twenty minutes until boarding. Leave me alone until then. Go sit somewhere else. I am getting on the plane. You don't need to be near me all the time."

Edgar got up and walked away. Steve turned to see where he perched himself. He was two rows over. Steve closed his eyes and pictured Max playing in the backyard and Heather watching him. He wanted to be back in her arms. He wanted his life back.

Steve stood and looked towards Edgar. Edgar stood and Steve held up his hand motioning for him to stay put. Steve pointed at the bathroom and began walking. Edgar sat back down.

ROAD RAGE

Steve walked into the bathroom and stood at the sink. He put his hands under the sink and the water automatically started running. He waited as the water began to get hot. Steve stared at the mirror. His eyes were dark with anger. He had not seen this side of himself since Iraq. Steve could remember how he felt back then when he would go out on sniper missions. He could remember thinking about his targets as non-human. They were the mission. There was no feeling attached. This time there would be feelings. He could feel the rage inside him.

CHAPTER 4

Mexico

They boarded the plane and got to their seats. Edgar was a few rows in front of Steve. The plane wasn't full. Who really goes to Mexico City on a Thursday night? Steve moved back a few more rows to a row with empty seats. He stretched out and tried to rest. He knew from the time that he hit the ground in Mexico until he got Heather and Max back would be nonstop.

Once he got that truck in his hands he would get control. Once he had the drugs he had bargaining power. Taking out Edgar, would be simple. One dark highway and hard shove and Edgar would be done. Steve closed his eyes as they took off. The flight attendant woke him to deliver his rum and coke as requested and in two swallows it was gone. Steve closed his eyes again adjusted his seat back as far as it would go.

Steve thought about Heather. He wondered where she was, where they were keeping her and how terrified she must be. Max must be scared to death as well. All he could hope for was that they were at least together. His whole body was tense as he visualized the two of them in some nasty basement or abandoned building. He would kill them all, if they did anything to either one of them. Hell, he was pretty sure he would kill them all even if they didn't. No one should ever have to go through this again.

ROAD RAGE

Steve jumped as the flight attendant touched his arm. "Sir we are about to land. Can you please sit up and put your seat belt on."

Steve stretched and looked over the seats to Edgar. He straightened his body and snapped the seat belt back on. The flight attendant smiled and kept moving. He looked at his watch. 10:45. He would wait until tomorrow to push for the phone call with Heather just to buy more time if he could. He knew Edgar would be checking in tonight but maybe he could wait.

As he came off the plane, Edgar was waiting. Standing in the concourse like an idiot.

Steve gathered himself together and focused on what he had to do. "Let's go get the truck!"

Edgar looked surprised. "Not tonight. We'll get it in the morning. That's the plan."

"Well fuck the plan, it needs to change. I want to be on the road within the hour. Better to cross the border at night, less guards. Make the call Edgar."

Edgar starred at Steve and slowly pulled out the cell and started dialing.

Carlos answered. "What now."

"Sir he wants to go get the truck now. He said there would be less guards at night on the border. Less trouble."

Carlos laughed. "Eagar bastard isn't he? Stick to the plan Edgar. If he leaves in the morning at 6a.m., he will hit the border during rush hour. The guards are busier then and they won't have time for inspections. Tell him this is not our first time."

"Yes sir. I will tell him."

"I like his eagerness though. Does he want to talk to his wife now?"

Edgar turned to Steve. "Sam said no. If you leave according to the plan you will hit the border during rush hour. The guards are busier then. It's better to stick to the plan. Do you want to talk to your wife now?"

Steve took a deep breath. "In the morning before I leave if that's okay. Please tell her that I love her and Max"

Edgar looked shocked. He relayed the message to Carlos and hung up the phone. He began to smile.

"What's so funny?"

"Sam said you had balls. He would tell your wife that you didn't want to speak with her."

Steve stopped walking. "Well can I speak to her in the morning or not?"

Edgar kept walking. "I don't know. He hung up laughing. I guess we will see in the morning."

He felt panic in his gut. "Edgar wait, call him back. I'll talk to her now."

Edgar kept walking. "No. I am not to call him until morning. Sorry that's the plan. No more changes. Sam said."

Steve started walking again, feeling like he would throw up. The panic wouldn't leave. Was Carlos going to kill her now, or would he wait. Had he just blown his last chance to tell his wife and child how much he loved them? He had to stay in control now. Fear and desperation would only get his family killed quicker. Control and being smart, was the only way to win this. He had to keep thinking that they were alive, all the time. All the way to the end of this. If he got there and they weren't, he would begin a new plan. For now, the plan was to get the drugs back to New Orleans as planned.

Edgar found the car he had left a few days before and they got in. Steve walked around the back making a mental note of the tag and as many details as possible. This was most likely stolen too, but at this point he wasn't sure of anything.

The two of them drove for about forty-five minutes until Edgar pulled into a small hotel. Edgar parked and went inside the lobby. He came back with the key to one room.

Steve held out his hand. "Where is mine?"

Edgar looked at him. "One room, from now on, you are not allowed to leave my sight. Sam's orders."

"I'm not sharing a room with you, asshole. I want my own."

Edgar smiled. "Forget it. If you want, you can stay in the car. I would remember where you are my friend. This is my town and it ain't so nice."

They pulled up to the room and Edgar got out. Steve sat there and watched him go in. He looked around the hotel and there were several groups of guys just hanging around. The last thing he needed was to get his throat cut by someone carjacking him. Steve got out and banged on the door. Edgar opened the door with a smile.

"Thought you might change your mind. Did you lock the car?"

"Nope. By the looks of the guys in the parking lot, it won't be there when we get up anyway!"

"Oh sure it will. They know who we work for. It'll be there."

Steve put his bag down and picked up the pen and paper on the desk.

"What are you doing?"

Steve turned to look at Edgar. "I am writing my wife a love letter. Do you mind? It's not like the hotel we are in is a mystery. I can see the sign from our room."

Edgar stood there confused. "I guess that's okay, but you're not mailing anything."

"I understand. Go to sleep Edgar. We have a busy day tomorrow."

Edgar got in bed and Steve sat on the other bed, propping the pillows up. He began to write everything he could remember from the day. Details about Carlos. Things he remembered about his voice. His accent. The cars in the warehouse. The van. Everything he could think of throughout the day that might help him or the police later track down these guys. He needed to clear his head of all this information so that he could be sharp for tomorrow.

Steve had made his mind up on the plane, no matter what happened he would end this deal with these guys. They would never take another family hostage, ever again. With or without the police he would put an end to this.

Edgar had begun to snore now as he wrote out every detail. He decided to do this at the end of each day. Somewhere along the road he would mail this back to his house just in case he didn't make it. He would get in touch with Tyrone somehow and tell him to give it to the cops if he didn't return. Somebody needs a history of what happened.

He finished his notes and got into bed. Sliding the notes under his pillow to ensure Edgar wouldn't read what he had written before he woke up.

Steve laid there for a while staring at the ceiling. He pulled the picture of them at the zoo out of his bag. He laughed as he found himself grateful to Carlos for including it in what he packed. He focused on the smiles on both of their faces that day. They had so much fun as a family that day. He could remember Max acting like a monkey for the rest of the day. Eating bananas and grunting instead of talking. He didn't want to miss raising Max. Tomorrow he had to get control. He had to get out of this with his family.

He fell asleep holding the picture on his chest.

The next morning Steve was awake before Edgar. He laid there waiting for the alarm to go off at five. He needed to be calm and cool until the truck was in his hands. Then he could begin to make a different plan. For now, he was at Carlos's mercy. At Edgar's mercy too. He was right, this was his town and he had no idea where he was or how to get any kind of help. As he laid there he knew it would not always be this way. He would do the research. He would find out everything he could about this little town just outside of Mexico City where the drugs came from. He would know the streets when he came back. He would speak more Spanish. He would be armed. For now, he was the lamb trying to avoid being slaughtered, but soon he would be the lion.

At five the alarm went off and Edgar jumped up.

Steve looked over. "Easy there Chico!"

Edgar looked back at Steve. "You been awake all night or something?"

"No, just a little while. I'm just ready to get this over with. Aren't you?"

Edgar rubbed his face. "Yeah, I am. Ready to be done with you for sure."

Steve laughed. "Man that hurts my feelings, we just slept together. I thought we were friends. Come on Edgar, we're in this together. At least you're by choice anyway, I'm not. That's the only difference. Either way, we were both chosen by Carlos. So you help me and I will help you okay. "

"Help me what?"

Steve sat up. "Get through this alive. You help me and I will see if you can get through this alive."

Edgar shook his head. "Man you're crazy. Carlos should keep you on his regular team."

"Careful Edgar. It's Sam remember."

Edgar stood and walked into the bathroom. "Yeah, whatever. We need to leave in twenty minutes."

"Yeah well hurry up then. I need to shower real quick."

Steve heard the toilet flush and the shower come on. He took the notes out from under his pillow and hid them in the bible in the night stand by his bed. He didn't need Edgar finding them while he showered. He got up and went over to Edgar's bag. His cell phone was lying beside it. He opened it and hit recent calls the words were in Spanish but he just needed numbers. Steve took the note pad and began to write down the numbers. He knew the last one was Carlos but the others were probably family or friends. That could help him later if he needed it. In his bag there was nothing. This guy really didn't know much. He had about a thousand in cash, a passport and a few pictures. Nothing else that would help. He heard the water turn off so he put the things back just like they were.

Steve laid back in bed stuffing the extra notes in the Bible with the others. Steve had written Heather a letter last night and he tossed it in the top of his bag. Edgar needed something to find while he was in the shower.

Edgar got done and it was Steve's turn. He took his clothes and hurried through a shower. The warm water felt good after the long day before. Steve went over in his head to stay calm today and make mental notes of everything. Street signs, businesses, hotels, everything that he could that would lead him back if he had to.

He finished and got dressed. He still hadn't gotten a tooth brush or deodorant. He would stop once he got the truck. He could get what he needed then. As he came out of the bathroom Edgar was reading the letter to Heather.

Steve looked at him. "Like what you're reading? That's private you know."

Edgar smiled and threw the letter back in his bag. "Whatever man. I'm the babysitter remember. I need to know everything you are doing and report it back to the Carlos."

"Well, you do that. You married Edgar?"

Edgar paused. "That's not your business."

"Just asking. I saw the pictures in your bag of the woman and girl. It would be a shame if someone was holding them hostage wouldn't it?"

Edgar looked shocked. He looked at his bag and then back at Steve.

"Relax Chico. I just looked in the top for a second. No big deal."

"You better do what you are supposed to. Don't forget who has your wife and kid. And quit calling me Chico. My name is Edgar. I don't like this Chico shit."

Steve picked up his bag. "Whatever Chico. Let's go do this okay."

As they began to leave Steve reached in and picked up the Bible from the night stand and stuck it in his bag.

"What are you doing? Put that back."

Steve closed his bag and zipped it. "I might need to do some reading later to keep my head clear. I'm sure they won't mind. I know God won't. Do you know God Edgar?"

He walked passed Steve and opened the car. "Let's go!"

Steve smiled. "I hope you do. You're gonna meet him soon?"

Steve got in and didn't say anything else on the ride. He just made notes in his head of everything he saw. Street names and places. This was a suburb of Mexico City and it was rough. If he had to come back, he would stand out like a sore thumb. They were in Chalco, Mexico.

The ride was only ten minutes and they pulled into a truck stop. Edgar pulled out his phone and made a call. The man on the phone told him what to look for. They pulled around to the side and next to a Peter built.

The men talked to Edgar for a minute and then came over to Steve. "You are the driver, yes?"

Steve looked at the faces of all three. "Yeah, you have some paperwork on this truck for me to look at?"

One of the men stepped forward and handed the manifest to Steve. He went through it and everything looked in order. He went over to the truck and opened the door to the cab. Steve put his bag in the sleeper and gave the cab a once over. Everything looked good.

The man in charge spoke. "Everything cool?"

Steve climbed down. "So far let's look in the back."

The man put up his hand. "It's fine. You go now. We have been here long enough."

Steve stopped. "Look I am not going through the border in a truck I have never seen in the back of. I need to know where the drugs are so I can try and keep a guard away from them. You understand? Now let's look in the back."

As Steve walked past the guy, he saw him slip Edgar a pistol. Steve thought that could be a problem later. He opened the back doors and there were lawn mowers stacked in box's floor to ceiling. There was a small space down the middle just wide enough for a person to get through. The men came around to the back and stood there looking in.

"Driver man, you satisfied. You are hauling a load of lawn mowers. The weight matches the count. You are well below the limits. Now let's go."

Steve took a deep breath and climbed out of the truck. He looked at Edgar and at the men. "It looks fine to me. I just need to talk to my wife now and we're ready."

Edgar spoke to the other men and they left. "Get in the truck Steve. I will call Sam and we'll see what he says."

Steve climbed up in the rig and shut the door. Edgar got on the phone and Steve rolled down the window to hear what he could. He had to learn Spanish. Edgar kept looking at Steve and waving his hands. Finally, he walked over and handed the phone to Steve.

Steve braced. "Hello."

"Steve its Sam, how do you like the truck?"

"It's nice. Can I talk to my wife?"

"You know Steve for you to be demanding is not very smart. I wasn't playing with you when I said I would kill your wife and kid."

Steve's stomach turned. "Did you? I have done everything you have asked."

There was silence for a minute. "No. Fortunately, I am a patient man. You guys always try and figure out how to get control of the situation. You won't. I have a GPS tracker on that truck and Edgar will be behind you the whole way. If you fuck with me Steve, at all, they will die. Do you understand?"

"Can I talk to my wife?"

"So angry Steve. Do the job and take some money for your home. For you, I tell you what. When you get back I am going to give you a little bonus. I have been talking to your wife, a lovely woman by the way, anyway, she told me that you guys struggle with the bills sometimes."

"Why would she tell you that?"

"What else did we have to talk about? She loves you very much too, did you know that?"

"Yes I do. Can I talk to her?"

"Yes. You do well for me on this trip and I will throw you five grand to help with the bills. You have twelve hours to make it to Laredo to the border. You need to be there between five and six pm. That's when they are very busy. Now hold on for your wife. It will be brief so say what you need to."

The phone rustled and Heather came on. "Baby are you there?"

Steve felt tears well up in his eyes. "I love you. Are you okay?"

"I guess. Why didn't you want to talk to me last night?"

"Just trying to keep you alive."

"Why are they doing this?"

"I don't know. I guess because I can drive big trucks. Is Max okay?"

"We are both okay. How long will this take. I want to go home."

The phone rustled again and Carlos was back on. "Okay. I kept my word now you bring me my drugs."

"Sam I want to talk to her again tonight. I am in the truck and about to head that way. If I don't talk to her I promise I will drive this truck right into a police station. You keep your word and I will deliver the drugs to your door step."

There was silence. "Sam!"

"Steve I will tell you one last time. You fuck with me and I will kill you and your wife in front of young Max here. Do you understand?"

"Yes, I understand."

The phone went dead. Steve looked down at Edgar and dropped the phone into his hands. He fired the truck up and put it in gear. Edgar took off running towards the car. Steve hit the interstate and headed north. The GPS on the dash already had the address plugged in and began to give directions. Twenty-five hours and twenty-three minutes. 1383 miles to home.

Steve brought the rig up to seventy-five and settled in. It was full of fuel and he was on the way. He now had control of the drugs. Getting control of everything else was going to take some time. He could see Edgar coming up behind him. Steve made note of the other cars driving around him. Surely Carlos was smart enough to have a second guy tagging along. At least to the border, maybe all the way. That would need to be dealt with as well.

Steve put the manifest in the front seat and began looking through the truck. There was nothing. No tools he could use as a weapon at all. He had to find the GPS tracker they had installed. At some point he would not want them to know where he was. He had installed several on big rigs so he knew what to look for. Unfortunately, he needed to get to the engine and that meant lifting the cab up.

He would need to get control of Edgar as well. Either take him hostage or kill him. To Steve it didn't matter. He knew nothing anyway. Carlos certainly didn't care about him so he was worthless as a hostage. That decision would be made in time.

ROAD RAGE

The road was quiet. Steve pulled out the note pad from the hotel and began to write the things he could remember. Anything he may need later but might forget. He hated the alone time. He had driven trucks for about six months when he got out of the army but hated the alone time. He needed the time to think though, so for now it was good. He needed a plan. He needed to get his wife and kid back alive.

He started going through the radio stations; the only thing he found in English was country. He laughed because Heather had always liked country but he never really did. Steve felt like it was Heather reaching out so he turned it up and sang along as best he could. He listened and thought about his wife.

The miles rolled past and twice Edgar pulled up beside him motioning for him to get gas. Steve pulled off and waited each time. Making notes of two other cars pulling off each time they did, both had two men inside. One was a blue Impala and the other a red Ford F150 truck. Steve was severely out numbered. He still needed to make good time to the border. Once he crossed he would sleep for a few hours and keep going. If Edgar dropped off what would it hurt? Steve was sure that once he hit New Orleans Carlos's men would show up. He had his number anyway; he could always buy a prepaid phone and just call him. Steve hoped that at the border the four goons would drop off. There would probably be new ones to follow on the American side though. Somehow between now and then he needed to get control.

CHAPTER 5

Losing the Tail

Getting control of Edgar was easy; it was the other guys that would be a problem. Steve looked at the GPS, a hundred miles to the border. He needed to lose the other two cars now in the middle of nowhere. It just needed to be him and Edgar going over the border. Steve knew they were armed and not afraid to kill. All four of the men from what he could see, were big for Mexicans. Not a fight he wanted out here in the desert all by himself. Four on one didn't sound very fun.

Crossing the border with weapons was dangerous though and they might not risk that. Steve's best chance was to cross the border, and then take a detour. Otherwise it had to be now. Steve could feel the anxiety rising up in his chest. His sniper training was long ago and he didn't have the calm he had back then. It wasn't just his life on the line this time.

Carlos would be expecting a Laredo crossing and if there were men waiting, they would be just on the other side of the border watching for the truck to come through.

There was an exit just ahead that had no signs other than the street name. No gas stations or food. Steve swallowed hard and took the exit. As he did, he could see the cars changing lanes behind him, first Edgar then one of the others.

As he down shifted on the exit, he saw the second car slow and stop on the ramp. This was a problem for Steve. Now it wouldn't just be one fight, it would be two.

Steve came to the end of the exit and it truly was a deserted road going into nowhere. To the left in the distance, he could see a building of some kind. Steve turned right and hit the gas. Shifting through the gears to put some distance between the car on the ramp and himself. Edgar was now flashing his lights and swerving behind the truck trying to pass. The second car was staying back, but not far. Steve could see the men in the second car reaching into the back seat, probably getting weapons ready.

A large clearing off the side of the road made for a good place to make a stand. Steve braked and pulled off. Edgar slid up beside the truck and jumped out like a mad man.

"What the hell are you doing Steve? This is not part of the plan." Looking back at the other car nervously.

Steve looked back as he stepped out of the truck. "Friends of yours?"

"Friends of Carlos's you dumb ass. You trying to get yourself killed?"

"They can't kill me, I'm the driver. I'm on the paperwork. I need to take a piss, my bladder is about to bust. Besides, something's wrong with the truck. I need to check it out. I don't want this thing to break down with a bunch of drugs on board. You know what I mean?"

Edgar's phone rang and Steve turned walking towards the bushes. He could hear Edgar as he walked away. "He's taking a piss! I don't know why it couldn't wait."

Steve walked over to the edge of the woods and tried to pee. He was so nervous, he couldn't go. He stood there for a minute and pretended, while going over the plan in his head. He would go back and get Edgar to the front of the truck. Steve had parked crooked so the guys in the car behind couldn't see the passenger door from their position. He would get Edgar out of sight and knock him out.

Once he was out, he would take his cell phone and gun. He would have to move quickly, putting Edgar in the truck and turning around before the guys could get to safety. After that it was a big truck verses a small car time. How he would deal with the other guys was not in the plan yet. Steve was running on all adrenalin as he walked back towards the truck.

Edgar was still on the phone as he got back. Edgar held out the phone, "It's Sam! He would like a word with you."

Steve stopped in front of the truck, squatting down, looking under the truck. He motioned to Edgar to come closer. "Bring me the phone then."

Edgar looked annoyed and stepped closer. Steve stood grabbing Edgar's hand and phone in one hand and hitting him hard with a right cross with the other. Edgar gasped for air but didn't go down. Steve blinked pulled Edgar hard towards him and hit him again square in the forehead.

Edgar's eyes rolled back in his head and he was out. Steve held the hand with the phone as Edgar went to the ground. He slowly let Edgar down and took the phone at the same time grabbing the 9mm from his waistband.

"Sam! How's everything in New Orleans?"

"Steve what the fuck are you doing and what did I just hear? That sounded a lot like somebody getting punched."

"Sir, Edgar is one dumb son-of-a –bitch. He just tripped over a rock here and I think knocked himself out."

"Bullshit Steve. Put Edgar back on the phone."

"I'm not kidding you. He's hurt. I will call you back in just a minute. Tell your goons not to do anything stupid okay."

"What's wrong with the truck? You shouldn't be having any problems, it's new. I hope you're not being stupid Steve."

"I am not doing anything. I got a low air pressure warning light and just stopped to check it out. I also took a piss, is that okay? Let me help Edgar up and we'll call you back in just a minute."

Steve hung up the phone and put it in his pocket. He looked down at Edgar who was still out cold. Steve picked him up and put him in the passenger side of the truck. He ran back around and waved at the guys in the car to come closer. They didn't move but Steve could see the driver on the phone.

He was at a point of no return now. Steve climbed up in the cab and fired up the truck. He looked in the mirror and he could now see the blue impala moving closer. If they got close enough he would just back over the car with the trailer. He had had enough of this shit and wanted control. The car came up within a hundred feet but it was not close enough. They sat in the middle of the road and Steve could now see clearly that the passenger was holding an Uzi.

Steve got back out and waved at them again to come help, pointing at the front of the truck. Steve walked out of sight and ran around to the passenger door and climbed in. Getting back in the driver's seat but staying low and out of sight.

"Come on guys. I know Carlos called you and told you what was going on. Come just a little closer to see what's up. I will show you twenty thousand pounds of what's up!"

The car pulled up again and was now fifty feet away. Steve rose up just enough to see in the mirror how far back they were. He needed them right at the back of the truck, for him to get the best shot.

The car was slowly moving forward when Steve decided to drop the hammer. He slammed the truck in reverse and gunned it, turning the wheel sharply, to swing the trailer back into the street.

He sat up to see where they were going as the trailer struck the rear end of the car. That spun them straight into the cab and the nose hit the rear tires. Steve kept on the gas as the rig of the truck drove over the front of the car. Steve's eyes locked onto the passenger's as the wheels rolled over him.

Steve quickly put the truck into first and drove off the top of the car. He needed to keep the damage to a minimum for the border crossing. He sure didn't want to be asked any questions. As he hit the ground the driver was now frantically trying to get out of the car. The rear wheels came up fast and finished the task. Both sets of wheels rolled up the back of the car and right over the driver. Two shots rang out as the wheels crushed the man. Luckily both shots went wild and didn't hit anything.

Steve swung the truck around pulling Edgar's gun from his waist band as he did. There was no one moving in the car that he could see. He swung the truck again and began to push the car off the road. The crushed car screamed as metal scraped pavement. As the car hit the dirt it began to roll over. Steve kept steady on the gas pushing the car over onto its top.

Edgar began to move slowly as Steve stopped. "What the…"

Steve hit Edgar in the forehead with the butt of the gun. Edgar slumped back down in the seat, unconscious again.

ROAD RAGE

Steve backed up and stopped the truck. For the first time, looking back towards the expressway. In the distance he could see the red F150.

Steve wasn't leaving any lose ends. He jumped down from the truck and ran towards the upside down impala. The passenger had begun to move slightly, trying to get the Uzi out from between the crushed seats.

With a clear head now and steady hands Steve put two rounds through the driver's broken window into the man's head. The Uzi fell to the roof of the car. Steve looked at the driver who was covered in blood and not moving. Two more rounds to the head would guarantee he wouldn't be following them.

Steve reached into the car and snatched up the Uzi for the fight that was coming. As he looked up from the wreckage the F150 was sliding to a stop in the middle of the road. Steve checked the safety on the gun and stood firing the Uzi wildly at the truck. Bullets riddled the F150, shattering glass and metal as the truck came to a stop.

Steve ran for the tractor trailer as the men took cover from the barrage of bullets. As he ran he continued to fire at the truck. The Uzi choked to a stop as Steve reached the cab. He tossed the gun to the ground as he frantically climbed back inside the cab.

The truck was still idling and ready to be his next weapon of choice. The F150 was not moving, as Steve slammed the rig into gear and hit the gas. Just as the front of the truck struck the F150, both passenger and driver began to fire.

As the front of the big rig began to crush the truck the firing stopped. Steve didn't stop until the front wheels had crushed the cab of the F150 flat. He put the truck in reverse and backed off the crushed truck. Surveying the damage, he felt he better give it one more good hit before he got out, to finish the job.

He drove past the F150 to let the trailer finish the job, less damage to the rig that way. Steve pulled up and began to back towards the F150. As he did in the mirrors he could see the passenger door begin to open. Steve pushed the gas harder as the trailer rear tires made impact. The screech of metal and glass braking was horrendous as the trailer pushed the truck for twenty feet before rolling up on top of the truck crushing it again flatter than before.

Steve got out of the truck and walked towards the F150. There was no movement. Both men were bloody and curled up in the front seats. Again he pulled Edgar's gun and put two rounds into each man for good measure.

As he walked away, Steve muttered. "The drug business is dangerous fellas!"

As Steve walked back to the truck he could see liquid draining from the front of the cab onto the ground.

"Shit!" Steve shouted as he began to run.

He shut the truck off and began to look at the damage. Bullet holes were obvious in the radiator at the front of the truck. Steve looked close, seeing two bullets that had hit the webbing of the radiator and now draining antifreeze onto the road.

"Shit!" He yelled out again. "I won't get very far like this."

Just then the phone rang in his pocket. He pulled it out. Sam was on the caller ID.

Steve stared up into the sky and flipped the phone open. "What's up Sam?"

Yelling. "Have you lost your fucking mind Steve? Your family is dead! Do you hear me? Dead!"

Steve hung up the phone dropping to his knees in the middle of the road. Tears began to fall down his face realizing what he had just done. The emotion, adrenalin and reality of everything that had just happen came crushing in. Down on all fours now crying out Heather's name then Max, crying out for God to help him. Crying out at what he may have just done.

Edgar woke up in the passenger seat dazed from the beating he had taken. Trying to figure out where he was and just what had happened. He reached for the door handle and began to climb out of the cab. Walking slowly, holding his forehead with one hand and his bloody nose with the other he saw Steve on all fours in the road.

"What the hell did you do?"

This snapped Steve out of his emotional breakdown and back to reality. He grabbed the 9mm from the street and stood wiping the tears from his face, pointing the gun at Edgar. Edgar stumbled to a stop putting his hands up in fear.

Steve took a breath and wiped his eyes again on his sleeve. "Don't you fucking move. I will shoot you in the face you piece of shit."

Edgar froze. "I'm not man. Don't shoot me, please. What the hell are you thinking?"

Steve stood there and then looked back down the road. Still no cars, still in the middle of nowhere. "I took control. That's what I'm thinking. No more of this bullshit. My family is probably dead by now. You give me one good reason why I shouldn't kill you just like these other guys?"

Edgar dropped to his knees. "Please man, don't kill me. I can help you. This is my country. I can help you hide."

Steve ran over to Edgar, who put his hands over his head in self-defense. Snatching Edgar to his feet, "Hide from what asshole? There's no one here. I killed your men and no one is coming. Carlos won't save you. He was probably going to kill you anyway when this was done you idiot!"

Steve let go, and Edgar fell to the ground, shaking in fear. He looked at the front of the truck still dripping antifreeze.

"I have to get the hell out of here. Somebody's gonna come down this road sooner or later and I need to be gone."

Steve reached down and grabbed Edgar's shirt pulling him back to his feet. Edgar held up a hand. "Wait. I do know some things that can help you. If you let me go I will tell you everything I know."

Steve looked at Edgar. "Go grab your shit out of that car and get in the truck. You tell me what you know and I will drop you off in Laredo before we cross the border."

Edgar paused. "Why don't I tell you now and I can just get back in my car and you can go wherever you want."

Steve aimed the gun back at Edgar. "Not a chance Chico. You're stuck with me for now. You fuck with me and I will tell Carlos what a help you have been feeding me information. You got it?"

Edgar headed for the car. Steve got in and started the engine. The temperature gauge was nearing the hot level but for now was holding. Steve headed for the building on the other side of the expressway.

As soon as they started moving Steve turned to Edgar. "Start talking."

Edgar blinked hard. "Okay. The guys following us were only going to the border. There are more guys on the American side. They are probably headed this way now because I was on the phone with Carlos as we got off the exit."

"Great. A busted ass truck and more guys on the way. Do you know where the GPS trackers are on this truck?"

"No. They handled all that down here. I doubt Carlos knows where they are. But he will be tracking us right now. He will have guys here soon. This is a bad plan man. You are going to get us both killed and your family and mine. You have no idea who you're fucking with dude."

"I don't care. If he so much as touches my wife or kid, I will not quit until his whole family is dead. I need to fix this truck, get rid of the GPS trackers and get hidden. He will keep my family alive as long as he doesn't know where the drugs are."

"I'm not so sure about that. Carlos is one crazy fucker. He has people everywhere. I bet you don't have more than ten minutes before someone is here. They will kill you and drive this truck back to Mexico and get a new driver."

Steve pointed the gun at Edgar. "Shut up. That's enough talking for now. Carlos will keep them alive until he has this truck back. You will help me or you will be dead too. Got it?"

Edgar nodded and was silent. The phone rang again.

Steve took a breath and answered. "Carlos we need to talk."

There was silence for a minute. "So, Steve, I see you have gotten Edgar to talk. It doesn't matter, he doesn't know anything. But I will kill him anyway for helping you, along with your wife and son. I thought you should say goodbye and tell your wife why she is about to die."

"Let's get something straight Carlos. If you don't let them go, you will never see these drugs again. If you so much as break a finger nail on my wife or son I will make it my life's work killing you, your family and anybody else that gets in my way."

Carlos laughed. "You think you're in control now don't you? You don't control shit! My men will have you out of that truck in a few minutes and execute you on the side of the road like the pig you are."

"What men Carlos? You mean the four guys you had following me that I just killed. Those guys are finished, just like your boy Edgar. This truck is mine now and so are the drugs. You want both of them back you better fucking keep my wife and kid alive."

Steve hung up the phone looking at Edgar. "There you happy? As far as he is concerned you're already dead. You want me to keep it that way you help me until I say so. Otherwise, I will make it true and dump your body in the bushes somewhere for the coyotes to eat. Got it?"

Edgar nodded. "I got it man but you're crazy. This truck is busted and he has other people on the way. It's a no win situation. Can't you see that?"

Steve pulled in to the parking lot of the old building. It looked like it had been vacant for years. "Is this your cell phone or did Carlos get it for you?"

Edgar looked confused. "Carlos gave it to me."

Steve shut the truck off and wrote down several phone numbers from the caller ID. He stripped the battery from the phone and threw it on the ground.

Edgar sat up in his seat. "What are you doing? That's the only way to get in touch with Carlos."

"He has GPS on that phone asshole. Did you really think he was only looking after me? He's watching you too. With that phone he can go online and tell his men exactly where you are, anywhere in the world. Now help me lift the cab up on this truck. It's time we disappeared completely."

They raised the cab up and Steve removed two other GPS tracker systems. Each were tucked away neatly in the engine compartment not to be seen. Steve had worked on enough diesels to know what wire belonged and what didn't. Spotting the battery connections was a lot easier than finding the devices. Find the wire the gives them power and trace it out. Within minutes the truck was clean.

Steve now turned his attention to the radiator and the two 9mm holes leaking antifreeze. Edgar stood there looking confused as usual. Steve told him to go find water or antifreeze or anything liquid if he could. Edgar stumbled off towards the building.

The building was one story brick and at one time had maybe been a grocery store of some kind. Windows along the front, now broken and partially boarded up, trash piled around the outside made it look like something straight out of an old western. The roof was still there but Steve could see light inside so it was clear this place had been abandoned for a while. Just like this exit. There was nothing here.

Steve looked at both holes and they were perfectly round about the size of his little finger. He would have to try and plug them with something to hold up under pressure. In the middle of nowhere finding tools to try and close the holes would be impossible.

Edgar was milling along the side of the building picking through the trash coming up with nothing. Steve looked around frantic trying to work out a solution. As he watched Edgar he was poking at the trash with a stick making no progress. As Steve watched it came to him. A stick! A stick the right size could be inserted into the hole. Wood is soft enough for the metal to cut into it and seal the hole. It wouldn't stop the leak completely but it would get them over the border and that is what Steve needed.

"Edgar, bring me that stick in your hand."

Edgar brought the stick exclaiming that he couldn't find any water at all. Steve held the stick up to the holes and broke pieces off until the stick fit perfectly. Steve picked up a rock and made the last few taps to secure the stick hard into place. Twisting it as hard as he could to get the radiator metal to cut into the soft wood of the stick. Quickly doing it again on the second hole and looking for any others. Now all he needed was a gallon of water to refill the radiator.

He made his way to the building ripping off one of the wood sections to gain access to the building. Edgar tagged along still rubbing his forehead from the hits Steve had given. Steve noticed and apologized feeling kind of bad now that there was a visible knot in the center of his forehead.

Once inside the building, there was not much to find. Whatever had been left behind had been picked through by vandals and the rest was just trash nobody wanted. Steve stood in the middle of the room and once again closed his eyes looking up to the ceiling. "God please, just a little help."

Edgar screeched from behind him. "I got it. I found something."

Steve turned to see Edgar picking up a milk jug with liquid about half way up. "Smell it! What is it?"

Edgar glared at Steve and handed the jug to him. "You smell it. Who knows what's in there. It could be piss for all I know."

Steve smiled as he took the lid off and smelled the liquid. Jerking back quick and making a face at Edgar. Wow that stinks, but it's not gas."

Edgar looked confused. "What does that mean?"

"You can't put gas in a radiator. But just about anything else will do if you don't care about the engine. You know what else will work?"

Edgar looked at Steve. "No, but I bet you're gonna tell me."

Steve smiled. "Piss will. You gotta pee?"

Edgar laughed. "Yeah, I guess I can."

"Okay let's get the hell out of here before we have company. We just need to get to the next exit or so and get some real water. The truck will take it, it's a tough old girl."

As they made their way out an old farm truck pulled up next to the rig. Steve stopped, holding his finger up to his lips at Edgar. Slowly he pulled the 9mm from his waist and checked the clip for bullets. One in the chamber and one in the clip.

An old man got out of the truck and started walking towards the truck. Steve waited until he was around the edge of the truck to make a run for it. As he came around the corner the old man was looking at the engine with both hands in his pockets. Steve aimed the 9mm at the man and yelled freeze.

The man didn't move his hands but slowly turned his head looking at Steve and then past him at Edgar. Steve yelled out, "Let me see your hands." The man still didn't move.

Edgar spoke in Spanish behind Steve telling the man to slowly raise his hands and be very still for the crazy American. The man slowly complied and held his hands up.

Steve turned quickly looking at Edgar. "What the hell does he want and why is he here?"

Edgar spoke again and the man pointed at the front of the truck. "Aqua?"

Steve understood aqua and said yes. The man pointed at his truck and turned to walk.

"What's he doing?" Steve spoke out.

Edgar laughed. "He is trying to help you. I think he has water in his truck. Steve began to lower the gun telling Edgar to go and see. The man pulled two gallons out of the back and handed them to Edgar. Steve stuck the pistol back in his waste and began to apologize to the man.

Edgar laughed. "He doesn't speak English man. He's just a kind old man trying to help a stranger."

"Tell him thank you and that we appreciate his help."

Steve pulled a twenty out of his pocket and tried to hand it to the man. He started shaking his head and waving off the money as he did. Speaking Spanish now quickly and just over a mumble. Steve looked at Edgar hoping for translation.

Edgar shook his head. "I am not sure. He said something about this store and being young. He lives near here. He saw us pull in. I didn't get the rest, something about the truck."

Steve shook his head. "We need to go."

Steve smiled and took the water pouring both gallons into the radiator and inspecting the wood plugs. Both looked to be holding for now and Steve capped the radiator and started pushing the truck cab back into place. With a loud clank the cab snapped back in position. Steve put both water jugs in the cab, noticing the cell phone lying on the ground where he had left it.

Steve bent down and picked up the phone and began to put it back together. "Edgar! I need you to distract this man for a minute. I need to hide something on his truck. Can you do that? Get him to tell you about the store and walk over there with him."

Edgar looked puzzled again, but began to ask the man what the story was about the store. They slowly walked over and began to look into the window. Steve turned and began to walk towards the man's truck. Snapping the battery back in the phone and turning the power back on.

In the back of the truck there were fencing tools and dirty rags scattered around. Steve silenced the phone and tucked it neatly under the rags. As he turned to head back, he for the first time looked back down the road towards the other cars. Black smoke was now rising up, soon to be visible for miles around. One of the cars Steve crushed must now be on fire and that was attention they didn't need. Steve began to run towards the truck.

He shouted loud for Edgar. "Edgar we have to go. We need to go right now. Tell the man thank you and to forget he ever saw us if he knows what's good for him."

Steve turned the key and cranked the rig and grinded it into first. Edgar began to climb in as Steve eased the clutch out and started moving.

Edgar got into his seat frantically. "What the hell is wrong with you?"

Steve pointed up the road as he pulled out of the parking lot heading for the expressway.

Edgar saw the smoke. "Oh shit!"

"Oh shit is right. That will get police attention in no time. We need to get the hell away from here."

"Why did you want me to distract that old man? What did you put in his truck?"

"Your cell phone. Carlos will send his guys to find that phone and it will lead them to an old farmer's house in the middle of nowhere."

"What if they kill him?"

Steve looked at Edgar and was quiet for a minute. "Shit! Why did you have to say that?"

Steve hit the brakes and turned the wheel to go back. Edgar started smiling. "You are a good guy aren't you Steve?"

"No I'm not, but I can't have this killer coming after this old man that just stopped to help a stranger."

They pulled back in to the parking lot and the old man was still standing by the store. Steve jumped out and ran to the man's truck. Pulled the phone out from under the rags and smashed it on the ground. Smiled at the old man and ran back to the truck. As they pulled away the man waved while shaking his head.

Steve got to the expressway and headed south. Edgar looked panicked at the wrong turn. "You're going the wrong way dude."

Steve laughed. "I am not crossing the border in Laredo. Carlos will be looking for the truck at the border now that I've removed all the GPS shit. We'll go back a ways and go further North up to the next town. I will cross there and then head towards New Orleans from the north side. Carlos will be expecting me to take a direct route from Laredo to New Orleans. I'll go through San Antonio and catch him by surprise. You gonna tell him any of that if you get the chance Edgar?"

"No man. He thinks I'm dead. If it's okay with you, I'll leave it that way and just disappear. I don't think any of this is worth it any more. I wish I was still waiting tables in Mexico City."

Steve nodded. "I bet you do. I want my life back too. I want my wife and kid back. You help me do that and I will be your friend for life."

I'll help you, but no thanks on the friend shit. You're a little bit crazy dude. I don't need any more crazy friends. That's how Carlos played it when we met. Talking about being friends and how he always took care of his friends. How I could make a lot of money being friends with him. My prints are all over that car back there thanks to you. I'll be wanted for murder by the time this is done. You ever seen the inside of a Mexican jail?"

Steve laughed. "No!"

"That shits not funny man. You go to jail for murder here it's bad. You're lucky if you get to eat."

"Nobody's going to jail. Just go live your life somewhere else and never look back. I don't think the Mexican police are going to do much investigating over four dead drug cartel guys."

Edgar sat back in his seat and put on his seat belt. "I hope not. I can't go to jail. I couldn't handle it."

"I can take you back to New Orleans. You can live there."

"What! I ain't living there. Carlos would find me and kill me for sure. Are you crazy?"

"When I'm done, Carlos won't be a problem."

Edgar looked at Steve. "Oh really? You gonna take care of it!"

Steve looked at Edgar. "Really! This shit will never happen again to another family."

Four exits later, Steve pulled into a truck stop and checked the makeshift plugs. They were leaking, but holding for now. Steve topped the radiator off with water and filled both water jugs full for the road. After topping off the truck with diesel they pulled around back out of sight to go in for some food.

Steve went to the counter and bought a prepaid cell phone with cash. A map of the border area with all border crossings marked. As they sat and ate, Steve planned the route and got the cell phone working. He still had Edgar's pistol on him but really needed to buy some more ammunition.

Steve hadn't seen any cars following him since they got back on the road and no one seem to be paying any attention. He would still be very careful to watch who pulled out when he did to be safe.

He still wanted to cross the border at rush hour, but he needed to change everything about Carlos's plan to be safe. For all he knew, Carlos may have guys at each border crossing by now. There were only three or four places in the area to cross. Getting across without being caught with the drugs was more important now than ever. If he was caught, Heather and Max would be dead for sure. This whole plan was risky, especially for his wife and kid.

They finished eating and headed for the border. It was an hour away and it was already five o'clock. He needed to make up some time.

He gave the truck a good once over and other than the holes in the radiator, things looked pretty good considering the truck had run over two cars earlier. Steve took out the knife he had bought inside and gently straightened out the fins of the grill to hide the bullet holes. Once he was done he looked at Edgar and smiled. "Good as new."

"Whatever cowboy. If we make it through this alive, it will be a miracle."

Steve laughed and climbed in the truck.

The place was busy, but no one left the parking lot as they did. So far they were in the clear.

CHAPTER 6

"A New Plan"

Once they were on the highway, they headed north towards Presidio, Steve pulled out the new phone and dialed Carlos's number. He looked over at Edgar, "Wish me luck."

Edgar shook his head. "You're gonna need more than luck my friend, you need a miracle."

Steve nodded yes as the phone rang. On the third ring Carlos answered. "Hello."

"Carlos, its Steve, are you ready to make a deal?"

"I'm talking to a dead man right now, that's the deal."

"No you're talking to a drug dealer and I need to trade this truckload of drugs I have for a woman and child. You still have my wife and kid?"

Steve heard Max scream and Heather yell out no. "You mean this little kid right here. Scream for your daddy kid."

There was silence and then the sound of a slap. Steve heard Max cry out and then Heather begging for him to not hurt Max.

Steve filled with rage. "Carlos, you piece of shit, if you hurt my kid or my wife, the drugs in this truck will be police property in minutes. Do you hear me?"

Carlos laughed into the phone. "I'm going to kill you. I am going to find you and kill you in front of your wife and kid. Then just for fun, I think I will fuck your wife and then kill your son in front of her. Wait, maybe I will fuck your wife in front of you and then kill them both while you watch, which way do you prefer?"

"You, listen to me. I'm not playing games here. You don't give a shit about my wife and kid. Let them go, and I will bring you the drugs. We're nobody to you. Let us go and go on with life. I will do the same and we can both just call this a bad experience."

Carlos screamed into the phone. "Where the fuck is my truck? You better get over the border in Laredo and hand it over. If you do that I just might make your death quick and painless."

Steve was quiet for a minute. "Carlos, let my wife and kid go and I will get the truck to New Orleans and hand it over. Give her this number and tell her to call me from a police station when she's safe. If I see your men anywhere near me I will drive this truck into the closes police station I can find. You hurt my wife and kid and not only will you not get your drugs back, but I swear to God, I will find you and kill you myself."

Carlos laughed loudly. "You got balls boy! What makes you think you can find me, you have no idea where to even start looking. I'm a ghost and you're a dead man. You just made sure that your wife and kid will die and when I find you, and I will find you Steve, you will die too."

"Carlos you won't find me and you're not going to kill anyone. Your drugs are worth way more than three lives and you know it. Now let's stop being angry and make a deal. Because if not, I will kill you and your family wherever they are no matter how long it takes. Do you understand me?"

The phone was silent and Steve's heart was pounding so hard he felt like he might have a heart attack.

Steve hung up the phone and looked at Edgar. "If that guy hurts my wife and kid, I will kill him and everybody he knows."

Edgar shook his head. "You don't know who you're dealing with dude. Carlos has got people everywhere. He has cops on the payroll in New Orleans. I saw two of them at that warehouse we were in before you came. You can't beat this guy. This game you're playing is going to get your wife and kid killed and you too eventually. I want to help you my friend but this is a suicide mission you're on. If you're smart and Carlos does give up your wife and kid, you better head for the hills too. Your life in New Orleans is over."

Steve sat back in the seat and quiet fell over the cab of the truck. His mind raced with regret, anger and question of what to do next. He still felt that Carlos would keep Heather and Max alive as long as he had the drugs. Once he lost control of this truck they were as good as dead. He had to stay hidden until they were safe.

As they neared Piedras Negras, Steve pulled off the highway and turned onto one of the main roads heading further north into Mexico.

Edgar looked at the map. "What are you doing? I thought we were crossing the border here?"

Steve shook his head. "I need to not be obvious. I know his men are waiting all along these border crossings. If they are and I cross, we're both dead. The more unpredictable I am, the safer we are."

"Look man, just let me out. I really don't want to die. I think I just want to get as far away from you as possible."

Steve laughed. "Come on Edgar, have a little faith in me. I won't get you killed, maybe wounded."

"Yeah, wounded in the head. Steve, these guys are crazy. There is no doubt in my mind that he has guys looking for us on both sides of the border. This ain't gonna end well for either of us. Seriously just pull over at the next exit and let me out."

Steve sighed. "Edgar I am just trying to save my wife and kid. This truck, is all I have. The minute he has control of it, they're dead. Hell, me too probably. Unfortunately for you, I'm not really sure I can trust you. Sorry Edgar but you're along for the ride."

"I won't tell. He thinks I'm dead. I'll disappear and that's that. I don't want anything to do with this anymore. I promise."

"Once my wife and kid are safe I will let you go. I promise. Until then, help me any way you can. Tell me anything you can remember about Carlos. His crew or the guys in Mexico we met. Anything you can think of."

Edgar began to tell Steve everything he knew, from the time he met Carlos until now. Steve had him make notes as they drove.

CHAPTER 7

Getting the Upper hand

Steve pulled out the cell phone and dialed Tyrone's number. On the second ring Tyrone answered.

"Who this?"

"Tyrone, its Steve."

"Man, where the hell you at. Mr. Jack is pissed. I told him you must be sick not to show up. You the most responsible dude I know man. Where you at?"

"Tyrone listen to me. I'm in trouble. Heather and Max are being held by this Mexican guy and I'm in Mexico in a truck full of drugs. If I don't make it home he's gonna kill them."

"Bull shit man. Where you at?"

"No bull shit Tyrone. This guy has Heather and Max and I'm riding in a truck full of drugs somewhere south of the border."

"Was it the white van?"

"Yeah. Look, you need to lay low for a few days. I don't want this guy to show up there and kill you guys. He's crazy and I don't know how this will turn out."

"What you want me to do? You want me to call the cops?"

"No. I don't know who I can trust. I may need you to go to my house and get Heather's car and meet me near Texas though. Would you do that for me?"

"Sho I will man. You my bro!"

"I need something else."

"Just name it man. What you need Steve?"

"I need some guns and ammunition. Serious guns. Like an Uzi. Can you get that?"

Tyrone was quiet. "Yeah man but you gonna get yo self killed trying to fight these dudes. You better go to the cops, man. I'm tellin you bro."

"Can you get the guns or not. Go to my house, when you get there, the key is under the planter on the back porch. In my room in the bottom drawer of the dresser there is about a thousand bucks inside a sock. Go get the money and Heather's car. Call me back on this number when you have everything. Okay?"

"A'ight man. I'll do it. You better call the FBI or something. These kind a dudes don't play."

Steve thought about what Tyrone said. "Hey you remember that cop who had the old bug we fixed?"

"Yeah I remember that guy. Pete, Paul, something like that. You want me to find his number?"

"It was Paul. Paul Thomas I think. Find his number, he gave us his cell. I will call him and talk it through. I still want you to go get the money and the guns. Find his number and call me back."

Tyrone said he would and the phone went dead. Steve looked over at Edgar, who was shaking his head. "What"

Edgar pointed at the side of the road. "Let me out man. You're gonna get yourself and your family killed. Now you will get that guy killed too. Carlos knows everything man. He is probably watching that garage, your house and everything else in your life. I want out."

Steve looked at Edgar and began to slow. The truck slowed to a stop in the emergency lane and Steve set the breaks. Edgar turned to get out and Steve grabbed his arm tight.

"Edgar listen to me. I could have killed you back there with the other guys. I'm begging you to just disappear. Don't tell Carlos anything. If you do I will find you and it won't be pretty. Are you gonna stay quiet?"

"Yeah, what would I tell him anyway? He knows you have the truck and he knows your still in Mexico somewhere. He thinks I'm dead Steve. That's probably the best thing for me. I will work my way to somewhere on the coast and stay there. Live my life and never trust a guy that says he can guarantee me big money for just a few days' work again. Good luck Steve, I hope it all works out for you and your family. I'm sorry I was ever involved."

Steve stuck out his hand and Edgar shook it. "Good luck Edgar. Watch your back."

"You too man. Stay alive."

With that Edgar was gone. Steve got out and checked the patches in the radiator. They were holding. He got back in and kept heading north. As he pulled away, he looked in the mirrors for Edgar, but there was no sign of him.

The phone rang and Steve answered waiting for Tyrone to give him Paul's number. Instead what he got was Carlos. In the background he could hear a woman crying. Steve grimaced at the sound.

"Steve, I am really losing my patience with you. This is the last time I will tell you. Tell me where you are and hand over the truck. If you don't, you're pretty wife is going to die, right now."

Steve took in a deep breath and stilled his insides before he spoke. "Carlos I know this truck load of drugs is all that's keeping them alive. If I give it up, they die. I don't want my wife or kid to get hurt. I just want my life back."

Carlos began screaming into the phone. "Bring me my fucking truck!"

Steve pulled the phone away from his ear. "I will Carlos, I promise. Just let them go and I will give up the truck. I don't want to be here and I want this to end. Please!"

As Steve said the word please, he felt weak. He felt like the victim he and his family were. Had he made a mistake taking a stand against Carlos? Would that mistake cost the life of his wife and son? There was silence on the other end of the phone.

Steve spoke again. "Carlos please, just let them go and let's end this."

A now calm Carlos spoke softly. "You have one hour. Find a truck stop and park the truck. Call me back and tell me where it is. You do that right now and I might let them go.

But you my friend are dead. I will find you no matter where you try and hide."

The phone went dead, as it did Steve dropped it in his lap. He felt the tears well in his eyes. Pressure built inside his chest. Fear, anger and anxiety flooded his body. Steve pounded on the steering wheel.

The phone began to ring again. Steve grabbed it up. This time it was Tyrone. "Hey man, I got that number for you."

Steve pulled himself together. "Give me the number."

Tyrone did. "Call me when you get Heathers car and the money. I am calling Paul now and I will call you back to let you know the plan. Don't leave New Orleans until we speak again. Just get the guns and wait for me to call."

"Ahight man. Stay alive bro."

Steve punched in the numbers. Three rings later, Paul answered. "Hello this is Paul."

"Paul this is Steve from Jack's garage. Do you remember me?"

A pause and then, "Yeah Steve. What can I do for you? I'm on patrol, can I call you back?"

"Paul, I'm in some trouble and I need help. I don't know who else to call."

"What kind of trouble? Did you get a ticket or something?"

"No, I am afraid it's much worse. My wife and kid have been kidnapped. Me too I guess."

"What? How are you calling me then?"

"I'm in Mexico in a truck full of drugs headed back to New Orleans. My wife and kid are there somewhere being held by a guy named Carlos. If I don't bring the drugs to him they die."

"Holy shit Steve. Are you telling me the truth? If this is some kind of joke…"

"I'm not joking man. The problem is, there are some cops involved and I don't know who to trust. You're the only cop I know. Can I trust you?"

"Yeah you can trust me, but this is FBI shit. Not New Orleans PD. Do you know where your wife and kid are being held?"

"No. They blindfolded us and took us down to a warehouse by the old airport. I was taken to the airport and sent to Mexico and she went somewhere else. They're gonna kill her Paul and my son too. Help me please."

Paul sighed heavy. "Shit Steve, I don't even know where to start. Did you see the cops involved?"

"No. Just the main guy and a few of his flunkies. There will be footage of me and one of the guys going through airport security but that won't help. The guy that was with me is a nobody. A hired babysitter to take me to Mexico and then follow me back. He didn't really know anything."

"Is he following you now?"

"No."

"What do you mean no? Did you kill him?"

"No, but the four other guys that were also following along.... Well let's just say the drug business is a dangerous business to be in. Bad shit happens to drug dealers. I have the truck now and no one is following me."

"Listen Steve, if all this is true you are talking about major drug trafficking. Kidnapping and homicide. This shit is over my head. I have a buddy that I went to the academy with. He's at the FBI now, we're still good friends. We need to get him involved right now. I can help locally but across international borders is out of my control."

"What's his number?"

"Yeah, hang on and let me get it. I will call him now and tell him everything. You call him in ten minutes and he will know what to do. Are you safe right now or are there people chasing you?"

"I'm safe but it can't last long. I know this guy has everyone looking for me and this truck. I'm sure there's already a price on my head."

"All right, give me ten minutes and then call this guy. His name is Blake Hardy. You with me Steve. Blake will know what to do."

Paul gave Steve the number and hung up. Steve again dropped the phone in his lap and gripped the steering wheel tight. He was in way over his head and hoped he had not just made things worse.

As he drove, all he could think about was Heather and Max. Would he ever see them again, had his stubbornness cost them their lives? Would it cost him his? Now he would unleash the FBI and lose all control. If Carlos found out it would definitely be the end. Ten minutes past and Steve picked up the phone. He was so scared, he couldn't dial the number. Fifteen minutes had past and the phone rang.

Steve didn't know the number. He answered. "Who is this?"

"Steve? This is Blake, Paul's friend. Don't hang up, I can help, I promise."

"Blake, no offense but contacting Paul was a mistake. I need to do this on my own. If I let you guys get involved my wife and kid will die for sure. You're probably tracing this call right now. Good bye."

Steve hung up. He began to hit the steering wheel with the palms of his hands. "Stupid me! Just call Carlos and negotiate a trade. This is suicide."

The phone rang again. It was Blake calling back. "Look I am serious. I shouldn't have called Paul."

Blake cut him off. "I am not tracing the call. I am walking down the street, it's after work and I'm going home. Steve I can help you get your wife and kid back. You're not the first guy this has happened too. We know about Carlos."

Steve paused at that. "You do?"

"We do. We didn't know him as Carlos but he uses a different name every time. Please let us help you. You need protection. You need help against this guy. He's pretty nasty."

"How many other guys have been in my position?"

"Three that we know of in the last year."

"How many got their families back?"

Blake was silent for a long minute. "None."

Steve's heart hit the floor. "Jesus!"

"Steve, listen to me. None of the other guys have managed to get the truck in their control like you. Only one made it out alive. You have got to let us help you and in turn we can get this guy."

"If you guys get involved he will see you following the truck and instantly kill my wife and kid."

"This ain't TV Steve. He will never see us. We can plant bugs on the truck and trailer and you that are undetectable. We can put agents on you so that if his men attack we can help."

"What about my wife and kid? You have to save them first."

"Steve, we don't know where they are, do you? How are you communicating with Carlos? By cell phone?"

"Yes. He just called me a few minutes ago and no I don't know where they are."

"Is it the same number each time?"

"Yeah. I only have the one number."

"Give me the number and we will trace it. I am already headed back to my office. What about you. Is this your cell phone, or one of the guys that was working with Carlos?"

"It's a prepaid. I ditched his guy's phone. I also went through the truck and found three GPS trackers."

"Ok good, here's what you need to do. Stop at the next place and ditch the phone you have. Get a new one. Keep your calls short to him. You and I will set up times to communicate. Keep the phone turned off with the battery out the rest of the time."

"What if he calls me? If he can't reach me then he may kill Heather assuming I have dumped the truck with the police. I think I should just take my chances with this phone."

"I'm sure he is tracing that cell already. Especially with cops on New Orleans PD in his pocket. You need to keep moving. Tell me where you are so I can get agents on the way."

Steve hesitated. "I'm scared Blake. This guy may have planes out looking for me right now. If he sees a bunch of black SUV's tagging along, my wife and kid are dead."

"Again, this ain't TV. He'll never see us coming. We can monitor the air and if he has a plane in the area we can let you know. If we have to take them out, they will never know what hit them. We also need to make sure that truck is clean. If we can trace his cell we can take him down but we need to make sure it's not a decoy. Right now we need to get you protected."

Steve gave them his location.

I will be in a plane in thirty minutes headed to you. I am sure there's a place we can land and get into a stealth chopper for surveillance. We are good at this Steve, you have to trust us. Steve you have to trust me. We will do everything we can to get you and your family to safety." I will call you in one hour to get a location again. Don't back track but be inconsistent in your travel. If you are headed north, get off and go west for twenty minutes. Then work your way back towards the border. I am in Houston so it won't take long."

"Blake one thing."

"Yeah Steve."

"I need some bullets. I am carrying a 9mm and all I have left is two rounds. I need to be able to fight my way out of whatever happens here."

Blake laughed. "I will see what I can do. Stay out of trouble. Get a new phone and get off the highway. Unpredictability is your best friend. You understand!"

"I do. I will call you with my new number. I'm gonna call Carlos one more time before I dump the phone. I will give him my demands and hang up. I'll make him let me talk to Heather one more time to make sure she and Max are still alive."

"Listen Steve; be careful with demands with this guy. He's radical and pissed. Your wife and kid mean nothing to him. The other victim's families were killed within hours of being kidnapped. It is a miracle that your wife and son are still alive. This truck must be loaded down with drugs. If he lets you talk to her call me right back. That will mean he is in the same place as she is and we can trace the cell and go in and get her. Timing is everything. Be careful what you say. One slip up and he will know you have help. Like you said earlier, if he knows that, they die."

"Great. Now I am scared to death. I've been really aggressive with this guy. I have hung up on him several times. He has been so mad at me that he just screamed into the phone."

"Then keep being that guy. He needs to think you're still out here alone and desperate. But most of all he needs to believe you are still bringing that truck to him. I will talk to you in one hour. Call my cell."

With that Steve hung up and began to dial Carlos.

Carlos answered on the first ring. "Steve. How good of you to call. I was just about to kill your son. Would you like to listen while I do it?"

"Carlos I told you. You hurt either one of them and this truck will become police evidence."

"Please my friend. Drive to the next police station in Mexico and turn it over. My drivers are already in the area and I will have my drugs within the hour. Either way, soon you will not be so brave. Soon my friend you will be dead, or you will wish you were dead."

"Let me talk to my wife please."

"She is busy right now with my dick in her mouth. I don't think she can talk and suck at the same time."

"Now I know you are lying Carlos, if she had your dick in her mouth she would bite it off. Now let me talk to her so we can arrange giving up this truck. I am tired of this game we're playing."

"Good. Now you're making sense. Just tell me where you are and my guys will be there in a few minutes."

Steve began to feel the panic rising up inside him. He checked the mirrors on both sides. Cars were all around him on the highway. Steve downshifted and bolted towards the exit coming up. One car began to swerve behind him and change lanes to match him.

"Carlos, I gotta go. I want to talk to my wife when I call back. If she and my son are not turned over to the police soon, your drugs go bye bye. Understand!"

Carlos was yelling into the phone as Steve threw it out the window. As he barely made the exit, a silver ford fell in behind him. Driver only as far as he could tell. One thing for sure though if this guy was Carlos's he wouldn't be alone for long.

Steve hit the gas and began accelerating up the ramp. The car stayed close behind. The light was red at the top of the ramp. Steve blew right through it getting back on the highway. The silver Ford followed. Cars swerved and horns blew as the truck and car blew through the light. As Steve cleared the intersection he hit the brakes hard. All the trailer wheels locked up and the truck slid to a stop. Steve jammed the rig into reverse and began backing up. The Ford did too.

Soon the Ford was entering back into the intersection and cars were still blowing and swerving to avoid wrecking into the crazy people running red lights and backing up on ramps. Steve reached for the 9mm readying himself to make the shots count.

The Ford turned into the traffic to avoid getting hit. Steve kept backing up fast. As the cab of the truck got even with the Ford Steve raised the 9mm and put both bullets through the windshield. The driver slumped over not moving. Steve slammed the truck back in first and hit the gas. Down the ramp he went going through the gears as fast as he could. So far there were no blue lights or followers. It had happened so fast that it would be minutes before people actually realized what had happened. Steve pushed the truck hard and started looking for the next exit. Now out of bullets and phoneless, he would need to get the hell out of there. Suddenly the thought of Blake helping sounded pretty good. He had to get a new phone and call Blake.

He had the truck up to 80 now and was constantly checking the mirrors. Steve knew someone would be giving a description of the truck to the police. It would just be a matter of minutes before there was a full on search happening. He had to get the hell off this highway. In a daring move, Steve hit the brakes and headed for the median. It was pretty flat and no one would be expecting him to be going south. There was the risk of going right back under the bridge he had just killed a man on, but the cops would be looking north. It was risky but it was unpredictable. Cars swerved as Steve rolled into the south bound lanes, but no one followed. He rolled through the gears bringing the truck up to a safe and quiet sixty-five. He pulled up beside another eighteen-wheeler to hide as they went under the bridge. He could see the blue lights on the bridge as he went under. "Please God, let me be invisible." Left his lips as he slowly passed the other truck. Steve watched the mirrors but no one came down the ramp. No cars or police.

Now it was time to find a phone and call Blake. It wouldn't be long before he needed help and probably in a big way. Whether it was Carlos's men or the cops, everyone was looking for him now. It had been thirty minutes since they talked but Steve wanted to hear Blake's voice now.

The next exit had nothing. Steve hesitated wanting to get off the highway but kept going. The next exit was eighteen kilometers away. Steve brought the truck up to eighty and tried to breathe. He realized he was sitting up in his seat, shoulders tense and jaw clenched. He forced his body to relax and sat back in the seat. Whatever happened over the next eighteen kilometers he would deal with? Hopefully it wouldn't be car loads of heavily armed drug dealers wanting to rip his eyelids off. Best case if the cops came he could call Blake from the police station and get them there before Carlos guys got there. He would just keep going until they forced him to stop.

As the kilometers rolled off no one came. At the next exit there was a decent size gas station and Steve pulled around back trying to hide the truck as much as possible. Steve went in and asked for phones, the man pointed to the back. Steve headed that way seeing the display in the corner.

Steve picked a phone and began to look for a charger. He bent down to see the chargers at the bottom of the rack. As he did he heard the door chime and the front door open with a creak. The man behind the counter greeted the customer in Spanish but nothing else was said. Steve felt his stomach turn. Was this the end? Would he stand only to catch a bullet in the face?

He stood to see one guy searching through the candy isle. He was by himself and didn't seem to be interested in anything but chocolate. Steve moved his way to the front and paid cash for the phone. He could activate it on the road by calling the service provider. Within a few minutes he was in the truck and back out on the road.

No one pulled out behind him and he was all alone on the two lane black top. He plugged the phone in and got it set up. It was time to call in the FBI.

CHAPTER 8

The FBI

After setting up the phone, Steve dialed the number for Blake. He answered on the first ring. "Steve?"

"Yeah. I had a little problem just now."

"What happen?"

"I noticed a car following me so I got off the expressway. He followed. I ran the light and he did too. I slammed on the breaks and started backing up pushing him back into the intersection. He turned to get out of the way and I put two in the windshield.

"Two bullets?"

"Yeah two bullets. These guys are trying to kill me Blake. I need help. Tell me what to do."

"Did you hit the guy?"

"I don't know for sure but I think so. He stopped following me and I doubled back and the cops were all over the bridge."

"What do you mean you doubled back?"

"I went a few miles and then crossed the median to head back south. You said unpredictability was my best friend. I am sure Carlos thinks I am headed north for the border."

"That's good, are you sure no one is following you now?"

"Pretty sure, I stopped and got this phone and nobody pulled off. Hell I don't know. Somebody could be laying back."

"Did you talk to your wife?"

"No. I think Carlos is with her but he wouldn't let me talk to her. I had to deal with the guy following me so I hung up. I'm afraid to call him back now. He's obviously tracking the phone."

"Okay, here's what you do. Use the phone when you need to. Take the battery out for the rest of the time. For you and I, turn the phone on at the half hour mark and at the top of the hour. Leave it on for five minutes and then shut it back down. He'll never get a good lock on you like that. You understand?"

"Yeah, I got it. How long before you get here?"

"We're in Del Rio now. They are fueling the chopper. We're getting clearance from the Mexican government to cross the border."

"What if he has someone on the inside?"

"The Mexican agency we are dealing with is solid. Are you still on fifty-seven headed south?"

"I am."

"Alright, get off the highway and head west. Set your GPS for Del Rio, once you're five or six miles away from the express way start the guidance to take you there. At the border crossing in Del Rio, we will have men working the gate to make sure you pass straight through without any problems. We're also watching the area now to see if anyone is lingering around, watching for you. If they are, we will take them down."

We'll intercept you somewhere out in the country. No real traffic and plenty of cover. We'll come in quiet and get you some help. Leave your phone on for now. I need to track you for the next twenty minutes so we can find you out there in the middle of nowhere. Carlos doesn't know this number yet, right?"

"No. I want to talk to my wife though. I am worried he may have hurt her or Max. Did you guys track his number?"

"We are, but so far it's leading us to a Costa Rica hub. He has to be running it through a switch located there. We'll send a local team, but it won't turn up anything. It may not even be a cell. This guy is no rookie. He knows how to stay off the radar. You'll probably have to flush this guy out for us with the drugs. If not, we'll wait for the drugs to lead us to him."

"Alright, I am off the expressway and headed west. No one is following so far. How will I know when you're close? You gonna spot light me or something?"

"No. We don't want to draw any attention. I will call you once we have a visual on you. We'll find a secluded area and get you stopped. Steve, you've done the right thing. I will do everything I can to get you and your family out of this alive. I will call you soon."

"What if someone shows up?"

"Just keep going like nothing's wrong. Make a turn or two to be sure they're following you for sure. If they are, when I call you, let me know. We will take care of it. He'll never know what hit him."

"Okay, hurry up. It's dark out here."

Blake let out a small laugh and hung up. Steve put the cell on the dash to make sure the signal was strong. There was nothing on this road. At five miles out he punched in Del Rio in the GPS. It calculated and directed the next right turn in twenty-two miles. Steve shifted in his seat taking a second to realize how tired he really was. He hadn't gotten much sleep in the last two days and when it got quiet he could feel it. He needed to sleep at some point. Maybe once the feds got there he could sleep for a few hours while they kept watch.

Fifteen minutes had past when the phone rang. Steve grabbed it and answered. "Hello, who is this?"

Blake laughed again. "Were you expecting someone besides me?"

"No, just tired. I hope you guys can stand guard and maybe let me get a few hours' sleep. It's been a long few days."

"I bet it has. We'll get through this. Hopefully we'll get through this with your family and Carlos behind bars. At the next road, make a right."

Steve looked out the window but couldn't see or hear anything. "Where are you?"

"About 500 hundred feet above you. What's wrong can't see me?"

"Hell, I can't see you or hear you."

"I know. We have some cool toys."

Steve made the right. "Okay, where to?"

"Go about five to six hundred yards and turn left onto the dirt road. There are some trees there that will give us some cover. You get shut down and dark and we will fly in and land near you. Once we talk a little you can climb in the sleeper and get some rest while we get to work on the truck."

"Sounds good. I guess I will meet you soon."

"Yes you will."

The phone went dead. Steve found the road and turned in. The trees were on his left as he made the turn. He got around behind them and pulled in a small clearing. He shut the truck off and got out. As everything got quiet he could hear the whisper of the helicopter but still couldn't see it. There were no lights at all. No flashing strobes like on most helicopters and planes. No sound like a normal helicopter. The wind began to blow all around him. Steve looked up to see the all black, sleek helicopter position itself between the truck and the trees. Even fifteen feet off the ground this thing was quieter than any helicopter he had ever seen. They touched down and the engine began to quiet. The side door opened and a tall lanky man stepped out. A flashlight came on and Blake walked over with his hand out.

Steve shook the man's hand and they walked towards the truck. "Steve I presume! I'm Blake. It's good to meet you."

Steve smiled. "I hope it's good to meet you too. I hope you guys can save my wife and kid for me."

"I hope we can do that too, and catch Carlos. What about you. Don't you want us to save you too?"

Steve laughed. "If it was just me in this deal, I wouldn't need you. I would take Carlos down all by myself."

"Well, let us take care of that. He is a bad guy with a lot of bad friends. It's a lot easier to take him down when you out number him 10 to 1. Thanks to you and this truck, we just might get that chance."

Four other men got out dressed in swat gear and heavily armed. They took positions at the truck and the road. One other man got out with a suit case full of surveillance equipment and headed for the truck.

Steve and Blake watched as the team acted in unison. Each man knew where he needed to be without communication. Steve was amazed that the men looked like they had rehearsed this a hundred times.

Steve looked at Blake. "Your team looks like they have done this before."

"They know what to do and they are good at it. We train our people very well. Now tell me how this got started and try and remember every detail."

Steve smiled. "I have been keeping a journal if you will. A lot going on, so I wrote it all down as I could. Come on, it's in the truck. I need to fill the radiator up with water anyway."

Blake looked puzzled. "What happen to the radiator?"

Steve shook his head. "It's in the journal."

Steve gave Blake the notebook and pulled out his water jugs. He raised the cab of the truck to fill the radiator. Blake stood flipping the pages speed reading as he went.

Steve spoke up. "Hey let me just tell you some of the things I am worried about and while I sleep you can read the rest."

Blake nodded. "Sounds fair, start at the beginning."

"Look, this thing has been crazy from the very beginning. I'm ex-army and I know how to take care of myself but when they took my wife and kid something snapped inside. I won't stop until Carlos is dead. If that's a problem with you, we need to stop now and you guys can leave."

Blake stood silent, looking at Steve's body language, studying his demeanor carefully. "You know I can't willingly let you kill Carlos. I am sworn to uphold the laws of our country. Committing murder is high up on the list of no no's."

"Well, then maybe you guys need to just plant your bugs and help me get across the border. Once this is over I will call you and tell you to go get the truck. What happens to Carlos will be a mystery. I assure though, he won't kidnap another family. Did you bring me the 9mm bullets I asked for?"

Blake crossed his arms. "Steve I know you want this guy dead. I would too if he took my wife and kid. We'll get him. But don't do something that will put you in jail for the rest of your life. Killing Carlos in cold blood will separate you from your wife for a long time. What good would that do?"

Steve stepped down from the cab. "Blake, Carlos is gonna die. Now I am pretty sure it will be self-defense on my part because he will be armed whenever I get to him. I know, and you know, that my life is over as long as he lives. No matter where you stick me and my family I will always be worried when I leave for work that he will find me, or that I will come home to a massacre. I'm not living that way and neither would you! I will get the bullets on my own if I have to."

Steve began to shut the cab as Blake walked towards the helicopter. Steve watched and shook his head. Thinking to himself that he should have just handled this on his own. Now the truck would be bugged and he wouldn't be able to find them like he did with Carlos's GPS trackers. Steve knew that Carlos would never be taken alive if they did find him. He was crazy as hell and would go out in a blaze of bullets before he ever went to jail. The fear was that Carlos would run back to Mexico and disappear with a new identity. If that happened, he would never forget that Steve made that happen. Carlos would have millions of dollars on his head and on Heather and Max too. It had to end with Carlos dead, no matter what.

Steve turned to see Blake standing beside him. "Shit dude! It's dark out here and you're sneaking up on me, are you crazy?"

Blake laughed and stuck out his hand. In it were two boxes of 9mm hollow point bullets. "Just make sure he has a gun in his hand without your finger prints when the cops get there okay. I may not be able to cover it up if I am not there."

Steve stared at the man for a long minute. "I will, thanks for reminding me."

Blake smiled. "Now why don't you get up in the cab and get some sleep. I can give you two hours and then we need to go. I will have a plan put together when you wake up."

Steve took the bullets, and climbed up in the truck. He opened one of the boxes and loaded the pistol, chambering one round and setting the safety. Steve pulled his overnight bag under his head for a pillow and pulled the picture of Heather and Max out. His flashlight put a blue tint to the photo and Steve wondered if they were okay. He decided to sleep first and then call as he was ready to move. Blake seemed to be pretty cool and he was feeling better about making the call.

His eyes got heavy and sleep came.

One and half hours had past when a knock came to the door. Steve sat up grabbing the 9mm tight. "Yeah."

"Steve it's time to go. We took out two guys at the border and a car has past by here twice. We think they may be close and we need to move."

Steve wiped his face with both hands, shaking off the sleep. He opened the door and stepped out. "So what's the plan?"

Blake smiled. "Kill them all!" And he slapped Steve on the arm.

"Well that's my plan but probably not yours."

"We have about ten hours of darkness left and about twelve hours to New Orleans. We want to get as far as we can in the dark. We can fly above you and never be seen as long as it's dark. Once daylight hits we will switch to surveillance by cars. Don't worry he will never know we're there. You have to call the shots once you get to New Orleans. We will be listening on this line now because I have cloned your phone. But how you deal with Carlos is up to you. Obviously you don't want to hand deliver this truck, he'll kill you on the spot if you do."

"I already told him to let my wife and kid go at a police station and I would call him once I knew they were safe and tell him where the truck was. I have to get them back safe first. I figure after I get them clear Carlos and I will have our time."

"I hope that happens, getting your wife and kid back safe. When it does I really hope you will just let us handle it from there. Carlos will never know what hit him. We have checked the amount of drugs in this truck and it's the largest shipment we've ever seen. Three quarters of that trailer is drugs, floor to ceiling. Its millions of dollars. That's the only reason you and your family are still alive. This is the mother lode for Carlos. He must want to retire."

"Then why do this much on one truck and take the risk of an unknown driver. Where I might get caught at the border with it."

"Maybe he has sleeper guys at the Laredo border that would have passed you through. We'll look into that for sure. Bottom line is, when you get to New Orleans, Carlos won't be far away. We need to hit him hard when he comes to check the truck. But listen don't do any kind of deal where he meets you with your wife and kid. He will kill them in front of you for sure. Make him set them free, as soon as they're in a police station or bus station or wherever we will pick them up. Once we have them it's all about the drugs then. You park the truck and make the call. We'll track the drugs from there and take him down hard."

"You guys don't even know what Carlos looks like. I know his voice; I know his face and will make sure he goes down with his drugs. You guys get my wife and kid in custody but I go with you until the end. That's the only way this is gonna go."

"Steve you know I can't take you with us. I will never get authorization."

"Then I guess I will drive the truck through his fucking front door. You guys sure better be there to back me up!"

"You mean clean you up, because if you do that you will be dead on the scene and Carlos will start hunting down your wife and kid."

"I don't know Blake; I can't let this guy go. It's personal."

ROAD RAGE

Blake grabbed Steve's arm slamming him against the truck. "My team has been chasing this guy for three years. I am not gonna have you fuck it up because it's personal. Now if you like I can put you into custody right now and we'll take possession of the truck right now. Your wife and kid will most likely die and you will to once you're released and go after him on your own. Don't be stupid. We're the FBI with unlimited resources. We have tracers on the truck, the cab and in the drugs. We'll catch this guy this time. Now be smart and play the deal to get your wife and kid back. We'll take Carlos down, you have my word."

Steve pushed Blake back off him and stood to his feet. He turned and got up in the truck. As he started to shut the door he looked down at Blake. "It will play out however it's going too. We'll just have to see won't we?"

Blake shook his head. "If you're gonna try and talk to your wife do it now. After you do, cut your phone off. Call me on the half hour. Go from here straight to the border. My guys are in the far right lane. If anybody gets on your tail, turn off and see if they follow. If they stick with you through three or four turns we will take them out. You good?"

With that Steve shut the door, cranked up the truck and began to back up.

Blake and his team scrambled for the chopper.

As Steve pulled out on the main road, he punched in Carlos's number and hit dial. The phone began to ring. On the third ring Carlos answered.

"Carlos, how are you?"

There was silence for a long minute. "Carlos are you there?"

Carlos spoke softly, "Steve I have never wanted to kill someone as much as I want to kill you."

"The feeling is mutual. I can't wait for us to meet again. Turn my wife and kid over to the cops and when I know they're safe we can arrange that meeting."

"I'll tell you what. How about you talk to your boy right now so that you know I have him here in front of me. Then I start cutting his fingers off one by one each hour until I have my drugs. How about that tough guy."

Steve pulled the phone away from his ear not wanting to think about that reality. On impulse he hung up and dropped the phone into the cup holder. Within seconds it rang. Steve looked at the number and it was Carlos. He didn't answer and the phone had no voicemail. He would have to risk it for now. Hoping and praying that if he wasn't the audience Carlos wouldn't hurt his son. The phone rang again and Steve didn't answer.

After five minutes, the phone quit ringing and Steve picked it up and called Blake.

"Yeah, what's up?"

"I just spoke to Carlos. It wasn't good Blake, I am not sure what to do."

"What did he say?"

"He told me if I didn't hand over this truck he was going to start cutting Max's fingers off one by one until I did."

There was silence on the phone for a long minute. "What the hell should I do Blake? I'm screwed either way. If I turn over this truck my wife and kid are dead for sure. If I don't, how the hell am I ever going to explain to my fingerless son why I didn't save him? What should I do?"

Blake was speechless. "I …..." "The sentence fell to silence.

"Blake, tell me what to do!"

"If you turn the truck over now Steve, your wife and kid will be dead five minutes after that. You have to keep going. Whatever happens now…… Is just gonna happen. I'm sorry. This guy is a real piece of shit. I'm surprised he hasn't already killed them. You have the drugs and the truck. He wants them both bad. This is a dangerous game you're playing with everyone's life. There are no winners here today Steve, just measured loss."

Steve hung up the phone and dropped it back in the cup holder. Tears began to run down his face. All he could think of, was little Max screaming in agony as Carlos cut into his finger. Heather surely fighting with all her might to save him, offering herself in his place for sure. This was the worst moment in his entire life.

He picked up the phone and dialed Carlos's number. It only rang once and immediately Steve's ears were filled with screaming. Max's screaming. Steve swerved in the road and slammed on the trucks breaks.

"No he yelled into the phone. Dear God no!"

Carlos's voice came back as the screams faded away. "See what you made me do. Your little boy is a tough kid. Your wife on the other hand is not so smart. If she tries to interfere with me again I may just have to kill her sooner than I would like. I really wanted to do that in front of you though Steve."

Steve's voice was low and the anger rose in it like a volcano. "What did you do to my son?"

"I told you. He will lose another finger in an hour if I don't have my truck back. How much pain will you make your wife and kid go through Steve?"

Speaking very slowly into the phone. "You listen to me mother fucker, if you don't turn them over to the cops right now I will set this truck on fire and your drugs will burn to the ground. I swear to God I will find you and kill you so slowly that you will lose your voice begging me for mercy."

"You do that my friend and I assure you the pain that your family will go through is not something you can imagine. Cross the border and my guys will pick you up. The only deal that I will make is that if you bring me the truck, yourself. I will trade your wife and kid for your life."

There was silence on the phone. "Do you understand what I am offering you?"

"Yeah, I got it. Don't touch my wife or kid again. Get my son some medical attention right now. I will cross the border in Del Rio by morning. Have your men there waiting. Here is the only way I'll do this. I drive the truck. Your men follow and I bring it straight to you. When I see my wife and kid drive away, I'll park the truck and I'm all yours."

Loudly into the phone. "No you listen to me asshole. You cross the border in Laredo as planned and one of my men will get in the truck with you. You will drive to where he tells you to. Once I know the drugs are clean and you haven't gotten any help, I will let them go. You fuck with me or my guys in any way and they die. You hear me asshole?"

"Yeah I hear you, but I gotta know their safe first. Nobody gets in the truck with me. Once your guys are following me, you let them go. She can call me from a police station and tell me goodbye. Come on Carlos give me something here. You've won. I am giving up my life for them. Do the right thing."

"Carlos laughed into the phone. "I tell you what Steve, you have the balls of a bull and I respect that. When you cross into New Orleans with my truck I will drop them both off at a nearby police station. I can always track them down later if you double cross me. At the city limits my guys take the truck. I know you're armed because you shot up my man a few hours ago. You'll get out and leave any guns in the truck. I will have the white van pick you up and my guys will take the truck. That's the deal."

"Done, I'll see you in New Orleans. Now get my kid medical attention."

"I can't wait. I have big plans for you my friend."

"I'm not your friend asshole!"

The phone went dead and Steve was exhausted. He had stopped the truck in the middle of the country road and was now standing on the double yellow line. There was nothing for miles in either direction. Steve looked up and knew that Blake was above him somewhere. Hovering above wondering what in the hell was wrong. He took a deep breath knowing that everything had just changed. He would probably die and Carlos would get his drugs. If he could just keep Heather and Max safe it would be worth it to him. He couldn't let anymore happen to them. If it meant his life, then he would give it.

The phone rang in his hand. He looked down and it was Blake's number. "Yeah man!"

"Want to tell me what the hell is going on down there. You're kind of a sitting duck."

"Yeah I know. We need to talk on the ground. The game has changed."

CHAPTER 9

A New Game

They met about three miles up the road in a small clearing. Blake's men took defensive positions around the truck while Blake and Steve talked. Steve explained that everything had changed and the bugs they had planted needed to come off the truck. Blake refused explaining that the bugs they had planted would not be detected. Steve told him that he would deliver the truck in New Orleans and be taken by Carlos's men. He would be unarmed and wanted to know just how Blake planned on rescuing him after he made sure Heather and Max were safe.

Blake's face was grim and he waived Steve to follow him over to the helicopter. When they got there, Blake opened a black case and took out a small capsule. He showed Steve how to engage it and instructed him to swallow it just before he was taken. The capsule would only last twenty-four hours in his stomach acid, so he needed to wait until the very last minute.

Steve put his hand on Blake's arm stopping him from talking. "Do you know how much damage they will do to me in Twenty-four hours? Seriously, you can't come in and get me quicker than that? What kind of outfit are you running?"

Blake smiled and lifted Steve's hand off his arm. "We will get you immediately but we want to make sure you are with Carlos when we do. We want him as much as you do. We'll be on you the whole time, either from the air or on the ground if not both. I promise, you'll never leave our sight."

Steve shook his head. "That never works out in the movies. There is always some secrete passage or car chase and the bad guy gets away. Don't let this son-of-a-bitch torture me to death."

"We won't. The minute you go inside a building or house, we'll move in for the kill. Carlos is gonna want you for himself. I am sure he will tell his guys not to touch you. He's pissed off and he won't wait to get his hands on you."

"Yeah, that's not a moment I am looking forward to. I am quite sure I will get greeted with several punches to the face."

Blake tightened his face into a painful look. "Yeah, that's gonna be a painful moment. You sure you want to do this. We could extract you as soon as we have Heather and Max. Might save you a lot of pain."

"No. I want this guy dead. I want to be in the room when it happens and watch him die for what he did. I can take the punches. I'm tough."

Blake held out the tiny glass cylinder and Steve opened his hand. Blake dropped it into his palm. "Remember, twenty-four hours is all this thing will last in your stomach. Hold off as long as you can before you swallow it."

"What if you can't find me in time? What do you do then?"

"Will find you. If he starts heading out of town with you then we will just have to track the drugs and get to him another way. We will rain hell down on wherever you are, I promise."

Steve closed his fist and turned for the truck. "Don't you fucking lose me Blake. I'll be pissed."

"Try and stay alive Steve, will be coming in hot! When the shit hits the fan you take cover. Lay flat on the ground, face down."

Steve turned with one parting comment. "Oh by the way, I am crossing the border in Laredo. Get your men there somehow and make sure it goes off without a hitch. I'd sure hate to have to shoot some innocent border guard and cause a scene when I cross. His rules not mine, but that tells me he has men there so be careful. You need to work that out with guards on duty that you can trust."

Steve waved a closed fisted hand in the air and took off in a jog for the truck. Blake cursed under his breath and pulled out his cell phone as he made a swirling motion over his head signaling the men to break for the helicopter.

Steve pulled back out onto the road and programed the GPS for Laredo Texas. It took about a minute to calculate and finally displayed a ten and half hour drive to reach the town. Steve exhaled hard and settled back in the driver's seat for the drive. In the distance behind him he could see the chopper lift off and begin to race across the sky. He stared into the night and began to think about Max and Heather. Wondering what kind of hell they were going through. He wondered what Heather had to do to stay alive. Steve realized he was gritting his teeth so hard that he might break one if he continued. He released his jaws and felt every muscle in his face spasm with the release of the tension. He would kill Carlos before this was over no matter what.

Heather opened her eyes as best she could. Her right eye was swollen so bad that it would barely open more than a slit. The left eye was open but almost completely red and blood shot. She was looking up at a concrete ceiling with peeling paint. She was lying on a dirty mattress on the ground. Her lip was shattered in two places and at least three of her teeth were loose from the repeated blows she took in the face from Carlos. As she sat up on the mattress her arm gave out from under her and she felt the intense pain starting in her wrist and moving up her arm.

Heather cried and fell back down, bringing her left arm up to her chest and holding it against herself to try and stop the pain. As she did she realized that her shirt was ripped almost completely off and even her bra was twisted in place.

Tears began to run down her face as she tried to pull herself back together. As she did she felt the lump at her feet and quickly sat up remembering that the last thing she had seen was Max being dragged by his hair out of the room. As she saw that and began to fight to save her son, one of Carlos's men had punched her square in the mouth. She fell back and started to get back up only to be kicked even harder right in the face. That was the last thing she remembered.

Even with the hurt arm, she scrambled to his side. His hair was matted from sweat and tears. His right hand was bandaged and heather could see the blood soaking through. She began to sob as she pulled him into her arms. Not even sure if he was alive at this point. She began to cry no as his limp body draped across her arms. Pulling his face towards hers desperately trying to see if he was breathing. Max's arms draped down over her lap with no life showing at all.

Heather tried to stand to get help when she felt Max begin to turn his head to look at her. She fell to her knees pulling him so tightly next to her she almost crushed his frail body. Max took in a deep breath opening his eyes fully now.

"Mom are you okay?"

Heather cried uncontrollably holding him close to her body, rocking back and forth while she kissed his forehead and face. All of her pain completely pushed to the back of her mind now that she knew Max was still alive. Max pulled his own arms up and around his mother's neck. Squeezing her as tightly as his weekend body would allow.

Maxed pulled his face away from the crazed kissing mother. "Are you okay mom?"

Heather nodded still not able to find her voice. The tears still streaming down her face at the relief that her son was alive.

Max smiled at that and squeezed her neck again. "Have you heard anything from Dad?"

Heather shook her head no.

That man was talking to him right before he cut off my finger. "Why isn't Dad giving him what he wants? I don't understand. Why hasn't he come for us yet?"

Heather crumbled inside hearing the doubt in his tiny voice. Such a brave little man he was in the face of danger. She took in a deep breath and found her voice once again. "Daddy hasn't given up Max. If he gives that man what he wants, he will kill us. Your dad knows that and I am sure he is figuring it out."

Max took his bandaged hand and wiped the tears off his mom's face. "I hope he figures it out soon, I don't have that many fingers left."

Heather let out a heavy sob again and wrapped her whole body around Max. "I won't let them hurt you again Max, I swear it. Your dad will be here soon. He has to be."

The lock on the door banged hard metal against metal. Heather stood forcing Max back into the corner of the room while she stood in front of him shielding him from whatever evil came through that door. No matter what, she would not let them take her son again.

The door opened and one of the men holding an Uzi stepped into the room. His eyes searching diligently everything that was going on. He motioned for Heather to step out from in front of Max so that he could see him. Heather stood her ground, holding Max in place defiant of the man's cold blooded stare.

As the man took a large angry step towards Heather she flinched in anticipation of the pain that would follow his attack.

Carlos stepped in behind him with a loud, "Stop!"

The man stopped immediately and began to back up out of Carlos's way. Carlos motioned for the man to leave the room. Heather's eyes darted from the man with the Uzi to Carlos and back. The guard took one last hard look at her and stepped through the doorway. Carlos opened his arms wide in a not understanding type of gesture. Tilting his head to the side as if he did not understand why Steve had made things so hard for them.

"Heather, your man has done this to you. Your son is missing a finger because of his arrogance. How far will he let this go?"

Heather began to shake her head no. "My husband did not do this to us. You did!"

The anger seething in her voice. "You chose us. You are the monster here not my husband."

Carlos's face flushed with anger and he took a short step towards her and then stopped as a grin ran across his face. An evil grin. "He is coming here now you know. He is trading his life for yours."

Heather gasped for air. "Please Carlos, why are you doing this to us. He is doing what you asked. Just let us go. We have suffered enough here. My husband is a good man. Please don't do this."

Carlos looked at Heather for a long minute and then stepped to the side in an attempt to see Max. Heather stepped as well to block the view.

Loudly she spoke. "No more! You will not touch my son again!"

Carlos's eyes shifted from Max back up slowly to Heather's. Looking closely at her torn shirt and battered face. "Mrs. Lawson you are a very strong woman. I admire that in you very much. Maybe I will keep you for myself once I kill your husband."

Heather stared back and straightened just slightly. "I don't think so!"

Carlos laughed. "You don't think what? That I am going to kill your husband or that I will keep you for myself if I want."

She smiled as much as she could. "Either. I think before this is done my husband will kill you with his bare hands. You have no idea who you are messing with."

Carlos thought about what she said. He didn't answer her but instead turned and walked towards the door. Speaking loudly in Spanish to the men outside the door, he went out and a guard stepped into the room and dropped a tray of food to the floor. Mac and cheese, milk in cartons and some sandwich meet bounced and hit the bare concrete.

Heather didn't move, still holding Max in place with one hand and tightly balling the other into a fist so hard that her nails dug into the palm of her hand. The man stepped through the door and slammed it hard. She heard the lock bang against the metal door and footsteps walking away from the room.

Heather collapsed down onto the mattress again and the tears began to flow. Max walked over and with his good hand picked up the milk and gave it to his mom. He then picked up the sandwich meet and the mac and cheese, placing them back on the tray and walked over to the mattress where his mom was.

Max sat beside her and smiled. "Dad will come soon. I know he will Mom. We have to be strong."

Heather pulled him in again for another long hug. Squeezing him so tightly that he could barely breathe. Max didn't fight it this time as he normally would, he let his mom squeeze and he squeezed back as hard as he could.

They ate every bit of what they had been given and were grateful. Heather knew that the plan was never to feed her and Max this long. The prepared sandwich's only lasted two days. From that point on, it looked like food that was gotten in some convenience store nearby. Heather knew that meant they were on borrowed time. Whatever Steve was saying to Carlos was keeping them alive longer than they were supposed to be. Heather smiled as she ate the cold mac and cheese knowing that no one could get under your skin like Steve Lawson could. Carlos had lost control of the situation and Heather prayed that Steve had some kind of plan. She didn't want to die in this place and was damn sure not going to let her son die in here.

She fell asleep that night holding Max tight against her. Tears continued to roll down her face long after Max had fallen asleep. Heather prayed and prayed long into the night. Asking God to spare their lives and protect them from this monster that had kidnapped their family. She asked God to protect Steve, wherever he was and to send him to kill Carlos very soon.

In the night in Mexico.

Steve stared into the night as he drove. He wanted to pick up the cell and call Carlos to see if he would let him talk to Heather. It had been a while since he had heard her voice and wanted to know if she was alright.

He dialed the number. Carlos answered on the third ring. "Steve, where are you?

"On my way to you."

"Good. I am ready for this to be over. Way too much drama, don't you think?"

Steve laughed. "Yeah, sure hasn't been your typical week for me."

There was a strange silence between the two men. Carlos spoke first. "So why did you call me?"

"I want to talk to my wife. I need to know she's okay."

Now Carlos laughed. "Your wife and boy are both just fine. You bring me my truck and I will let them go. I promise you can talk to her before I kill you."

"The deal is you turn them loose and I bring the truck. We need to be clear about that before I cross the border and your guys pick me up. Did we not agree to that earlier, my life for theirs."

Silence again on the line. "Yes Steve, we did. In the morning I will take your wife and son to the police station and set them free but only after you cross the border and my guys are following you. I would be crazy to do it any other way. That's the deal."

Steve thought about the plan and how many ways it could backfire, how fast things could go bad and Heather and Max still lose their lives in this. It was a mess and Steve knew it.

"Carlos I'm not crossing the border until I know for sure they're safe. You know once I am on the states side of the border you have control. Just let them go now. Give Heather this number and tell her to call me. Once she does I will cross the border and the truck is yours. I'm tired Carlos. I've had about two hours sleep in the last few days and I am tired."

There was silence on the line. "Carlos are you still there?"

"I'm here. I am trying to keep myself from going into that room and killing both of them right now. Who the fuck do you think you are telling me what you want! You're tired! Who gives a shit if you're tired. I want my fucking drugs back right now. Bring me my truck or I swear to God I will kill your wife and throw her body off a bridge into the morning rush hour traffic. Do you fucking hear me asshole?"

Steve held the phone away from his ear as Carlos shouted. "Carlos stop yelling and let's talk. I'm bringing you the truck right now. I'm not playing any games with you, I'm headed to Laredo as we speak. I'm doing what you asked, but I have to know that my wife and kid are safe. Do you fucking understand me?"

ROAD RAGE

Carlos slammed the phone down on the desk and stormed off to get Heather. Steve panicked at the silence and called out to Carlos. He could hear the man screaming in the background so he knew he had not hung up the phone. Would this be an opportunity for him to hear a conversation that might help him figure out where they were? Steve hung on the silence now trying to make out any sound he heard.

The next sound was not what he wanted. Heather was screaming as she came into the room. Carlos was dragging her by her hair punching at her every time her weight slowed his pace. Carlos grabbed up the phone and slammed it to her now bleeding face.

"Talk to him you bitch and make it good. It will be the last conversation you ever have!"

Steve's breathe drew in sharply as he heard Heather whimper from the pain. "Baby is that you?"

Heather's voice cracked as she answered. "Steve, oh my God where are you? Give him what he wants so this will all be over."

"I am baby I am. I love you so much!"

"I love you too. Max and I are okay for the most part. Are you okay?"

Steve began to cry and his voice was cracking now as well. "I'm, I'm coming for you right now. He is going to let you and Max go, I made the deal."

Heather braced against the desk as she realized what Steve had just said. "What deal?"

Carlos snatched the phone away from her as Steve was speaking. "I think that's enough. She doesn't need to know our business. That's enough, your wife and kid are just fine, now bring me my truck."

Steve took a deep breath. "The deal is you take her before I cross the border and let her and Max go. Once I know she is safe the truck is yours. You have my word on the life of my wife and child. I will give up I promise. Now let them go, please I am begging you Carlos. Just let them go and I will go along I swear."

Carlos calmed himself. My men will be on the Mexico side of the border. They will follow you across. When they call me I will let them go. You so much as change lanes after that and I will find them and kill them so badly that no one will recognize their bodies. Do you fucking hear me?"

"I got it Carlos. I will do everything you ask once they are safe, I promise."

Carlos held the phone to Heather again. "Say goodbye to your hero!"

Heather sobbed into the phone. "I love you Steve, I love you so much."

Steve felt the pain through his whole body. "I love you to sweetheart. You take Max and get as far away as you can from New Orleans."

The phone was dead and Heather was gone. Steve dropped the phone back into his lap and slammed his head against the headrest. Why had this happened to his family? What in the hell had caused this maniac to pick his family? What had he done so wrong to deserve this? He screamed up to God to fix this for him. To save his wife and child from the grip of this maniac. To save his own life from what would surely be an awful death if Carlos got his hands on him. So many things could go wrong with the plan. Letting himself be captured was a bad idea either way but he had no choice in the way it was going down. It's what had to be done to save his wife and child. He knew he would do it gladly for their safety.

The GPS showed just under three hours to the border now and Steve settled in for the long drive. He couldn't see Blake at all above but knew he was there somewhere. He would call him about an hour out and maybe have one more rendezvous before he crossed. Steve figured Carlos's guys would be within a mile of the border to make sure they didn't miss when he came through. Steve really hoped Blake had managed to get everything fixed at the border for him. He sure didn't need some border guard tearing the truck apart at this point. He felt like driving through the border at seventy-five miles an hour and watching everybody dive out of his way. Once he knew Heather was safe, nothing after that would matter.

CHAPTER 10

The Release

Steve shook his head to fend off the sleep that had been chasing him for the last several hours. It was almost five am now and he would be at the border in less than an hour. He needed fuel and he needed to call Blake. Carlos's men could be anywhere at this point and he had to play it safe. He had to know that Blake had everything arranged before he got too close to that border.

An exit was just up ahead and Steve changed lanes to make the stop. He watched every car around him to see if anyone followed. No one did and he took the exit. Steve pulled into the truck stop and pulled into the diesel pump area. As he began to pump the fuel he pulled out the phone and called Blake.

The phone rang five times before a sleepy Blake answered. "Hello... what time is it?"

Steve was pissed. "What time is it? What the Hell Blake, why are you sleeping?"

Blake slowly laughed. "Well dude I'm sleeping so that when you need me I'm ready. Don't be pissed. I'm not the one driving a truck into my own death, you are. I can sleep for a few hours right now. What's up?"

Steve laughed now. "What's up? Are you fucking serious right now? I'm about to cross the border in forty-five minutes and I need to know everything is okay. Is it?"

"It is my friend. We have people all over it. Carlos has two guards that we know of in place as well."

"Before the border?"

"No, working the border crossing. Two guards called in sick this morning and two new guards came in for them from the union. We know them both to be dirty. They are for sure Carlos's men. Carlos should tell you to take the center lane. If he does then we will have confirmed that they are his men."

"What about other cars hanging around the border. Have you seen anyone?"

There's a rest area about two miles before the border. There are two cars there that have been there for the last hour. Four men total. We have people on both sides as well watching the last two miles of highway to pick up any predators. We will let you know if they move as you pass. Hang in there buddy, this thing is about to get a little crazy. I sure hope you know what you're doing."

"I'm doing what I have to. I'm gonna make the call to Carlos now and make the final deal. Before I cross the border he is to take Heather and Max to some police station in New Orleans, and give her my number. I need you to get her as soon as she hits that station. She and Max need to disappear do you hear me. I have to know they're safe."

"They will be. I have a chopper standing by and ten men on the road watching every station in New Orleans. We'll get her and Max out of there immediately."

"Alright then, I'm going to make the call. Get awake, it's time to party!"

"Stay safe and remember we're with you the whole time. If you want to abort this plan just make the call."

"I want Carlos, I am going all the way with this truck right to his front door."

"Remember this guy's not stupid. When we swoop in and grab Heather and Max he's going to know that you've had help. He's gonna know that we've bugged that truck."

"I'll tell him that I am calling the FBI to report a kidnapping after he drops her off. I don't want this guy to get away. I want this son-of-a -bitch to die. I want to watch the life leave his body. I hate this!"

"Look, we have people on the NOPD that we trust at every station. When she gets delivered we will get our man to put her and Max in a car and run like hell. We'll be in the air and can make sure that he gets away clean. The ground units will run interference if they need to. We'll get her and Max away safe without too much show. You stay the course and play along. When she calls you, you tell her that a cop is going to say, "I am the safe way." When he does she and Max need to leave with him and him only. Each Captain at the precinct will know the deal. I'll start making calls now, okay?"

"Okay that sounds pretty good. Just protect them Blake. I don't want this to be for nothing."

"It won't be. You keep your head and be ready for anything. There is no telling what Carlos's men will do once they have you back. They may force you off the road immediately or just kill you right away. This is a dangerous deal you're driving into."

"I know it is. I'm not stopping until I get to New Orleans. Carlos may think he is getting back control but this truck is big and heavy. I will stop when I am ready."

"Go get em tiger. I'll call you back to let you know we are set at the stations. Don't worry about Heather and Max. You keep that tracker I gave you close. If this shit goes south, you down that thing and keep your cool. When it activates, I'll know you're under their control."

"How long does that take from the time I swallow it until it is active?"

"About five minutes."

"Alright Blake, good luck."

"Good luck to you too my friend. I'll see you on the other side."

Steve laughed. "Here on earth or in the next life either way."

The phone went dead as Blake hung up. Steve finished pumping the fuel and noticed a car pull in the lot across from him. One man behind the wheel but he didn't get out to get gas or anything. He sat watching Steve. Steve knew that his time alone was gone. Soon there would be more and he would have to be careful about any further phone calls to Blake.

Steve paid the attendant and got back in the truck. He was going to go in and clean up a little but now he wanted to be moving. No leaving the truck now. Steve pulled out back on the highway and noticed the car fell in behind him. Although the man was keeping his distance Steve knew he was Carlos's boy. Steve picked up the phone and dialed Carlos's number.

After several rings he answered. "Well Steve, how good of you to call so early in the morning. Where are you?"

"You know where I am. Your man just picked me up at the truck stop and you know it. Don't you?"

"Ah Steve you are very smart for a mechanic. I do know where you are and I can take you at any time now. You keep heading for that border and soon our business will be finished."

"Well, as we discussed you take my wife and kid right now to the police and I won't kill your man back there like I did the others. You do it or I will burn this truck to the ground where I sit and disappear forever with only one goal in life."

"And what's that?"

"Killing you and your whole family Carlos. Now we made a deal. You need to keep your end of the bargain or I'm gone and I will take your man with me."

"Fine! I will have them taken right now. But trust me it won't do you any good. I also will only have one goal once I kill you and that will be to kill your wife and kid. So I guess we're alike in many ways aren't we Steve?"

"We're nothing alike Carlos!" I wasn't a murderer before now. You made me this way. You started this not me."

"You just keep coming to the border. When you get there you stay in the center lane and there will be no problems. Your wife will call you from the police station."

"When I know she is safe I will cross the border but here's the deal. I drive the truck alone all the way to New Orleans. Your guys can follow and I will not cause any more problems, I promise."

"That is not the deal! When you cross the border there is a rest stop about three miles from the border. You will pull in and one of my guys will ride with you. You will give your gun to the border guard when you cross. Do you understand me because if you don't, I will kill your wife and kid right now."

"Fine. I understand. I won't fight you once I know they're safe. You know I will have to stop at the weigh stations between the border and New Orleans right. Your man better be a CDL driver or he can't be in the truck."

"He will have the proper documentation. This is not our first time."

"I'm waiting on my wife's call."

"Goodbye Steve, I look forward to seeing you again in person."

"So do I Carlos. I'm going to enjoy killing you when I get the chance."

"You won't get that chance my friend. But I will, and I promise it will be so much fun for me. Not for you though. Not for you my friend."

"Just keep your end of the deal Carlos and you can do whatever you want with me. My wife and kid mean that much to me."

"See you in a few hours."

The phone went dead. Steve dialed Blake's number but kept the phone in his lap out of sight. Through the speaker Blake answered. "What's the deal?"

"He is taking them now. I have a guy on me in a red Ford mustang. He's alone but I have to think he won't be for long."

"What about the border. Did he tell you center lane?"

"He sure did. I'm to give my gun to the guard and at the rest stop after the border I will be taking on a passenger. This shit is either gonna go down right there or they will take me all the way."

Blake paused a minute "Are you sure you want to do this this way. As soon as we have your wife and kid we can pull you out of this and be done with it. We'll follow the drugs and eventually get Carlos Steve, you have to trust me. You don't have to put your life at risk man. Just walk away and let us do our job."

Steve paused for a minute. "You'll never catch Carlos if I don't take this all the way to the end. He wants to kill me personally and I know his guys are not going to do it for him. He hates me with a passion for what I have done to him. It's the only way to get to Carlos and you know it Blake. Now do your job and stay close okay?"

"I will, but this whole thing has me nervous. For Carlos to give up your wife and kid so easily makes no sense for what we know about this guy and I have to think he has something else planned."

"I hope not but if he does I am going to have no mercy on his men out here I tell you right now. I will kill every one of these guys with my bare hands."

"You better leave that up to us if it comes to that. You sure don't want to end in prison at the end of all of this do you?"

"You won't let that happen to me. It'll go down as self-defense or something else you come up with for the authorities. I trust you Blake. Keep your eyes open."

"Will do man, keep safe and keep awake. Call me when Heather makes the call. My guy will call as well but call me anyway."

The phone was quit and Steve checked the review mirrors again. The Mustang was there and a Chevy pickup had fallen in close behind the Mustang. Steve shook his head, not liking the way this was turning out. He had not heard anything from Heather yet and he was now twenty minutes from the border. He picked up his phone and called Carlos.

Carlos didn't answer and Steve tried again. Again no answer. Steve sat the phone down in the console and focused on the car and truck following him very closely now. Steve's heart began to pound thinking the deal was about to get ugly when the phone rang.

Steve jumping at the sound. "Hello!"

"Steve!" Heathers voice came over the phone.

"Oh my God baby tell me you are at a police station."

"I am, but Steve they kept Max. Why did they keep Max?"

"Jesus Heather that was not the deal I made with him. There will be a cop that comes up and tells you he is the safe way. You leave with him right away. Don't do anything else do you hear me. Don't go pee, don't leave a statement or anything. You leave with that cop only, no one else."

"Okay Steve but what about Max. What are they going to do to him?"

"Nothing I promise. You go with the cop and I will get Max back."

Steve dropped the phone and checked the mirrors for the Mustang and the truck. Both were on his left fifteen feet back from the end of the trailer. Steve slammed on the brakes and cut hard to the left. Crashing into the Mustang's front end and crushing the car under the rear tires. The Chevy swerved off into the median and into oncoming traffic.

Steve kept control and pulled the 9mm from beside the seat. The Chevy came back across the median but kept his distance from Steve. Steve down shifted and headed for the approaching exit ramp. The Chevy followed. Steve's phone rang again. This time it was Carlos.

"Where is my son mother fucker?"

"Steve why did you just run over my man. We have a deal."

"The deal was my wife and son. Not just my wife. Did you not understand the deal?"

"Steve listen to me, if I gave you your wife and son back you and I both know I would never see that truck again. Not only that but you have FBI bugs on that truck that I want gone before you bring it back to me do you understand me."

"What. What are you talking about?"

"I have a lot of friends Steve, in a lot of places. When the FBI asks for access to Mexican air space for one of their choppers I know about it. Now I gave you half of the deal. You tell your friends to debug that truck and you cross the border or I promise your son won't have any fingers left when I am done."

The phone went dead. Steve pounded the steering wheel screaming at the top of his lungs. He looked for the Chevy in the mirror and found him hanging with him but staying very far back. Steve picked up the phone and called Blake.

Blake answered immediately. "What's up, we saw you run over that car. The driver isn't dead but he's in custody so we will see what he knows."

Steve cut him off. "Listen to me Blake. You guys have to take the bugs off this truck. He knows you guys are helping me and he only released Heather not Max. I am pulling over in the first open area I see. There's a truck following me so let's do this in plain sight so he can report it back to Carlos."

"This a bad idea. This deal is gonna get away from you at the end and I am not sure we will be able to get you out. These guys are going to be all over you when you cross that border in that truck. If we take the bugs off, you and the truck may disappear forever. And the chances of you getting Max back alive, goes to zero if you give up the drugs. You need to think this through man."

Steve came up the ramp silent. "Just land and get the bugs off the truck and trailer. I have the tracker for me and I will swallow it when I cross the border."

Blake was Silent for a long moment, then spoke one word. "Okay!"

Steve pulled the truck into a large gas station and into the back lot that was large and clear. The pickup pulled in as well but held at the corner of the lot so that he could escape if needed but still see the rig and Steve as he climbed out. Steve looked over and the man had a cell phone to his ear. Steve knew it was Carlos on the other end of that call.

The chopper landed to the right of the rig in the grass surrounding the station. Blake and his men poured out all looking towards the pickup. The man closed the phone and backed the truck up as far as he could without backing into the road. One of Blake's men took a covered position and trained his very mean looking AR15 right at the man in the pickup. Only two words were spoken. "Got him"

Blake walked up to Steve. "Alright Steve, we'll do whatever you want here but I am begging you to let us leave at least one tracker on the trailer of this truck. They will not detect it and I promise we will not act on it until you and Max are safe. Otherwise dude, I'm afraid all of this will be for nothing and you and Max will both end up dead."

"Blake I'm at the end of my rope with this guy. If I don't go along he will kill Max or worse cut more of his fingers off. I can't do it anymore. I have to just give up and do what he says if Max has any chance. Do you understand that? Now get the fucking bugs off the truck so I can go."

Blake turned to his men and nodded his head. Three of the men went straight to the truck and started removing bugs. Steve turned and walked out into the parking lot trying to clear his head of all that was happening. He pulled the phone from his pocket and dialed Carlos.

Carlos answered immediately. "Well Steve, I am glad to hear you are following my rules for a change. Now I have a few more."

Steve stayed silent.

"Are you there?"

"What are the rules Carlos? I want my son released and I will do whatever you want from here on."

Carlos drew in a breath as the anger built inside him. "You arrogant prick how dare you tell me what you will do. I am sick of you thinking you're in control of me!"

Carlos was now just below screaming into the phone. "Carlos I'm sorry but if you were in my shoes you would have done the same thing to protect your family. I just want this to be over. I want my wife and kid and for you to go away with your drugs. I will start a new life and never come after you I swear. Just let my son go and I will do whatever you say."

Steve fell to his knees in defeat giving into Carlos. "You should have done this in the beginning my friend and we wouldn't have these problems. It was a simple deal, 3 days and you would have been done with your wife and kid safely back in your arms."

Steve shook his head. "I don't think so Carlos. You always kill the families and the driver. The FBI knows all about you and how you operate. They told me."

"They don't know anything about me. I am a ghost to them! They search around like idiots when I am right in their face. They're a joke and you are a dead man for bringing this down on me."

"What about my son?"

"You get rid of the FBI. My contacts will tell me when they leave the air space. You pick up my driver across the border and you do exactly as you are told all the way to New Orleans. If I so much as smell a cop your son dies one finger at a time do hear me!"

"Yes. If I do this will you let my son go?"

"Bring me my truck with no police and I will let him go."

The phone went dead and Steve dropped his arms down by his side. Tears began to fill his eyes, knowing he would never see Max alive again. Doubting that he would ever see

Heather again. Blake walked slowly towards the man trying to give him some time.

Ten feet away Blake stopped. "Steve we need talk if you're okay."

Steve wiped his eyes and stood up. "Listen Blake, you guys have to go away. I have the bug you gave me. I'm going to New Orleans alone. Just set up there and wait. When the truck stops you need to give me a little bit to make sure Max is safe. After he surfaces wherever then you come in and get me. Hopefully Carlos won't kill me by then. Will the tracker stop working if I'm dead?"

"No, it will work until the acid eats through. What's the deal with Max, did you guys negotiate his release or what?"

"No. He told me he would kill him by cutting off one finger at a time unless I got rid of the bugs and you guys and went along with the plan. He knows you're helping me. Someone on the Mexico side told him that the FBI requested air space. You need to clean that up when this is done."

"I will. Steve this is a suicide mission for you and Max. Carlos is not gonna give him up or you. Hell, even Heather will be in danger for the rest of her life if we don't get this guy. No one has ever seen him and gotten away. This is not going to end well."

Steve starting walking away. "Get done, I need to go."

Blake stood there shaking his head. "Shit! Steve wait. We'll do it your way but I'm not okay with you just giving up. This guy's a killer and it won't change. Whatever he's telling you he will do, is a lie. Your walking into a death trap and what you're doing will not save Max. You need to think about that."

"I'll be in the truck, let me know when you're done."

Blake stopped and watch as Steve walked to the truck and got into the cab. He pulled his cell out and called into the SAC to report in. He informed him that the mission had reached critical failure not only for the witness but for the truck as well. The man listened with no interruptions for fifteen minutes while Blake talked. Blake asked about Steve's wife and if she was in protective custody. He wanted to be able to give Steve some good news.

Quietly the man spoke. "Agent Hardy this is the closest we have gotten to Carlos and we're not letting this truck go because your witness is giving up."

"But Sir,"

The man cut him off. "Agent, listen to me right now. You will leave one bug on the drugs and one on the trailer and I don't care about Mr. Lawson or his son. They are collateral damage. Our job has always been and always will be to take down this fucking maniac that fills our streets with drugs. Are we clear?"

"But..."

"Are we clear agent Hardy or do I need to relieve you of your position with the Bureau?"

"Yes sir, we're clear. What about his wife sir is she safe?"

"Yes. We have safely put her away and you can inform Mr. Lawson that she will never be hurt by Carlos. We'll see to it that she is put into the witness relocation program when this thing is over. Do not get emotionally involved agent Hardy. Your mission here is the drugs and saving lives second. I'm sorry it's that way but we're fighting a much bigger picture here and you know that. Stay focused on the better outcome for everyone not just Steve Lawson. Are we clear?"

"Yes sir, I'm clear. I will report back in when we hit New Orleans."

"Good. I want eyes on the trackers here at the main office asap."

"Yes sir."

The phone went dead and Blake slid it back into his pocket as one of his men approached.

"What's up Ron?"

"You okay sir?"

"Yeah just on the phone with the SAC."

"We're almost done. We have a few in the cab to get and we are good to go here."

"Ron listen, the SAC wants two bugs to stay. One on the drugs and one on the trailer. Be quiet about it and make damn sure they can't be found. This guy is walking into a death trap and we can't let the drugs get away from us. You understand what I'm saying?"

"I do sir. I'll take care of it myself right now."

Blake nodded. "Good man."

Blake walked to the cab and stood where Steve couldn't see Ron slipping back into the trailer for the bug for the drugs. Steve was laying back in his seat with his eyes closed. Blake shook his shoulder gently.

Steve opened his eyes and looked at Blake. "You all done?"

"Not quite but soon. Listen, I just talked to my SAC and he wanted you to know that Heather is safe in protective custody."

Steve sat up with that. "Oh thank God. Where are they taking her?"

Blake shook his head. "I don't know and I wouldn't tell you if I did. You are walking into a shit storm and I am begging you to do this another way."

Steve laughed. "What other way Blake? He has my son. If I don't do what he wants he will kill him for sure. The only chance I have is to go there with the drugs and beg him to do the right thing. I'm dead either way at this point. If he doesn't get these drugs he will never stop hunting me. Hell Blake he knows what the fucking FBI is doing in Mexico what makes you think he won't know where you're putting Heather right now? This guy is a monster and I have really pissed him off. I don't know what I was thinking. I should have just driven the truck and kept my mouth shut."

"Yeah, and your family would be dead right now. Wake the fuck up! He doesn't let anyone live Steve, and the fact that we have Heather right now is a miracle. So try to not be so hard on yourself. We have never gotten this close to him and that is happening because you had the balls to fight back. Don't stop now. Hell Steve, you have beat this guy and you still can with Max. These drugs are worth far more to him than Max is. Carlos knows that if he kills Max you have no reason to give him these drugs. Now fight damn it. Don't quit now or you and Max both are dead and Carlos gets away with that and the drugs."

Steve pushed the door to the truck open knocking Blake down to the ground. Blake stumble trying to catch his balance but Steve was on him in a flash pushing him down to the ground face first. Landing hard on Blake's back grabbing him by the back of the head and forcing his face against the pavement.

"Don't you think I want to fight? I want to kill this son-of-a -bitch so bad I can't think straight. He has my son and he has already proven to me that he will hurt him. I can't stand it Blake, but what the fuck am I supposed to do?"

Two of Blake's men began running towards them but Blake put up his hand telling them to stop.

Blake mumbled out against the concrete. "I will help you!"

Steve let go of Blake's head as the tears began to fall. Crying now. "How can you help me? This guy's knows our every move. He has a man right there who is probably telling him everything that is happening right now and I am sure that there are more on the way. This thing is over. The only hope I have of getting Max out is to hand him these drugs and beg for my son's life."

Steve slid off Blake's back to the ground next to him. "It's over."

Blake raised his head and brushed the dirt and gravel from his cheek. "It's not over Steve. You have the drugs. Max will stay alive as long as you have the drugs."

"Yeah, he'll stay alive and Carlos will start cutting off more fingers as soon as I don't comply. I can't have that Blake. What if it was your son, what would you do?"

Blake sat up next to Steve and shook his head. "I don't know. I can't imagine how bad that would be. I do know that if you give up this truck, you and Max are dead. We may still be able to track Carlos down eventually but that won't save you and Max."

"You're not helping. All I can do is try and save Max. You guys will have to be ready to come in as soon as I get to Max. I need to be able to communicate with you. What do you have to solve that problem?"

"Unfortunately nothing that will work for this. Not with me, anyway. If we had more time we could plant a bug in your teeth that would allow us to listen to the conversation and you would communicate by just talking out loud but I don't have it with me and we don't have enough time to go get it."

If I try and get away again he's just going to hurt Max until I get back in line."

Blake shook his head. "Steve, I know it may be hard to consider right now but a hurt Max is better than a dead Max. You need to think about that before you send us away."

Blake stood and walked to the back of the truck. Ron came around the corner and gave Blake that knowing nod telling him the two bugs were in place.

"How did that go with the Vic?" Ron asked.

Blake shook his head. "Bad. That guy is fucked no matter what happens now. They're gonna torture his kid and then kill them both."

"You can't make the guy see that. As soon as he gives this truck to them he's toast."

"I know, and the SAC doesn't give a shit about him. It's not good either way. This is the part of the job I hate. A no win situation."

"We could take the guy over there in the truck and just take the truck. Take Steve into custody and stop this thing right here. We would be taking a lot of drugs off the street that might end up getting away from us."

"Jesus Ron you sound like the SAC. That guys kid is being held and tortured. What if it was your kid?"

"I don't have kid's sir. I'm sorry I wasn't trying to be cold hearted, but there are millions of dollars of drugs in this truck and if we take it down it will hurt Carlos financially as well as his reputation with the Mexican drug cartel. Somebody may come up here and ice his ass saving us the trouble. There's no way to save this guy's kid but we can save him and our streets right now. How many kids will overdose because of the drugs in this truck. A hundred? A thousand? Those are all somebodies' kids too."

Blake turned to face Ron and saw Steve standing right behind him listening. "Oh shit Steve I…"

"So the SAC doesn't give a shit about my kid and neither do you guys."

"Steve that's not true. Ron is just seeing this like everyone is, but you. Max is dead either way and you will be to if you drive this truck over the border. Carlos is not going to let Max go when you get there. He's most likely going to kill him in front of you and make it very bad so you suffer the most. I think you need to see the bigger picture here and fight this guy now while you still have some control. I'm sorry you heard us talking. The truck is clean. You're free to go!"

ROAD RAGE

Blake walked to the chopper and got in. The other men began to clear away from the truck as Steve stood there going over the situation in his head. He knew they were right. There was no way to save Max in any scenario. Carlos would kill Max in front of him, and he knew that he wouldn't be able to bear that.

Steve pulled out the phone and dialed Carlos. As he did he motioned for Blake to come back.

Carlos answered on the first ring. "Steve get in the truck!"

"Carlos you and I had deal. Both my wife and kid were to go free."

Blake walked up to Steve, with a what now look on his face. Steve mouthed take out the pickup truck now! Blake looked at the pickup and then back at Steve. Steve made a gun out of his finger and thumb and pointed at the truck and simulated pulling the trigger. With animation he mouthed again, now!

Carlos yelled get the kid, in the background. "Steve, if you don't get in that truck your kid loses another finger right now."

Steve yelled at Carlos. "Enough! You so much as touch another finger and I will hand the keys to this truck to this FBI agent standing next to me do you fucking understand me?"

"Give me the kid's hand. I have your son here Steve, you want to tell him why his daddy would rather see his son hurt than just do what he's told. Tell him why Steve, you have five seconds."

The phone rustled and Steve heard the heavy breathing of Max's voice filled with fear. "Daddy!"

Steve fell to knees at the sound of Max's voice. "Max, I love you son so much."

"Why are they doing this to me, just give them what they want, please..."

The phone was snatched away and all Steve could hear in the background was Max screaming at the top of his lungs. Steve dropped the phone and pulled the 9mm from his waist band. The FBI agents still had not fired at the pickup but Steve aimed and opened fire at the driver. The guy slammed the truck in reverse and began backing over the curb into the street. Three of the other agents looked at Blake for direction and Blake pulled his own Sig Sauer and opened fire. The three agents did as well. The pickup splintered into pieces and went across the road into the ditch. As it did a huge fireball erupted and the pickup engulfed into flames.

Steve bent down and picked up the phone. "Carlos!"

He could still hear Max screaming. "That's another finger from your son. How many more do you want me to take?"

The anger in Steve was pouring out of him. "You might as well put a bullet in his head because there is no fucking way you were ever letting me or him go."

Carlos screamed into the phone. "You mother fucker! Bring me my truck or I will kill this kid and kill you and your wife. Do you hear me?"

Steve calmed his voice before he spoke. "The only thing right now that will save your drugs is to take my son to the nearest hospital and drop him off. If you don't, you will never see these drugs and I will hunt you down and kill you with my bare hands. I swear to God! Your man is dead by the way. His truck is burning as we speak but don't worry he's full of bullets so he's not suffering but I promise you will Carlos."

"Your son is dead my friend. You have killed him."

The phone went dead. Steve closed the phone and put it in his pocket. The three agents ran toward the truck to make sure the driver was dead and Blake walked to Steve.

"I am not sure what to do right now for you man. Are you okay?"

Steve turned and faced Blake. The tears streaming down his face. "He will kill Max now for sure."

Blake stepped closer and wrapped his arms around Steve. "I'm sorry man."

Steve's legs gave out and he collapsed against Blake. Blake held him up as one of the other agents came to their side. Both men got under Steve's arms and carried him to the cab of the truck. Steve climbed into the front seat and wept.

The agents gathered at the back of the truck knowing that they would not let another thing happen to this man or his family. Each man knew that he would give up his life before Carlos got these drugs or got his hands on Steve Lawson.

Nobody spoke and nobody had to. It was understood that this was now a battle to the end. A battle that would only end with Carlos dead at the feet of Steve Lawson.

Blake got into the rig and drove for the next thirty minutes getting them away from the burning truck and off the grid so Carlos no longer knew the location. They sent the helicopter back to the airport and Blake and three men stayed with Steve to plan the next step. All four FBI agents assured Steve they would take this fight all the way to the end.

Once it was safe, they stopped to put their heads together and came up with a plan. Blake stepped away from the group and called the SAC. "Sir its Agent Hardy checking back in, sorry for the second call but some things have developed."

The man cleared his throat. "I'm listening."

"Mr. Lawson has decided that he will not be driving the truck into the hands of Carlos. There is little hope that his son will make it out of this alive at this point, and he wants to use the truck as a decoy to try and lure Carlos out."

"No. Take the truck and Mr. Lawson into custody. We will have a team at the border to process the truck and we will join Mr. Lawson and his wife back together until we get Carlos. Nothing we can do about the kid at this point."

"Sir, you know that's not the right way to handle this. This man has been through hell these last few days. He has listened to Carlos cut off his son's fingers over the phone. He listened to Carlos beat his wife over the phone. This is a unique situation that if we play out we may get Carlos tonight dead or alive."

A long pause on the other end. "Agent Hardy you know the regulations here."

"But sir you don't know..."

"Let me finish agent Hardy before you speak. You know the regulations so I am going to pretend that the last call we had was me telling you to bug the truck and follow. You will follow my last directive as far as the New Orleans office knows. Do I make myself clear agent Hardy."

Blake stood speechless. "I am not sure I do sir."

"You do have a unique situation there and if it were my son I would want to kill everyone involved. So I am going to hang up now and I will expect a full report on my desk when this thing is done, are we clear? Do not let those drugs get away from you."

"Yes sir!"

"Agent, that report will detail an operation that was by the book do you understand me?"

"Yes I do sir, loud and clear."

"Good luck agent Hardy, try not to make too big of a mess okay. You're a good agent and I don't want this thing to blow up in your face."

"Got it sir. I'll do my best."

"You always do."

The phone went dead. Blake slowly put the phone back in his pocket and turned to face the other three agents and Steve, who now had come out of the truck looking more put together and calm.

One of the men spoke. "Well, what's up?"

Blake began to smile looking at Steve. "Looks like you have your own personal kill squad, courtesy of the FBI! Where to captain?"

Steve smiled back. "New Orleans where else?"

CHAPTER 11

In America Again

Blake made the call to take down the center lane guy at the Laredo border. Blake's man stepped into place to let the truck pass through without issue. Also ignoring the three FBI swat agents tucked in the sleeper part of the cab fully armed. He had also called ahead to the Texas State Patrol and they had arrested six men waiting at various places across the border who were also heavily armed and now being questioned about their connections to a New Orleans and international drug smuggler named Carlos.

Although, there was no plan at this point, Steve knew that having possession of the drugs was the only way this thing would turn out remotely good. Steve prayed that Max would survive long enough for him to get there.

He had not heard from Carlos in over an hour, and wanted to call. Blake urged him to wait until they made sure they were clear of all of Carlos's men on the states side of the border. Blake constantly worked his phone, arranging additional manpower for New Orleans and verifying the safety of Heather throughout the drive.

They quickly got off the main expressway and began back road travel to avoid detection by Carlos and weigh stations. There was no way for the FBI to get every weigh station covered between Texas and New Orleans. It would slow them down and create problems they didn't need.

Each man checked his weapon and checked his ammo over and over. Each on the ready to attack and conquer whatever situation arose. Each man taking turn sleeping as they could. The drive to New Orleans was ten hours taking the express way. This trip would be more like twelve.

Blake had arranged to change the tractor part of the truck out in Houston since the one they were in still required water every few hundred miles from the multiple gun shots in the radiator. The new truck had a few additions that would help them as they fought their way clear of Carlos. A metal plate was positioned in front of the radiator to prevent damage. Bullet proof glass and run flat tires. This was one of the FBI's tractors that normally pulled one of their command centers. This unit was older and was not in current use. The Houston field office was more than glad to help. This thing would take everything Carlos had to give with the exception of a hand held rocket launcher. It was also equipped with an FBI computer console and communication center.

Just as they got back underway in Houston, Steve's phone rang. It was Carlos. "Carlos, good of you to call we need to negotiate."

"Do you care about the life of your son?"

"Very much. I suggest you do the same."

"You have killed my men, taken my drugs and involved the FBI. Do you know how much trouble you have caused me?"

"Yeah, I do and you know what Carlos?"

Carlos coughed a laugh. "No Steve, what? I can't wait to hear."

"You picked the wrong guy to fuck with this time. I'm coming for you Carlos and before this day is done I'm gonna kill you myself. Do you hear me? You have fucked around and now you are going to find out."

"You my friend, don't even know where I am. How the fuck are you coming for me. I have your son and I will torture him to death if you don't give me my drugs right now."

"I already told you Carlos, take my son to the nearest hospital and I will give you your drugs. That's the only deal I am willing to make. Do it right now and give me a place to meet you. I will trade my life for Max's."

Carlos screamed. "Do you think I am stupid? If I give up Max you have no reason to give me my drugs and I am sure your FBI buddies will not allow you to hand over that truck. You have created a no win scenario for all of us."

"You give up Max and I swear to you Carlos, I will meet you anywhere you say and I will come alone with the drugs, no trackers from the FBI."

Silence for a long moment. "Where are you now?"

"You don't know?"

"No Steve, your FBI pals have helped you quite well. You have killed six of my men and there are eight in custody at this point. You have caused me considerable pain."

"You have no idea what pain is you son-of-a-bitch. I have listen to you beat and torture my family for three days and I will not let you hurt them anymore. Last offer Carlos. Tell me where to meet you and turn Max loose. When I know he is safe, I will give you my location and you can take the truck."

Silence again. "The only way I will do that is if you put one of my men in the cab of that truck with you. When he verifies that you are alone and unarmed I will release your boy. Any FBI agents or cops anywhere in sight and you and the boy die."

"Where do I pick up your man?"

"Where are you?"

"About a hundred miles east of Houston. On back roads."

"I will call you back."

The phone went dead and Steve looked to Blake. "Okay what the hell do we do now?"

Blake shook his head. "I don't know what to think. He is planning something but he has to know we will have trackers on this truck. Hell this FBI cab has GPS, satellite sensors and three other trackers I can't even tell you about."

"So he has to be planning on ditching the truck. He will probably split the drugs up into smaller trucks that can disappear into the city and hide."

"He's also gonna know that we're watching. This guy's not stupid."

"Look if he turns over Max, I don't care about me. I don't want to die but Max is more important. If I can get Max out safe, I will take my chances alone with this guy. I'll have the tracker inside me and you guys can find me as soon as you have Max. I'll try and stay alive as long as I can, just be quick about coming to get me okay."

Blake laughed. "Be quick! This guy is gonna tear your head off as soon as he sees you. Being quick is not going to help."

"Look Blake, I appreciate everything you and the FBI have done to help me but I have a chance to get my son out and I have to take it. You have to back off and let me take this thing home."

"Do you really think he will give up Max?"

"I think he will make it look like it and that's why I need you guys there so that when he does, you can protect Max and get him out safe. Once I let his man in this truck all bets are off."

Blake shook his head. "It's a suicide mission for you."

"It's my son's life. I don't care what happens to me."

"Okay, it's your show then. When Carlos calls, you play it however you want. We'll do what we can."

"I'll tell him it has to be River Oaks Hospital in New Orleans. You guys can be there, and get Max."

"Okay. I'll make the call and get us a ride. One of us could try and hide in the cab here and take the guy out as soon as we have Max."

"No, you know that's not gonna happen. That guy is gonna check this truck top to bottom when he gets in here. Hell I am sure Carlos will have an army of guys there when I stop."

"Tell Carlos only one man. Unarmed and when you know Max is clear you will hand over your weapon and control of the truck. No army of men, no bullshit. At least that way it's a one on one fight. Once we have Max, you find a way to get the hell away from this truck. I have a backup piece that you can have on your ankle. We won't be far away. We can track you by the tracker in your stomach. I think that's the safest bet to get you both out alive. I'll have a team of guys I know at the hospital. We'll take the guy down and get Max as soon as he shows. I'll have them call your cell as soon as Max is clear. From there you fight your way out and we'll be on top of you in no time."

Steve was nodding as Blake talked. "I like it. It lets me keep control until Max is free. I'll tell Carlos that you guys will handle the guy getting into the truck to make sure he's not armed and that there's no army of guys. That way he'll also see me drive off and leave you behind. Just have a chopper wait until I leave."

"You think he'll go for that?"

"I won't give him a choice. These drugs are worth more to him than Max. Besides this guy's ego is so big, he thinks he can get to us even if he does let us go. What he doesn't know is, I'm an old country boy and we know how to disappear if we need to. He won't find me."

"Okay then, we wait for his call."

Steve continued making his way to New Orleans. Three hours past when the phone rang. Blake was driving at this point, and Steve was asleep. He jumped up grabbing the phone from the console.

"Yeah."

"Steve is that you?"

"Yeah Carlos, I was sleeping."

"Sleeping while driving, that's not good at all. You wreck that truck and the FBI won't be happy."

Steve looked at Blake and then looked out the window to see who may be following. "No probably not. Have you released my son yet?"

A laugh. "No Steve, he is right here, but he will need to learn to write with his left hand. Maybe even his mouth if you keep this game up you are playing."

Steve hung the phone up and set it back in the console of the truck. Blake looked shocked. "What the fuck dude? You just hung up on the man. He'll go into a rage."

"I'm not listening to my son scream again. I can't take it. I don't have any control over what he does to Max but I don't have to listen."

Blake sat back in the seat. Eyes a bit wider than normal. "Shit!"

The phone rang again. "Carlos listen to me."

"No you listen to me asshole. I will do this deal but you do it how I say and where I say. My man will get in the truck and my men will escort you to where we want. When I have control of the truck we will turn your son loose. But, you my friend.... You and I are going to have a long talk about how much trouble you have caused me."

"Yeah well, that whole plan ain't happening for me. Here's what you're gonna do. It's fair for both us. I will meet your man with my FBI buddies. They will disarm him and put him in the truck with me. They will also make sure that no one follows us. They will stay behind when I leave with your man. That way you know that the FBI is not along for the ride. As soon as we are gone from them you take Max to the River

Oaks Hospital in New Orleans and drop him at the front door. I will have some friends there to take him into protective custody and get him medical attention. With me so far?"

Carlos screamed. "Who the fuck do you think you are?"

Anger rose up in Steve's throat. "I'm the guy with millions of dollars' worth of your drugs Carlos. Wake up asshole! You hurt my son one more time, and I will hand this truck over to the FBI and walk away. Now, are you listening to me?"

"I will kill you so slowly you will beg me to die."

"We'll see about that."

"Yes we will. I'm listening, tell me what you want."

"Good. Once Max is safe I will hand your man my gun and you're in charge. I've told the FBI that they are not to follow and not to interfere in any way. They have agreed to let you go for now. They seem to think they can catch you now without much effort."

"They have no idea how to catch me. I have smuggled millions of dollars of drugs across their borders and sold them in every town. They're a joke to me."

"Well that's the deal Carlos. That's the only way I can know for sure that Max will walk away from this alive. What happens after that is up to you."

Silence on the phone for a long minute. "Carlos are you there?"

"Yes. I can agree to your plan. You drive on I-10 until you get to the Mississippi. There is an exit just before, Par rd. You know it?"

"I do."

"My man will be waiting on the ramp. He will drive."

"Okay, I'm fine with that. He does know how to drive a big rig right?"

"He does. When you get the call about your son, you give him your gun and he will give you handcuffs to put on."

Silence for a moment. "Okay, Par rd. in three hours."

The phone went dead and Steve looked at Blake. "What do you think? That seemed a little too easy."

Blake nodded. "I agree. He has something else planned."

"But what. There's nothing between the Mississippi line and New Orleans. He'll be in plain view from the air and you know he thinks the FBI will be watching. Hell, I think he knows we changed cabs too."

"What do you want to do?"

"Go through with it. If he gives me Max I will wreck that truck and take off running."

"Do you want us to stay close in the air?"

"No. He'll be watching you guys take off. You need to fade off into the distance. Now once you guys have Max. Come get me and the drugs."

"Alright. We'll have an unmarked team following you the whole time. I'm not letting this thing get away from me."

"Blake you can't be seen. If I lose my son because of the FBI I am gonna be pissed."

"He won't see us. It will be multiple cars and they will rotate off so he never knows. Don't worry about that. You need to be worried about handing that guy your gun. I hope his orders are not to shoot you in the face as soon as you do."

"I don't know what Carlos's plan is here but I do know he wants me for himself. I will deal with the guy in the truck. Hell, I'll unload the gun and hand it to him empty. He probably won't check it."

Blake smiled "You'll have the back up. This guy won't search you or just don't let him if he tries. Move over to the passenger seat and never get out of the truck. We'll clear him and off you go. Hand him the empty 9. If he asks tell him you ran out of bullets back in Mexico killing his friends."

Steve laughed. "I hope it goes that well. This seems too easy to me. Carlos is smarter than that. Tell your surveillance guys to be ready for anything. He may fly in with a chopper and pick the truck up cab and all. Who knows?"

From the back. "Dude if you make it out of this alive, it will be a miracle."

Steve turned to look at the man. "That's not very positive man. You need to stay quiet until we get there."

The man sat back. "I'm just sayin."

"Well don't say anything else damn it!"

Blake laughed. "Alright enough. I'll drive for the rest of the trip. Everybody get some sleep. Especially you Steve. You've damn near been up for three days. You need to be alert and rested when you turn over this truck. I have a feeling the shit is gonna hit the fan."

Steve settled back in his seat and closed his eyes. Just as he began to drift off the cell rang loud in the console.

Steve jumped, startled by the call. As he looked at the caller ID it was all 0's. He looked at Blake. Blake smiled. "Answer it dummy!"

Steve hit the button and put the phone to his ear. "Hello."

"Baby it's me!"

Heathers voice filled his ear and he fell back in his seat with relief. "Oh thank God you're okay. You are okay, right?"

"Yes. I am in a FBI safe house somewhere. They told me not to say just in case. Are you okay?"

"I'm fine baby it so good to hear your voice."

"Steve they kept Max!"

"I know, I'm trying to get him out. It will be okay."

"How will you get him? What are you doing? Is the FBI helping you?"

Steve paused for second. "Are you sure you're safe. What are the names of the agents staying with you at that house?"

"I don't know, they told me but I don't remember."

"Ask."

"Alright hold on."

Steve looked over at Blake and shook his head. "I don't like this deal man. They have her in a house somewhere and she is asking questions like she is being prompted. Do you know these guys that have her?"

Blake shook his head no. "I don't know who has her now. My guy picked her up at the police station for sure but after that no."

Heather came back to the phone. "Agent Samuels and Agent Rains. Why are you so worried? I'm safe."

"Hold on babe. Agent Samuels and Agent Rains. Do you know them?"

"I know Rains, not Samuels."

"Babe listen to me. This guy Carlos has people everywhere in New Orleans. I don't trust anybody but the guys I have with me. I want you to get Agent Rains on the phone for me. Stay close to him okay."

"Steve what the hell is going on? Where is Max?"

"I will get Max, I swear, but get Agent Rains for me. I love you very much."

"Why do you sound like your saying goodbye to me? Don't you fucking say goodbye to me. You talk to me and tell me what's going on with Max. Tell me what you're planning."

"Babe I will, but right now I need to make sure you're safe. If this guy Samuels is good that's one thing, but if not you might be in danger. So get agent Rains on the phone right now!"

Heather dropped the phone on the bed and called Agent Rains. Steve listened as he began to hear shouts and then Heather scream. Gun shots rang out through the phone. Steve sat up straight in his seat shouting into the phone. "Heather!"

Silence on the other end. Steve looked at Blake as he heard the phone rustle as it was drug across the bed and picked up. "I got your woman asshole. Now we have your woman and your kid."

Steve took a breath and began to speak when he heard shots through the phone. The phone dropped and hit the ground. When it did the line went dead.

Steve dropped the phone from his hand. "Jesus! They took her Blake. How the fuck could this happen."

Blake snatched his own cell from his pocket and dialed his SAC. Two rings. "Blake what's up?"

"Sir who has the women under protection?"

A short pause. "One second and let me pull the information."

Blake waited two seconds. "The safe house has been compromised sir. We were just on the phone with the woman and shots were fired. Get a team of our men there asap. We don't know the status and we don't have any way to get back in touch. Please Sir hurry."

The phone went dead and Blake looked back over at Steve who was now pounding the dashboard of the truck.

At the safe hose

Heather dropped the phone on the bed and called out for Agent Rains. As she did Agent Rains looked at Samuels as Samuels pulled his weapon and fired. Rains was hit and went down. Heather turned screaming running back towards the phone. Guns shots rang out striking the wall behind her as she ran. Samuels lunged after her, striking her in the head with the butt of his 9mm.

Heather fell to the floor in a lump unconscious from the blow. Samuels spun around to check Rains who was also not moving. He went for the phone on the bed.

Heather in agony, feeling the blood and the bump on her head beginning to swell laid very still while Samuels checked Rains and went to the bedroom. She slowly began to crawl backwards away from the door of the bedroom. She stood quietly when she looked over at Rains.

Rains was hit in the chest and bleeding badly. In his outstretched hand his 9mm was aimed at Heather. She froze in place. Her heart was beating so hard she could feel it through her shirt.

Rains waved the pistol and spun it in his hand now presenting the hand grip to Heather. She breathed in finally after what seemed like minutes and took the gun. Rains collapsed on the floor.

Spinning back towards the bedroom Heather took one step, two and then three. Samuels came into view. His back to her with his gun in one hand down by his side and the phone to his ear in the other.

She cleared the door frame with the 9mm, raised and aimed at the back of Samuels head. As she stepped through the door Samuels began to turn.

Bam...... Bam....

The shots rang out so loud in the small bedroom that they were deafening. The phone flew from Samuels hand as he pulled his weapon up to fire.

The room was in chaos. Gunpowder and the smell of blood filled the room. Silence fell throughout the whole house.

The phone lay on the floor shattered into pieces from the six foot fall from Samuels's ear. A hazy smoke lingered in the air.

In the truck

"Fuck! Fuck! Fuck! Flew from Steve's mouth. Jesus Blake do you guys screen anybody before they become an agent. I think I just heard my wife get killed."

Blake shaking his head no. "No man. I know Rains. He would know if his partner was bad. Rains is a good Agent. I'm sure the shots were from him taking Samuels down."

"Jesus Christ man, this is a fucking disaster. We're walking into some kind of trap and Carlos is clearly in control."

"I can stop and we can try and do this another way."

No, came from Steve's mouth. "What way. No one is safe from this guy. I'm going through with it Blake but I want you at that hospital. You guys. I'll be fine. Get my son and get him somewhere that Carlos can't find. Get someone to wherever my wife is and I pray to God that she is okay."

Blake's hands raced on the surface of his phone searching for Rains cell number.

"If I lose both my wife and kid I swear to God I will hunt this mother fucker down if it is the last thing I do. I will tear his body apart while he is still alive. Then I will find his family and kill every one of them too."

Steve felt a large hand from the back touch his shoulder firmly. Steve looked back at special agent Tom Scott.

"You won't be alone!"

The man let go and sat back in his seat. Special agent Vince Carter leaned forward and put his hand on Steve's shoulder.

"You won't be alone!"

The man sat back in his seat. Special agent Ed Kennedy leaned forward and put his hand on Steve's shoulder.

"You won't be alone.

As this finished happening Blake looked back at his men and then at Steve. "I will get your kid and then come get you. After that the four of us are going to take a little vacation for some well needed rest. You won't be alone!"

Steve felt his chest tighten and he looked away from the men out into the swamp lands of Lafayette Louisiana. His life was swirling in his head. In the background he could hear what seemed like all four men talking all at once. The sounds blurred and drifted off into the distance as he pictured his wife being shot in the chest or worse in the head. She wasn't used to this kind of life in any way. Steve had at least been in the war in Iraq and knew what it felt like to have people want to kill him. He knew how to prepare for the fight of his life. He knew how to be ready to face death if it came. Heather didn't.

It seemed like hours had passed, but in reality it had only been about twenty minutes. He felt the truck slow and looked up to see the Par Rd sign showing one mile to the exit. He turned and looked at Blake.

Blake looked over at him. "Sure you want to do this?"

Steve nodded. "Give me the backup piece."

Blake pulled it from his ankle and handed it to Steve. "It's a small 380 auto. Six in the clip and one in the chamber.

Cocked and ready to rock my friend. Safety is beside the trigger. It won't do major damage, but up close it'll hurt you."

Steve emptied the 9mm clip out and handed the shells back to Tom. "Hang on to those for me brother. I'll be back to get them in a little bit."

"Will do! Don't lose your head. We'll get your boy and your wife. You focus on what goes down and don't get dead okay."

Steve smiled at all three of his new crew. "I'll do my best. Save my family."

All three men nodded yes and readied their weapons.

Ahead of them on the ramp there was a black BMW. Steve recognized it from the warehouse and new it was Carlos's men. Two men stood behind the car with arms crossed looking very casual for drug dealers.

Steve was pointing at the car. "That's Carlos's BMW right there."

"What, no way Carlos is here for this."

The agents in the back raised three muzzle up straight at the two men as they pulled to a stop twenty feet away.

Both men uncrossed their arms and raised their hands in defensive motions. Blake was quickly checking the mirrors and surrounding areas for any sign of other men, snipers or hostile looking vehicles. There were none.

Blake turned to Steve. "You ready?"

"Let's get on with it."

"Okay you know the drill. Stay in the truck. When I call you, try anything you can to get away. Oh yeah, swallow the tracker now"

The phone rang and Steve snatched it up barely one ring. "Heather?"

"No my friend it's Carlos. Were you expecting your wife? I think maybe she is tied up at the moment."

"You son-of-a-bitch, you better be on the way to that hospital with my kid right now or I swear we will kill your two men here."

"So hostile Steve. We have a deal. He is on the way right now. As soon as my man is in control of the truck we will drop him off. Tell your friends to leave."

The deal is one man unarmed. When I get the call from my guys that they have my son I will turn over my gun and go along. No FBI no bugs, the drugs are yours. Now where the hell is my wife?"

"What? What do you mean where is your wife? The FBI has her."

"Yeah well I'm not so sure about that. Your man Samuels has her."

"Steve I don't know what you're talking about. I don't have your wife. Not yet anyway but when I do this time I will have my way with her. Over and over and over."

Blake and the others were out of the truck now and searching both men. Blake turned and gave Steve a thumbs up. Steve motioned for the guy to get in the truck.

"Carlos I'm tired of fucking around with you. We made a deal now let's get on with it. Your man is getting into the truck now. Release my son and you better not have my wife."

"I will do as I say. Your son is being dropped right now at the front doors of River Oaks and is alive and well. Well minus a few fingers because of his father. I made sure he understood that before I got rid of him. Too bad you won't get to explain that one to him. You'll be dead by then."

The Mexican driver stepped up into the doorway and Steve pointed the 9mm at his chest. He rows his hands in surrender and climbed into the seat.

"Tell your man in the BMW to get lost. Nobody follows us until I hear my wife and son are safe."

"He will leave as soon as the FBI goes."

"Carlos he will leave right now or I will put a bullet in your man's brain and my friends will shoot your BMW and your other man so full of holes that there won't be anything worth burying. Tell him to go now."

Carlos sighed. "As you wish Mr. Lawson. I will be talking with you soon."

The phone went dead.

The man at the BMW pointed to the phone laying on the trunk lid and Tom motioned for him to answer it with the muzzle of his AR. He nodded and got in the car. The car went into gear and drove up the ramp getting back on I-10.

Steve looked at Blake and nodded good to go. Blake waved and all four men ran towards the chopper waiting in the grass to the side of the ramp. Steve looked back at the driver.

"You speak English?"

The guy nodded yes. "Good. You wait right here until I get the call. You make a move I don't like, you die. You understand?"

The man nodded.

Five minutes later the phone rang. "Is this Mr. Lawson?"

"Yes it is. Who is this?"

"This agent Remy Labelle. I have your son. I am a friend of Agent Hardy. I know he is on the way but he wanted me to call you and tell you it was okay."

"Is he okay?"

"Yes sir. The doctors are working on him now. He'll be fine. Do you know about his fingers?"

"Yes agent I do. Don't trust anybody. You keep your guard up 100% of the time. When Blake gets there you get my kid out of that hospital. Let me talk to him."

The phone shuffled and Max's weak voice came on. "Dad is that you?"

"Max buddy. I am so sorry."

"Where are you? I want to go home."

"I know you do. Everything will be okay soon. You go with my friends from the FBI and I will see you soon okay."

"Okay."

"I love you son."

"I love you too daddy"

Steve hung up and handed the driver the 9mm. He slid the weapon to his left in the door and began moving up the ramp. He pulled the handcuffs out of his pocket and handed them to Steve. Steve complied knowing that his wife may be back as a hostage or worse, dead. His son was safe though and that's what mattered for now. If he could escape he would. If not he would hope for the best and trust that Blake would take care of him.

Steve studied the driver and he seemed very nervous. "You okay man?"

He never took his eyes of the road. They were on the bridge now crossing the Mississippi doing about 45 in the slow lane. He found that odd as well since the speed limit was 55. Steve started looking around waiting for something. Not sure what, but it was coming and Steve knew it.......

CHAPTER 12

Not the Plan

At the safe house, Heather slowly opened her eyes. She had fallen next to the bed as Samuels had shot. She had pulled the trigger twice before diving to the ground. The house was silent now and she was hurting all over from the impact. The gun was still in her hand ready to fire again.

Heather looked back through the door towards agent Rains. He was not moving. She turned to try and see over the edge of the bed without being much of a target. She could hear two different cell phone rings almost starting at the same time. One from agent Raines's direction and one from the other side of the bed. Neither phone was being answered. She lifted herself slightly to look over the bed. No sign of Samuels. Slowly she stood until she could see agent Samuels. Her first shot had struck him in the neck and now the man lay in a large pool of blood still holding his gun.

His eyes were open but she couldn't tell if he was alive or not. She raised the gun aiming straight at his head. He still didn't move. Heather took a step but didn't take her eyes off the agent.

In a flash she saw the man's eye move toward her and the grip on his gun tighten. She fired again striking him just above the nose this time. His head exploded against the hardwood floor. Heather gasp at the sight, and fired again into the man's chest.

The gun in his hand fell to the floor. It was over for him. Heather ran back into the living room to check agent Rains. There was blood everywhere. He was dead. Heather slid the gun in the back of her jeans and pulled the man's cell phone from his jacket pocket. From his pants she felt for keys. There were none.

Heather looked toward the bedroom. "Shit!"

She stood and walked back into the bedroom. The smell of blood and death had filled the room. Samuel's body had not moved since the shooting. He was dead for sure now, she was terrified. She had never seen a dead body other than at a funeral, much less been responsible for the death. Her hands shook uncontrollably.

Heather slowly walked around the end of the bed and looked down at the man. She gasped and quickly put her hands over her mouth at the sight. The blood was everywhere, so much of it. His head was gone at the top and most of that was on the floor behind him.

Suddenly she felt her stomach up heave and she began to throw up so fast it shot straight out. This added to the already gruesome seen on the floor. Heather turned and ran out of the room. The hell with the keys she thought. She had the cell phone she would just call the police instead. She had to get out of this house. She had to get away. If this was Carlos's man they would know where she was.

Heather ran from the house. As she came outside, nothing looked familiar. She had come there in the night and had no idea where she was. She ran past the FBI car and down the driveway. She looked both ways and saw nothing but residential streets and houses.

The phone rang in her hand. She answered and Blake spoke. "Rains, where the hell have you been?"

"This is not Rains, he's.... dead. The other agent shot him."

"Is this Heather?"

"Yes. Who is this?"

"Heather I'm Agent Hardy, Blake. I have been with your husband for the last day. What happened there?"

"I don't know, I was talking to Steve and all of sudden they started shooting at each other. Agent Samuels shot Agent Rains in the chest. I started running and he hit me in the head. I didn't go unconscious but I faked it. He got on the phone with Steve and I tried to sneak away. Agent Rains was hurt bad but still alive. He gave me his gun."

"It's okay Heather, what happened then?"

"I shot him."

"You shot who?"

"Agent Samuels. I came back into the bedroom and he turned to shot me but I already had the gun up and pointed at him. I just pulled the trigger and dove to the ground. I was so scared. I thought I might have missed and he would kill me for sure but I...."

"Heather you did fine, okay. He was a bad guy. He was working for Carlos and he would have kidnapped you again. Now listen you have to hide. Don't tell anybody where you go. Keep the phone that you have, it's safe to use but don't. Don't call anybody. You need to get away from that house. It's not safe."

"Where is Steve and what about Max? Is there any news?"

"Steve is in the truck but we will get him out I promise. Max is safe and I am on the way to get him right now. He's at River Oaks hospital. They are working on his hand but as soon as I get there we are going to take him somewhere safe. I need you to get the hell out there right now. Take the FBI car and go. I will call in the shooting and let my people know that you are clear. I don't know who else might be involved so I need you to get in that car and get out of town. I will call you and bring Max to you somewhere safe. Do you understand me Heather?"

Heather was crying now standing in the middle of the road. "Yes but the keys are in his pocket and I don't know if I can do it. There is so much blood."

"Heather listen to me. You have got to go. Carlos's men are coming. They will hurt you and in turn they will hurt Steve. Run!"

Heather heard the screech of tires before she saw the car turn onto the street. She slowly took the phone from her ear. "They're coming. Oh my God they're coming."

Heather closed the phone and took off running. There was no time for the keys at this point. She didn't know if the men in the car saw her or not but she wasn't hanging around to find out. She just ran. Heather pulled the gun from her waist band to be ready if she had to. She ran through the back yard and through the neighbor's yard. She crossed the next street and ran through the yard across from that. She had never run so hard in her life. Her lungs were burning but she kept going. After the fifth or six yard she stopped to catch her breath. Finally looking back to see if anyone was following. She saw no one.

She bent over to catch her breath and try and make her side stop hurting. That's when she heard the car door slam in front of her. As she straightened she saw two Mexican men coming up the driveway. Heather raised the 9mm and fired wildly at the two men. Both ran for cover and Heather did too. She ran around the house and crossed into the neighbor's yard. As she looked back she saw one of the men take aim and fire. The bullet hit the house right beside her head. She screamed and fired back at the man.

Running again, she crossed the street and began going back through the yards. She couldn't see the men now, both were heavy set and would never keep up with her. Her adrenalin had to be off the charts now because she was in a dead hard run and nothing was hurting.

She approached the safe house and ran in through the still open front door. She would only have seconds but she had to have the keys. She ran into the bedroom which now stunk of all kinds of smells. She grabbed at both front pockets and hit pay dirt on the left. She grabbed the keys and his gun laying on the floor. Heather had no idea how many bullets these guns held but she didn't want to run out.

Pausing at the front door to see if the men were there, luckily, the coast was clear. She ran for the car. The crown vic was big and Heather was not used to this size car, but she could do it. She shoved the key into the ignition as the back window exploded. She screamed again but got the car cranked. With one hand she put the car into drive and with the other she began to shoot back through the back window at anything she could hit.

The car lurched forward as she hit the gas and began driving in the same path that she had run. Things like swing sets and small pools were an annoyance more than an obstacle at this point.

She slid out of the next yard sideways onto the road and floored it. The big V8 surprised her and the car spun sideways in the road. As it did she saw the Mexicans coming straight at her? No time left to roll the window down, heather floored it and began firing at the car. The driver's side window shattered and bullets began hitting the windshield of the approaching car. She was now headed straight for the front of a house and had to drop the gun in the seat to manage the wheel. The car fish tailed throwing mud and grass everywhere. As she spun around the Mexicans were on her and hit the tail end of the Crown Vic. This spun her again and slammed the two cars together door to door.

In the spin Heather had lost her grip on the wheel and the gun went to the floor. The bullets were hitting the roof and door of the car. One passed inches from her head and shattered the passenger side window. She reached up and through the car into reverse and jammed the pedal to the floor.

The sound of metal against metal was ferocious. The Crown Vic was twice the size of the BMW the Mexicans were driving and twice the weight. It pushed them against the front porch of the house as she backed away. She felt the Crown Vic jump the curb and heard the tires squeal on pavement. She slammed on the brake and looked up to see where she was.

The car was diagonal across the road. Heather knew she wouldn't outrun the BMW if she took to the street, it was lighter and faster. But she was pissed and had had enough. She reached to the floor and grabbed the 9mm that had now slid back into reach. She threw the car down into drive and floored it. The tires squealed and the big Ford raced forward. The BMW was not freed from the porch yet and both men were still dazed by the side swipe. The passenger raised his gun just as the front end of the car stuck the passenger door driving the BMW hard up under the porch.

ROAD RAGE

Heather shoved open the door and came out of the Crown Vic with both guns. She shot the very dazed passenger three times at least and emptied the rest of both clips into the BMW where the driver should be. When both guns emptied she dropped them and ran.

It was two blocks before Heather noticed the blood on her arm. She had been hit in the shoulder, but with so much adrenalin, she had not felt it when it happened. She stopped running and put her good hand over the wound. The phone in her pocket had rung several times during the fight but there was no time to chat.

Staggering now, not from blood loss as much as just sheer exhaustion. Heather stumbled to a large area of bushes and trees between two houses. She collapsed on the ground and pulled the phone from her pocket. There were four missed calls. Three from Agent Hardy and one from an SAC, whoever that was.

Heather scrolled to Blake and hit send.

Blake answered immediately. "Heather are you okay?"

Heather out of breath now. "I don't know. I think I just killed two more men and I wanna go home."

Blake tried not to laugh out loud. "I know you do and we will get there. What happened?"

"They came after me. I couldn't get to the car so I ran. We ended up in some yard and we shot at each other a little. I ran back through the yards and got the keys. I got in the car and we shot at each other some more. I drove like a maniac and finally pinned those son-of-a-bitches against a house. When I did, I got out and shot the shit out of them...... Is that okay?"

Blake pulled the phone away from his ear looking at it in disbelief. "Yeah that is fine, I'll take care of it."

"Well that's good, because I think I am gonna pass out now."

Heather fell flat back in the bushes unconscious from either blood loss or adrenalin overload. Blake called for her several times with no answer.

"Shit she's out."

He hung up and called his field office. The shift operator answered with the standard, thank you for calling the New Orleans.... Blake cut her off.

"Cindy, its agent Hardy. I need an immediate trace on agent Raines's cell phone. When you get it call me back with the location."

"Does your SAC know what's going on or should I clear this through him first?"

"Cindy I have people dying right now. I need that location yesterday. I will call the SAC. Can you get it?"

"Right away."

The phone went dead and Blake called Steve. The phone rang and rang. With the throw away there was no voice mail.

At that moment they landed on the roof of the hospital. Blake and his team came in strong and loud. Everyone they came in contact with, immediately sucked against a wall to stay out of the way. Nurse after nurse pointed towards ER as the asked where Max was. Blake found Max in a back corner of the ER. The doctor was sewing up his hand where his finger had been.

The doctor turned as Blake and the team came in the room. "What the hell? You can't be in here."

Blake showed his badge. "Doc I need you to wrap that up right now. He's coming with us."

The doctor stood. "I don't think so. This young man needs surgery, like yesterday."

Blake looked at Max. "How you doing little man?"

Max smiled. "It hurts. Where's my mom and dad?"

"We will take you to your mom. We're still working on getting your dad safe. Soon though, don't you worry. Right now though, we have angry drug dealers looking to hurt you to get at your dad. That's not gonna happen on my watch."

The doctor sat back down and finished sewing up Max. He wrapped the hand and gave Max a shot for the pain. He reached into a cabinet and took out a bottle of pills. "Give him one of these every four hours for pain if needed. What this man did to this boy was brutal. You need to get this guy Agent Hardy."

"I will!"

They went to the roof and got into the helicopter and took off. Blake got the headset on Max and got him secured. He took the seat next to him.

Blake smiled. "You know you have got some pretty awesome parents."

Max smiled. "I know. They still make me do my homework though."

Blake laughed out loud and put his arm around Max. "How's the hand?"

"It hurts but the doctor shot it full of some kind of pain killer so it's not too bad now."

Blake smiled again. "You know your dad has been fighting like crazy trying to get you and your mom to safety right."

Max looked down at the floor of the chopper. "I don't understand why he didn't just give that man what he wanted. He told me if he did he would let us go."

"Hey, that's bull shit kid." Tom blurted out.

Blake gave Tom a hard look. "Max, he would have killed you if your dad gave him those drugs. He would have then killed your dad. Your dad is a hero for what he has done. He traded himself for you. So don't ever think your dad wasn't doing everything he could to get you free. Carlos is a bad man and I will see to it that he gets everything he deserves."

Max looked back up at Blake. "He traded himself for me. What does that mean? Will they kill him now?"

Blake took a breath. "Awe shit. What I meant was he traded the drugs for you and he is in the truck but don't worry kid, we'll get your dad."

Tom looked at Blake with the same hard look. "Nice."

Blake's phone rang and he answered. It was Cindy with coordinates for Raines's phone. It was six miles from their location and by air they could be there in a matter of minutes. Blake gave the pilot the address and he put it into the GPS system. He then banked hard to the right and powered up the throttle.

Blake gave Max a pat on the back. "We're going to get your mom kid. We'll be there in few minutes.

Max smiled and nodded yes.

Heather woke to the sound of a helicopter landing in the street ten feet away from her. She sat up as she saw men begin to pile out wearing swat gear with big FBI letters in yellow across their chest and backs. She forced herself to her feet and one of the men spotted her immediately. He rushed to her and put his arm under hers almost lifting her completely of the ground.

As she got the helicopter max sprung from his seat and hugged his momma tight. She winced but put both arms around his neck and squeezed him as tight as she could.

Tears rolled down her cheeks as she spoke. "Oh Max baby, I thought I might never see you again."

As soon as she was in the door they were lifting off at full speed. Blake dialed Steve again with no answer. He called his SAC next.

One ring and he picked up. "Hardy you better have a good fuckin story to tell because you've got dead bodies all over the damn place."

"I know sir and I was gonna call you about that, but I've been a little busy."

"Damn it Blake, I've got dead agents to answer for. You kill a few drug dealers and it's no big deal, but when agents get dead careers end son."

"Sir it's not like that, I promise. I've got both the kid and the wife in protective custody with me and I am trying to get them to safety. She needs medical attention from a gunshot wound and the kid needs surgery on his hand."

"What the hell happen to the kid's hand?"

Carlos cut of two or three fingers sir, I'm not really sure."

"Oh shit! Are you serious?"

"Yes sir. Mr. Lawson is still with the truck but we have lost contact by phone. I have a tracker on him that is still working but everything else is gone."

"What the hell do you mean everything else is gone? Did you not put trackers on the truck and those drugs like I told you?"

"I did sir. But they're gone off the radar. I have surveillance on the truck but I haven't had time to call yet to follow up. I've sort of had my hands full."

"I understand and let's put a stop to that. I will get a full SWAT unit deployed out immediately. Get your surveillance guys on the phone and tell me where that truck is, I want those drugs agent Hardy."

"I understand sir. So do I. I want this kid's father back too."

"Yeah me too, but right now we need to lock down that truck. I'll get the guys in the air you call me back and tell me where."

"Will do sir, thanks for the help. One more thing sir."

"Yeah?"

"I need a medical chopper to meet us when I get eyes on that truck. I don't have time to transport the girl and the kid. I need a team I can trust to get them to the hospital and watch over them. Carlos has got people everywhere including the Bureau."

"What the hell are you talking about Hardy?"

"Agent Samuels was one of Carlos's men. He shot Rains and Mrs. Lawson shot him. Rains didn't make it sir."

"I know he didn't, we have a team there now cleaning up. I am assuming she also had the car chase and killed two other Latino men in someone's front yard about two blocks away."

"Yes sir. She took a bullet to the shoulder during that exchange. It's not bad, through and through clean. We've got it packed but she needs surgery too."

"Alright agent, get me that address and I will have medical there when you are. Sounds like you've had a busy morning. How much sleep have you had in the last thirty-six hours son?"

"I'll sleep later sir. Right now, I have a hostage to rescue, a truck load of drugs to apprehend and a drug dealer to take down. It's been busy sir."

"Carry on!"

Blake dialed one of the surveillance agents and the guy answered the phone in a panic.

"Holy shit! I can't believe this."

Blake trying to understand. "You can't believe what?"

"He just went off the bridge."

"What do you mean he went off the bridge?"

"I mean the mother fucker just took a hard right and drove right off the bridge.... Like in the water off the bridge."

"Where?"

"Lake Pontchartrain Bridge on I-10. The truck is gone. It went under and no one is coming to the surface."

"Shit. Get eyes on the surface under that bridge. Don't take your eyes off the water. Somebody is coming to get those drugs. I am on the way."

Blake sat back in the jump seat shaking his head. "Check the system. Are all the trackers gone now?"

Tom opened his Ipad. "Yep, all but your boy. And he's moving out into the lake. How the fuck is that?"

Blake slammed his fist against the side of the helicopter wall. "He's under water! That fucking Carlos planned this shit all along. He's got divers in the damn water and they're taking those drugs out of that truck right now."

Get on the phone with NOPD and see if they have a water patrol boat in the area. We need divers and..... hell I don't know what else a crane I guess. We have to get down to that truck right now. Tell NOPD to get patrol units at every boat ramp"

CHAPTER 13

A Hard Right

Steve looked over at the driver as he accelerated on the bridge crossing the edge of Lake Pontchartrain. The guy was sweating.

"Hey man, are you okay? I can drive if you want."

Steve's hands were handcuffed in his lap. He could feel the weight of the backup gun on his ankle. Even with his hands cuffed he could still pull the piece and shoot. Doing it while on this bridge would not be good, but right after was fine with him. Max was safe now and Heather too hopefully. It was time to get the hell off this crazy Carlos ride.

He looked over again and the guy looked like he was about to shit himself. "Hey man seriously, are you okay or do I need to drive?"

What happened next, Steve had no way to prepare for. The guy swerved left and in a hard jerking motion turned the truck straight for the guard rail. The last thing Steve saw before they hit the rail was a big red x. Steve braced for the hard impact of the concrete wall but it didn't come. The truck barely flinched as it went straight through the rail.

The next thing he knew he was weightless as the truck began to flip over as it headed for the water. Steve could feel himself screaming but nothing came out. He was belted in and that kept him in his seat, but everything in the cab of that truck was flying through the air including the 9mm which hit the roof and then the front windshield. Everything in Steve's mind was moving in slow motion. The last thing he saw before they hit the water was the look of desperation on the Mexicans face. Steve thought this crazy son-of-a-bitch is trying to kill us both. I go through all of this shit, and I'm gonna die by drowning in a wreck.

With extreme force. The truck hit the water hard, mostly upside down but as the nose hit first it slammed the rest of the truck over putting the full length of the truck in the water upside down.

Water began filling the cab immediately. This older truck's door seals were long gone. Steve was hanging upside down still in the belt. Now locked from the impact and trapping him head down. The water was already covering his forehead and filling fast. Soon he would not be able to take a breath. Steve looked to his left and the Mexican was already out of his belt and sitting on the roof of the cab like it was no big deal.

Steve couldn't believe his eyes. "Hey amigo, help me." He yelled as water was passing his eyes.

Steve's hands frantically worked to unfasten the belt so he could right himself and have a few minutes more of air. Blake had given him a handcuff key and it was in his pocket but there was no chance of getting to that.

He took one last breath before the water covered his mouth completely. The truck was sinking fast and the cab was violently rocking back and forth as it plunged to the bottom of the lake. Steve fought to find the release of the belt but the seat had broken during the impact and now the release was behind him. He would die here just like this, and it made no sense. What the hell had just happened? This crazy Mexican drove that truck right into the guard rail. Feeling his lungs starting to burn the last thing he thought was about the red x on the concrete below the guard rail. This was no crazy random deal. This was on purpose, this was Carlos.

Just then the door of the cab opened and Steve felt water rush over his entire body. The seat belt was cut away and a regulator was shoved into his mouth. Air filled his mouth suddenly and he began to breathe with a few water filled coughs. A hand grabbed his arm and pulled him from the cab. His mind raced trying to manage what the hell was happening around him. This couldn't be the FBI. It was too fast. The x was marking the spot. The guard rail was cut away otherwise the impact would have been much worse. These divers were in the water. This was Carlos taking control.

How was it possible for him, in just a few hours, to plan this or had he planned it as soon as I had taken the truck Steve thought. Maybe he had planned on forcing the truck off the road at this moment but instead was able to put a driver in that would do it for him. No doubt some other pour waiter guy that would walk away from this with fifty thousand in his pocket and be happy as hell.

A second diver had joined the other and both now had Steve by the arms. They each had an underwater propulsion unit and they were now flying through the water. Under normal circumstances, this would be very cool, Steve thought, and he had to hand it to Carlos for pulling it off, but this was not going to end well for him.

He probably wouldn't get the chance to get to the gun on his ankle before he was searched or knocked unconscious. He sure hoped Blake could figure out where the hell he was right now. Hopefully the tracker he swallowed was working. Hopefully it worked underwater.

For ten minutes or longer, they were underwater. Steve was so cold by the time they surfaced he couldn't move. The last thing he saw was Carlos standing over him drawing back to punch him straight in the face.

Blackness overcame him as he went unconscious.

In the chopper, Blake and the other men were trying to get an understanding of what was happening on the ground. They had New Orleans Police moving and a wrecker service with huge wreckers on the way. The nearest diver they could get in touch with was twenty minutes out.

Blake threw his note pad to the floor of the chopper. "This is a fucking disaster."

Heather began to put the pieces together now. "Steve is underwater isn't he?"

Blake looked at his men and then at Heather. "Yes, which means Carlos had divers waiting and they now have Steve and the drugs."

"But how are you tracking Steve?"

Blake realized, Heather didn't know all the details of what had happened over the last two days.

"We gave Steve a tracker for him to swallow for just this reason. When the other trackers hit the water, they quit. There not waterproof. Steve's will work for about twenty-four hours. After that we have nothing."

Panic covered her face. "Well what the hell are we doing? Go get Steve, I don't care about the drugs or Carlos."

"I understand Heather. But I can't take you and Max into a potential gun fight."

ROAD RAGE

"Bullshit, we both have been through worse today! Go get my husband!"

"We will drop you at the bridge and a medical chopper will take you and Max to a hospital for treatment. As soon as you're safe, trust me we will go get Steve. We will do everything we can to save your husband. He made me promise to take care of you first."

Heather grabbed Blake by the shirt snatching him almost out of his seat. "You better get my fucking husband back do you hear me!"

Blake sat back in fear. "Yes ma'am."

Heather looked over at Max. "Honey we don't use that kind of language do you hear me. It's not nice but mommy is a little upset right now."

All four men and Max tried to keep from cracking a smile. Max nodded his head and didn't say a word.

Three minutes later they were landing on the bridge. NOPD had stopped traffic and the wreckers were approaching. There was no sign of the truck or Steve. Blake, Heather and his men all stared down at the water.

Heather turned and looked at Blake. "What the hell are you waiting on? My husband is underwater somewhere!"

Blake and his men took off in a run. Five seconds later they were in the air. Blake pulled up the tracker on his lap top and it showed Steve's location about half a mile to the west of their location. Blake scrambled for his head set. "West Mac he's going west. Push this bird as hard as you can."

Mac gave the thumbs up and the chopper banked hard. Blake looked at Tom and pointed at the AR15 laying across his lap now. Tom laid his hand on the weapon and patted it like a good dog. It was understood that if he got a shot at Carlos he was to take it. No permission needed.

As they came up on the tracker location they could see two boats racing at full speed across the lake. As they made visual contact the boats split apart. Steve's track began to move left with the boat on the left. Mac looked back at Blake for direction. Blake pointed left knowing Carlos was probably in the boat on the right.

Blake motioned for Tom to get in the gunner seat and ready himself to take out the boat. Mac began to descend and Tom took aim. Fifty feet above the boat and going sixty miles an hour, Tom opened up. The AR15 was set on three round blast and Tom was burning through his first thirty round clip. The boats front end began to splinter.

Blake looked out over Tom's shoulder to see Steve curled up in a ball at the back of the boat. From the chopper he couldn't tell if Steve was dead or alive.

As the first bullets hit the bow, Juan the driver of the boat killed the throttle and the boat immediately slowed. As that happened the helicopter shot past the boat and Tom let off the trigger. Mac yelled to hang on from the front and banked hard.

Juan grabbed Steve, still unconscious and threw him over the back of the boat. Steve was barely in the water when he hit the throttle again on the boat. Steve's face was two inches from the prop when he did. Blood filled the water as the boat screamed away.

Mac banked hard and came around just as Steve hit the water and the guy took off. Blake knew they had just thrown Steve in and to save him they would have to get him immediately. As Mac maneuvered over the drop site Tom took aim, flipping the selector to fully automatic. Thirty rounds began to scream out of the AR at the boat.

Blake knew what had to happen and took his cell phone and wallet out of his pocket and through them down on the seat, kicked off his shoes and jumped out while they were still 20' above the water.

Steve, barely conscious, at the time he went into the water, opened his eyes and saw the prop of the boat begin to turn. Jerking back as much as possible, put his shoulder in direct contact. Steve felt the pain through his entire body as the 5000 RPM turning prop took his shoulder skin down to the bone. Steve screamed under water as he went end over end in the rush of prop water. Disoriented and in pain, he gulped in a huge moth full of water.

Blake hit the water like a ton of bricks. His plan was to hit feet first, but with the slowing momentum of the chopper and his speedy jump he landed sideways, slamming his face hard against the surface of the water. As he righted himself and tried to get his bearings on where Steve had gone in, he heard the splash of another man behind him. Agent Ed Kennedy had jumped in also when he saw that Blake took a hard hit on entry. Two seconds after that he heard a massive explosion in the direction the boat had gone.

Blake looked up at the helicopter to see Tom give him the thumbs up and point towards Ed. Blake spun and Ed was surfacing with Steve in Tow. Blood was everywhere and Steve was choking both spitting out water and taking it in with the rough surface of the lake. Blake got to the both of them and they each took an arm to stabilize Steve.

Mac looked back at Tom and quickly told him that he was going to set the chopper skids in the water. He would have to pull the guys in. Tom unbuckled, secured his AR and gave

Mac the thumbs up. Mac opened the window in his door and hung his head out to see the water. Like the pro that he was, he eased the chopper down right beside Blake. Tom, with his massive upper body strength reached down and pulled Steve straight up onto the floor of the chopper. Blake and Ed both climbed in on their own.

Mac turned around to see everyone in safe, and lifted back off. Steve, was still spitting water out and writhing in pain from his shoulder. Blake, Tom and Ed went into action as if they had just left the battlefield with an injured soldier in tow. Tom ripped Steve's shirt off the shoulder while Ed got gauze, to pack the wound. Blake was on his phone to report that they had Steve and had blown up one of the boats.

The director wanted to know about the drugs. Blake had nothing to tell him.

Blake's boss screamed into the phone. "What do you mean you have nothing? I told you to get trackers on those drugs that we couldn't afford to lose them. What happened Blake?"

Blake closed his eyes. "Sir they drove the fucking truck into Lake Pontchartrain. We were all over it with trackers and surveillance. Nobody could have expected that. How do you plan for something like that?"

Steve reached up and grabbed Blake's leg. In a harsh whisper he spoke. "I know where."

Blake looked down and Steve nodded his head yes. "Sir I have to go. I will call you back as this thing develops."

Blake hung up and bent down next to Steve. "Tell me what you know man. I could use some good news right about now."

They had wrapped Steve's shoulder now and gotten the bleeding to stop. Steve sat up with his back against the cockpit wall. Taking in several deep breaths as he let the pain subside. "Irish Bayou. Carlos himself was on the other boat. He pulled me from the water and punched me straight in the forehead. I hit the ground hard and pretended to be out. They were hauling ass in those boats and Carlos was screaming orders to the other men. I heard him say something about tonight and the Irish Bayou marina."

Blake grabbed Steve by the shoulders in excitement forgetting about the wound for a minute. "Dude you are my hero!"

Steve screamed out. "Owe! My shoulder!"

Blake let go and began to laugh. "Sorry man, but I swear your family is the toughest bunch of people I have ever met."

Steve looked up at Blake. "Tell me you got Heather."

Blake smiled from ear to ear. "We got her. But not before she killed three of Carlos's men. One of them being an FBI agent. Y'all are a trip."

Steve smiled. "That's my girl. Thank you guys for saving my family. I think I will pass out now."

As Steve said that he closed his eyes and began to slowly fall over. Blake reached out and caught him before his head hit the ground. Blake looked up at Mac. "Mac, let's get him to the nearest hospital, in a hurry!"

Mac nodded as the helicopter leaned forward picking up speed. Blake and Tom got Steve up and strapped into a seat. Blake got a headset on so that he could talk with the whole crew.

Jeff Stein came on the radio, Mac's co-pilot. "Sir, we will be at East Jefferson General in four minutes. I called ahead and they have a trauma team on the roof waiting. Is he gun shot?"

Blake took a second to look over Steve one good time to make sure it was just his shoulder. He couldn't see anything else bleeding. "No. Tell them it is a deep wound to the shoulder and possibly a concussion. He's lost a lot of blood."

Jeff held a thumb up as he transferred the information to the hospital staff on the radio. As soon as that was handled, Blake got back on the phone with the director. When the yelling stopped, Blake informed him that Steve had heard the rendezvous point during the boat ride. They didn't know a time but, Steve had heard him say it would be that night after things calmed down.

Blake and the director agreed that surveillance needed to be going on at every place along the lake that had a private dock, boat ramp or beach area. They couldn't let these drugs get away again. Blake hung up and looked at his men. "What a day."

Blake called the agent he had put on Heather and Max to find out what their status was at this point. They also were at East Jefferson, being the biggest hospital in the area. Blake sat back smiling, knowing that soon the three Lawson's would be back together safe, but a little bit worse for the ware. All three would recover and make it out of this thing alive.

Two minutes later Mac was setting down and the trauma team jumped into action. Blake grabbed his phone as soon as he was in a quiet area began to call in for reinforcements so that he and his men could go after Carlos. Tom shook his head no. Blake stared at him confused.

"What do you mean no? No what? Don't call in for backup? I can't leave these folks unprotected. Carlos will know we came here, it's the biggest hospital in the area."

Tom spoke first. "Get some new guys, and you go find Carlos. I'm staying here to protect Steve."

Ed stood his ground too. "Then I have Max."

Blake looked at Vince. "I guess you get Heather then."

Vince smiled and leaned against the wall. "Yep."

Blake laughed. "You might miss catching one of the biggest drug dealers in New Orleans."

Tom shook his head. "I doubt it. He's underground now and will stay that way for a while. We got close today, and he knows it. But boss, we have the rest of our lives to catch bad guys. This family has been through enough. I made Steve a promise that he wouldn't be alone, and I meant it."

Ed and Vince stood silently nodding their heads. Blake smiled and shook each of their hands. "You guys are damn good men. Get some food and get on them and don't let them leave your sight. If they go into surgery you go into surgery. If Carlos has got cops and FBI agents on the payroll he damn sure could have a nurse or staff member on payroll too. Hell, you're probably right about Carlos too, but I have to stay on the hunt. Keep me posted with their conditions. As soon as we can, we need to get them on a bus and the hell out of New Orleans. You guys will stay on that all the way. Hopefully we can get them secure and I can have you guys back tonight. If you can get them all in one room, you guys take turns getting some sleep."

With that, Blake took off running for the helicopter. Mac powered up and off they went.

When Tom and the crew got inside there were two agents standing outside the ER area waiting for Heather and Max.

Tom approached and asked their names. Each man answered and showed his credentials. Tom looked casually and told them they were dismissed. Both guys stood their ground. Tom shifted his AR15 slightly and both men took a step back.

Tom smiled. "Call Agent Hardy and he will reassign you. My team has been with this thing for days and we will protect them from now on. Got it?"

One of the agents pulled out his phone and dialed Hardy. Blake answered on the first ring. "What happened?"

The agent stuttered. "Sir, sir, there are three big swat dudes here that say we are relived. You told us to stay on these people no matter what. I need to hear that from you and I sure hope they're telling the truth."

Blake laughed. "Agent Barnes I'm sorry. I should have come down and told you myself. Those three guys are my team and they will stay with the Lawson's from here on. Return to headquarters and we'll regroup. Tell my guys to quit being bullies!"

The guy hung up the phone and smiled at Tom. "They're all yours."

Tom nodded back. "Where is Heather and Max?"

The agent pointed. "In the ER, they told us to wait out here."

"Who told you?"

"The Nurse, she said we couldn't come back there."

Tom shook his head. "You're and idiot! Don't you know this drug dealer has people everywhere trying to kill this family?"

All five men came through the ER door with guns drawn. Two nurses hit the floor screaming and a security guard stepped around the corner to see why. As he did he was pinned to the wall by Tom, who passed him off to Vince as he kept walking.

Tom in a loud authoritative voice said. "Heather Lawson are you in here? Max Lawson are you here. It's the FBI!"

Two doctor's stepped out from behind curtains, looked at each other, and then at the two large men coming their way.

One of them spoke. "Gentlemen, you can't be back here, it's staff only."

Tom reached both of them and grabbed an arm each. "I am going to protect these people and that means I don't leave their sides. Now where are they?"

Heather spoke softly from behind the curtain. "Doctor it's okay. Agent come in here and show me some ID."

Tom let go of the doctor and straightened out the wrinkles in his jacket. He leaned down to the doctor's ear. "Sorry about that, it's been a long day."

Tom pulled the curtain back only to have a Beretta 9mm pointed straight at his head in Heather's right hand. Tom flinched instantly, moving his right hand to his AR resting across his back.

"Don't do it! I have had a really bad day today, and everybody I have been around has tried to kill me. So you stay real still and slowly show me some ID."

Heather was lying in a hospital bed with a stich needle hanging in her arm still in mid stich. While Max was in the bed next to her with the curtain open between them. Heather looked up at Tom. "Don't I know you from earlier in the helicopter?"

Tom handed his badge and ID to her very slowly. "Easy now Heather. Yes, you do. I came with Agent Hardy to get you earlier today.

Tom pulled out his cell phone. "I'm gonna get Blake on the phone so you can talk. Take it easy."

Heather lowered the gun to bed and sat back relaxing now that she remembered. "You shouldn't come charging in on a woman who has been shot at, hit, and killed people all in the same day Agent. That's not good for your career."

The phone began to ring on speaker. "This is Blake, what's up?"

"Hey boss its Tom. I got you on speaker here with Heather. She needs to verify who we are. She didn't quite remember me, and stuck an agency issue Beretta 9mm in my face when I came in. I guess you missed that on her when you helped her to the helicopter."

Blake was silent for a moment. "Heather is everything okay now?"

"Yeah, I'm sorry about that. Where is my husband?"

"He's there, we got him back."

Panic now all over her face. "Why isn't he down here? Is he hurt?"

"He's fine, but needs surgery for his shoulder."

"I want to see my husband right now."

"Heather I think they took him straight into surgery, but Tom will get you to him as soon as he can. No more guns okay. Please give that gun to Agent Scott."

Tom leaned over palms out and picked up the 9mm from the bed, laying the phone in Heather's lap. Gun in hand, he took a step back from Heather. Dropping the magazine out and finding no bullets in the gun or the clip. He began to smile and looked up at Heather smiling back at him.

He turned to look at Vince standing to steps behind him, gun in hand ready for whatever happened. Tom smiled showing Vince the empty gun. "She was bluffing! Damn I like this girl."

Heather picked up the phone and took it off speaker. "Blake, is Steve hurt bad, tell me the truth. What happened?"

Blake took a deep breath. "Heather he'll be fine. They threw him off the back of a boat and his shoulder got in the prop a little. Not bad, but it took some skin and meat off down to the bone. He lost a lot of blood and will be hurting for a while, but he's fine. He's gonna be just fine. Tom, will get all you guys together in one room and watch over you. You have Tom, Vince and Ed. Three of my best guys."

Heather laid back in the bed now seeing the doctor standing there terrified at all that was happening. "Okay, I have to go. The doctor just got the crap scared out of him and may tell us all to leave. I'll talk to you later."

Heather handed the phone back to Tom. "Good to meet you again. Sorry about the whole gun pointing thing. I've had about enough of people trying to kill me and my son today."

Tom nodded his head to Heather. "You're one tough lady."

Tom looked over at Max whom had not said a word during any of this. "How about you little man, how you doing?"

Max smiled and said. "Okay, the doctor said he would try and fix my hand up as good as he could but I might only be able to throw curve balls. I'm not really sure what that means but at least it doesn't hurt anymore. They gave me medicine for that."

Tom smiled. "Doc can you finish her up?"

The doctor came in holding his breath as he walked past Tom. "Can you wait outside, this is a sterile environment."

Tom looked at Heather, then Max and then at the doctor. "Nope. This is my post now and I don't leave their side. Sorry doc."

Tom looked back at Vince and Ed standing further back. "You guys go find Steve and make sure he's protected. I got this. I'll call you when we're done here."

Both men nodded and disappeared. Tom turned back to Heather who was now trying to cover her exposed bra up with the blanket.

Tom stared down at her for a second and realized that she was embarrassed by the lack of clothing. "Oh shit! Sorry ma'am. I……." Turning quickly.

Tom turned putting his back to her, now facing Max. Tom's face turned red as he looked down at the boy laughing at his embarrassment.

Max giggled.

Tom shook his head. "Shut up kid."

CHAPTER 14

Family Reunited

Heather was sewn up and wearing a blue scrub top since her original top was torn and bloody. Max's hand had been treated and sewn up, minus two fingers on his right hand. The doctor talked about surgery, but the bottom line was, the fingers were gone and there was nothing that could be done.

Steve, was still in surgery getting tendons put back, and a skin graph done. Unfortunately, for him the scar on his shoulder would be a permanent and constant reminder of probably the worst day of his life. Tom remained with Heather and Max in a hospital room resting while Ed and Vince took turns standing inside the surgery suite watching over Steve through the window at the scrub sink.

They had decided, that once Steve was out of surgery and recovery, that they would transport them to a hospital just over the state line for the remainder of the hospital stay. Once that was done, they would be moved to a witness relocation home in Georgia. They would send a team to sweep their house for bugs and pack it all up. The cars would be sold and new ones purchased under their new identity. When they left for Georgia it would be to start a whole new life. What they had done here in New Orleans, the friends they had made and the enemies now would be left behind.

Tom was on and off his phone during most of Steve's surgery making the arrangements including new passports, driver's licenses and paperwork needed for the Lawson's to disappear. Tom was explaining to Heather how the process would work including testifying at a trial about what Carlos had done, once they caught him.

Heather laughed as he finished that statement. "You really think there will be a trial? Carlos will never be captured. You know that right?"

Tom grinned and patted the AR15 leaning against the wall next to him. "Just stating the possibilities so you know."

Heather looked up at the ceiling and sighed. As she did she put both hands on her face. "My husband won't rest until that man is dead. You do know that, right?"

She now looked at Tom in all seriousness. "You know that don't you. I have never seen this side of him. The man I've seen these last few days is not the man I have known for all these years. I am afraid he may do something stupid when he wakes up from surgery."

Tom shifted uneasily. Not really sure what to say. "We won't let him Heather."

She laughed. "You won't let him? Unless you put Carlos in the ground, there will be no letting him. That man is fierce about protecting Max and I. I can't imagine what he will be like now. Carlos woke something up inside of him that I've never seen before."

Tom looked at Max asleep on the bed and then back at Heather. "Don't worry, we'll end this when the time comes. Carlos won't survive it. I promise. I got to know your husband pretty well over the last few days. I know he won't stop until this is done. Neither will we."

Tom's earbud chirped in his ear, and Vince's voice came over the mic. "Steve's good. We're headed to the room now. He's awake but still pretty out of it. We're here for the night."

Tom stood and shouldered the AR.

Heather jumped to her feet. "What is it?"

Tom stuck out both hands for her to hold. "Steve is good, and coming here to the room. Stay in here and let him come to you please. I'm going to the hall to make sure everything is good. Just stay put.

Heather crossed her arms and looked at Tom with the look.

Tom shook his head. "I said please!"

Heather held the gaze with Tom, but sat back down on the bed. "Okay. But hurry up."

Tom stepped into the hall and looked both directions. There were a few nurses standing at the nurse's station at the end of the hall but otherwise the place was calm. Tom could hear Vince talking to Ed as the elevator doors opened. Tom instinctively looked back down at the nurse's station that was now empty.

Tom paused at that, and began to step that way as Vince, Ed and an orderly pushing Steve's bed came around the corner. The nurses had just been there working. Vince and Ed immediately went on guard when they saw Tom pull his AR in front of him.

Ed looked at the orderly. "Quick, in the room."

Steve looked up at Ed and then the orderly. "Is there a problem?"

Ed patted Steve on his good shoulder. "Nothing to worry about. Just being careful."

Tom took two more steps towards the station, when a doctor came into view. Tom's fingers tightened on the AR. The doctor stopped and stared at Tom. Tom didn't raise the AR but held his ground.

The doctor had his hands crossed behind his back like he was on a leisurely stroll in the park. "Is there a problem officer?"

Tom stared and noticed that the man didn't raise his hands as any normal person would in the situation. Tom started to speak when the muzzle of the silenced weapon flew out from behind the man.

In an instant Tom was hit in the chest. The impact slammed him against the wall and to the ground. Ed ran forward pulling his AR up and fired.

The first shot hit the doctor in the chest but he didn't go down. Ed raised his aim and was now pulling the trigger as fast as he could. He felt the doctors second shot fly by his head as his bullets began to hit the man in the neck and face.

Vince, was pushing Steve's bed hard now trying to make the turn into the room. The orderly had stopped pushing when the bullets began to fly. Ed was running now towards Tom on the ground, not taking his eyes off the gunman.

The orderly came back up on the opposite side of the bed from Vince, with a syringe in his hand. As Vince went for his Glock, the man plunged the syringe towards Steve's chest. Vince knew he couldn't draw his weapon fast enough. He would kill this guy for sure but not before he stuck Steve.

Screams were now filling the halls. Ed was yelling out for Tom and the nurses were in a panic at the end of the hall. Vince was reacting to the orderly, but it wasn't going to be enough. The scene was playing out in slow motion to Vince, who was the only one realizing that the gunman was a distraction. As the syringe came down, Vince cleared his weapon and shot the man straight in the face.

The orderly flew back in a splatter of blood and brains against the wall. Vince closed his eyes and lowered his weapon to his side. The hallway went silent.

Steve looked down at his chest to see Vince's left hand protecting him. The syringe was sticking out of the top of Vince's hand with the plunger fully depressed. Vince took a step back, holstering his Glock. As he did Steve pulled the syringe clear of Vince's hand. Sitting up now he began to scream as loud as he could.

"Get somebody in here right now!"

Tom grabbed Ed's hand looking up at him from the floor. "I'm fine go get some help."

Vince fell against the wall. With each second that passed he could feel his body weakening from the drug. He grabbed his wrist as hard as he could to try and stop the blood flow but it was to late.

Steve was trying to get up to help but was so weak he could barely move. Tom rolled over grabbing his chest where the bullet proof vest had been struck by the first shot. The bullet was still hot as he touched it.

Vince felt his knees go out from under him as Ed came running back down the hall. Vince looked up at Ed as he approached. He reached up grabbing at his body armor gear. Pulling him down close. He could see the doctors and nurses coming but he knew it was too late. His breathing was shallow now, and getting harder to take another breath. Ed was now right on top of him holding him up in a sitting position.

Vince smiled at Ed. "Make sure you get this fucker for me."

Ed grabbed Vince's face. "Don't you do this to me. You better fight it. Doctor!" He screamed.

Tom stood now trying to get his breath. Holding his AR at the ready if anything else came around the corner.

Vince began to lose consciousness as the doctor fought to get Ed out of the way.

The doctor laid Vince down trying to find a pulse. "He's coding, get the crash cart!"

In the room Heather heard the first shot and jumped in panic. She instantly grabbed Max from the bed and ran into the small bathroom in the room. She shut the door and locked it. Pulling Max behind her as they both got down on the floor. She could hear the gunfire and the screams of both FBI agents and others.

When the sounds stopped and the quiet came her heart began to pound in her chest. With no idea what had just happened. Had Steve been shot after all of this, so close to getting back to her? Was everybody dead now or was she about to have the door to that bathroom shot all to pieces killing her and Max?

She began to pray.

Ed backed away from Vince slowly looking up at Tom. Tom looked once more both ways in the hallway as people began to flood around them. "We got to get the hell out of here."

Ed nodded and they pushed Steve's bed into the room. As Tom came in, Heather and Max were gone. He stopped instantly and looked under the other bed and then back up at Ed.

Ed looked confused. "What?"

Tom looked at the bathroom door. "Heather?"

Heather heard her name but was afraid to answer not a hundred percent sure it was Tom.

Tom spoke again. "Heather, it's Tom. Are you guys in the bathroom?"

Heather stood slowly to the side of the door. "Is it safe?"

"Yes, come out. Steve's okay."

Heather rushed the door slamming into Tom as she came flying out of the bathroom. Tom recoiled holding the AR back to keep her from hitting it and him. She dove on top of Steve kissing his face all over.

Steve screamed in pain as he reached up with his good arm to squeeze her as tight as he could. Max came out a little slower sort of hesitating.

Steve looked down at him and smiled. "Hey little dude. You okay?"

Max began to cry.

Steve easily pushed Heather off of him and started getting up out of the bed. Tom stepped towards him putting a hand on his chest. "You better stay in bed."

Steve reached down and picked Tom's hand up. "You better help me up or get out of the way."

Tom laughed and helped him up. He held on to Steve as he took the few steps over to Max and bent down.

"Max buddy, I'm so sorry for everything that has happened to you and your Mom. This guy that did this to us is a really bad guy. Everyone he has kidnapped before, he's killed. If I had given up, he would have killed you and your mom instantly. I couldn't have lived with that."

Max wiped his tears away. "He's done this before?"

"Many times."

"Did you kill him?"

Steve looked up at Tom. "Not yet, but I will!"

Max stared at his dad. "Good." As he said that he hugged his dad as hard as he could.

Steve grimaced in pain but didn't say a word. He put his good arm around Max and squeezed hard. "I love you son. I would have died before I let him kill you. I'm so sorry I couldn't keep him from hurting you."

Max crying harder now. "It's okay daddy. I'm okay."

Heather crying as well pulled Max slowly away from Steve. "Baby let's let Daddy get back in bed okay. He's hurt pretty bad too."

Max stepped back and noticed the bandage on his shoulder. "What happened?"

Steve smiled. "They tried to run over me with a boat and I got caught by the prop. I'm tough though don't you worry."

Tom laughed. "Y'all are all tough. But right now we need to get the hell out of here. This place is compromised."

Ed motioned back at the hall. "I'm gonna see how Vince is."

Tom nodded. "Stay alert. Nobody comes in here."

"Roger that. You calling Blake?"

"Right now. We're out of here in five either way.'"

"Roger that." And he walked back into the hallway.

As he did, they were still working on Vince. His gear was gone now and his shirt was cut up the middle. He heard the doc yell clear, as Vince's body jumped.

The doc looked up at him and shook his head no. He was gone.

Within five minutes of that there were cops all over the place. New Orleans PD had shut the hospital down and most of the roads surrounding it.

Ed stepped back in the room. "Vince didn't make it. We have got to get out of here now and it has to be by chopper. NOPD is all over the place."

Just about that time a knock came to the door. Ed spun bringing his weapon up to the ready. "Who is it?"

"New Orleans police. Can we enter?"

Tom stepped forward and pointed at Steve and Heather. "You stay in here. I will go out."

Tom turned to the door. "I am agent Tom Scott, FBI. I will come out there."

Tom went out and there were a dozen cops standing in the hallway. Tom looked at a young Latino officer standing in front of him. One hand resting on the butt of his pistol. Tom looked over his shoulder to see four more officers now starring at him and wondering what the hell was going on.

The officer spoke first. "Is everyone okay in there?"

Tom focused back on the officer. "Yes. You need to clear this hallway."

"Sir, do you mind if I come in there and take a look. Get some statements."

"Yes I mind. These people are under federal protection. Anybody comes in this room, they will be met with extreme prejudice. Are we clear officer Rodriquez?"

The man's name badge was on his shirt and he looked down at it as Tom said his name. His grip tightened on the butt of his gun. Tom took a step towards the officer now invading his personal space.

"Is there a problem with my instructions? Clear the hall. No one enters this floor until we are gone. Do you understand me?"

Tom now looking down at the officer having a good six inches on the guy in height. Whispering so only he could hear. "You better take your hand off that weapon and back away.

Your department is corrupted by this drug dealer and nobody is getting near this family again."

The officer moved his hand slowly, and took a step back. "What drug dealer?"

"Carlos. That's all we know. So far three FBI agents are dead including one of my men just now. Luckily I had on a vest with a plate or I would be on the floor too."

Rodriquez looked at Tom's chest noticing the bullet hole in his gear. "Can I get a quick statement from you so I can do the report of what happened here today? I got three dead guys on the floor. I need to do my job too."

Tom took a breath and eased his stance slightly. "The people in this room have been held hostage for the last three days by a drug dealer named Carlos. One of the victims, was in surgery here. As we were bringing him to the room, one assailant dressed as a doctor fired at us from the end of the hallway. (Pointing at the guy dead on the floor.) As that happened I was struck in the chest by the first round, knocking me to the floor."

He looked down the hall at the dead doctor. "Who fired the shots that killed him?"

"Agent Kennedy with the FBI."

"Okay where is he?"

"He's in the room and not available right now."

As he said that his ear piece went off and Tom held up a hand. Touching his throat pod to speak. "Go ahead."

It was Blake. "Tom we just touched down on the roof. Where are you?"

Tom turned to look at the door number of the room. "Third floor room 345. Hurry!"

As Tom got off the radio he scanned the area once again. Most of the officers had begun to clear out. Several working with the hospital staff checking the downed men for life. As he scanned each office one stood out. A taller white guy that really wasn't doing anything. Tom noticed the man was sweating. His body language was tense and rigid. He kept watching Tom and then looking at the door. Tom swore and looked back at Rodriquez.

"Get these guys out of here right now. We'll have to do this later."

Rodriquez started to object. "But I have to know what went down here for the report."

Tom raised his AR15 up pointing right at the other cop. As he did he flipped his com unit to the VOX position so he broadcasted by just speaking without pushing his throat mounted com.

As Tom did this four officers drew their weapons now aiming them at Tom. Voices began to raise in the hall. "Lower your weapon sir."

Tom's eyes didn't move off the guy sweating. Tom speaking to Blake on the com set, more than anyone now. "You, keep your hands where I can see them."

The officer turned to fully face Tom. "What the hell are you doing man? I'm a New Orleans police officer. Lower your weapon."

Tom, repeated himself. "Keep your hands where I can see them. Officer Rodriquez will you please go remove that guys weapon from his belt, including his Taser."

The guy looked at Rodriquez and took a step back. "Nobody is taking my weapon. Jesus dude, what the hell is wrong with you."

Rodriquez turned back towards Tom. "Agent Scott you need to stand down."

Tom spoke. "Blake you need to be here right now, hot!"

Rodriquez took another step back. "Let's just all calm down, okay."

Tom's eyes never left the officer. "Drop your belt to the ground, now."

Ed came on the com. "Tom what the hell is going on out there? Do I need to come out?"

Tom spoke sharply. "No hold your position in the ready."

Ed immediately directed Heather and Max back in the bathroom and stood with his AR up and ready between Steve and the door.

Blake's voice next in Tom's ear. "There in two seconds. Me and four guys. Three in the elevator and two coming down the stairs. Weapons out correct?"

Tom quickly shifted his eyes back and forth to assess all that were in the hall. "Yes but slowly."

Rodriquez looked confused. "What the hell are you talking about? Put you gun down and let's calm down."

Just then Tom heard the elevator ding and the doors open. Rodriquez turned to see who was coming, but the other cop didn't move. He and Tom were locked in a death stare now.

The officer's eyes shifting from Tom to the door behind him. Sweat was now beading up on the man's forehead.

"Whatever Carlos has got on you, or threatening you with, it ain't worth dying over man."

The guy shook his head slightly acknowledging that Tom was right. His hand dropped slightly from a defensive stance towards his gun.

Tom aimed the AR straight at the guy's head. "I will drop you like bad habit man. I not fucking around."

Just then the hallway flooded with Blake and the other FBI guys. All had weapons out and ready. Tom's eyes never left the sweating cops eyes. Blake looked at where Tom was aiming and nodded to one of the agents behind him.

Agent Derrick Thomas charged the guy fast, body slamming him face first to the ground. Two other agents took positions next to Tom. Blake looked at the other officers now looking more confused than ever.

Tom lowered his AR and looked at Rodriquez. "Your man there is connected to Carlos. It may be that he's just on the guy's payroll or something else but whatever it is, he's dirty."

"Bullshit. I've known Bill for ten years. He's a good cop."

"Not today he's not. Blake we need to find out what he knows."

Blake agreed. "I will leave two guys here to deal with that. Right now, let's get them on the chopper and out of here."

Blake noticed Vince on the floor for the first time and looked at Tom.

Tom shook his head. "In the first attack the orderly went to inject Steve with something and Vince stuck his hand out to block it. Vince took the injection in the hand as he shot the guy in the face. He was dead within minutes."

The cop on the ground spoke as he was being man handled by the FBI agent that tackled him. "You can't beat this guy. He's everywhere. I'm a dead man so you might as well shoot me now."

Blake stepped over to the guy. "Tell us what you know."

"I know that my family is dead now. Carlos doesn't care about human life. He doesn't care what you know. Cause he's a ghost. You'll never catch him."

"Where does he stay here in New Orleans? Where have you met him?"

The guy shook his head. "I've never met him. A guy walked up to me outside and showed me a picture of Steve, his wife and kid. Told me if I didn't kill the three of them, they would kill my family. The guys then showed me a picture of my own fucking house. Who's going to protect my family? He handed me a card with a phone number on it and told me to call the number when it was done."

The guy began to cry as he was cuffed. Blake looked at Tom and then at Rodriquez. "You need to get guys to his house right now."

Tom stepped back into the room. "Get ready to go. We need to get you guys out of here right now."

Blake cleared the hallway and questioned the Officer more on what he knew. But he really knew nothing. He was approached and threatened and reacted. A decision that would cost him his career but no real reason to push the issue on a criminal level. He told Rodriquez to take him down to the station and get the full statement but to cut him loose after that. The FBI was not going to press it. Rodriquez understood and cleared out.

They got a wheel chair for Steve to make it easier and started heading for the roof. The entire trip up was like a military operation. Seven men now guarding them like they were the royal family under siege.

Blake, Tom and ED were the only ones in the chopper as they took off. Blake sent a car for the other guys and they took care of Vince. Blake would have to go see his wife when this thing was over. Vince had been a great team member and a loyal friend to all of them. It was time to catch this guy and put an end to it all.

The chopper lifted off and climbed to altitude safe from sniper fire or any other crazy possibilities this last few days had proven to be possible.

Mac turned around and smiled at the Lawson's. "Welcome back. I hope all you guys are okay?"

Heather and Max both said they were but Steve was still pretty out of it from the surgery. He managed a thumbs up as he leaned against Heather.

Mac turned to Blake. "Where to?"

CHAPTER 15

Recovery Time

The chopper cruised for a fairly short flight landing at a small airport outside of New Orleans. There they boarded an FBI jet. The flying was much smoother and Steve could lay down instead of sitting in the chopper. As they boarded Tom and Ed helped Steve in and got him situated.

After Steve was good, the two men sat down and both began to safe the weapons for the flight. Blake started to complain but just dropped it knowing the two men and how their loyalties ran. He stood there looking at both shaking his head.

Steve looked over at both of them and smiled. "Guys. You don't have to stay with us all the way. I am sure we'll be fine once we're out of New Orleans. Go with Blake and kill this asshole. You know where he will be tonight. Even if he's not there capture his men and make them tell you. These guys will know more than anybody we have dealt with so far. Besides you need to get the drugs. So go!"

Tom smiled. "We told you we would stick with you."

Heather looked at Blake. "Do you know these other two agents on the plane?"

Blake nodded. "Sure do. They are two guys I have known since coming to the FBI. They're solid."

Heather looked at Tom. "Thank you for saving my husband and our lives today and the last few days. Go do what you do best. We will get hidden away somewhere and be fine. You can come check up on us later. Go kill this guy for us. You are with us by doing that."

Tom nodded and looked at Ed. Both men stood.

Steve said. "Get this guy for Vince. He took that syringe today knowing it meant his life. He gave his life up for me."

Steve put his hands over Max's ears. "Fuck their shit up, Okay."

Both men nodded and got off the jet. Blake gave instruction to the other two agents and introduced them both. He shook Steve's good hand and hugged Heather. "You take care of these two men." Looking at Max and Steve.

Heather smiled. "I will. Watch your back Agent Hardy. And thank you for everything."

With that, he was gone and the plane took off.

They flew for a few hours and landed in a small town near Nashville Tennessee. The two agents on board met with the local agents there and checked everything out. From there they went to a local hospital and were each checked again to make sure no wounds were open or looking infected.

For the first time they were introduced as the Stevenson family from Georgia. Steve was now Clark Stevenson. Heather was now Patricia Stevenson and Max was now Jake. The agents had given them all new passports, birth certificates and Heather and Steve drivers' licenses issued by Georgia.

Once the doctor was gone Steve asked the agent. "We're in Nashville, are we living here or in Georgia?"

The agent smiled. "You'll be in Georgia, Clark. But we wanted to do a small detour just to make sure we were not being followed in any way. All air traffic will be grounded for thirty minutes when we take back off. This is not our first time. The FBI has witnesses all over the world. We'll keep you guys safe."

Steve laughed. "Clark! Who came up with that?"

He laughed. "I don't know how they pick names at Whitsec. We don't ask those guys many questions. They're kinda shy about what they do."

He laughed. "Well, Clark ain't too bad. Could have been worse. Could have been Harold and Maude with our son Tex."

He laughed. "That would be bad. But you're going to Georgia. I could make a call and see if Bubba and Sissy are available with your son Junior to round it out."

They both laughed as Heather and Max just looked at them both like they were stupid. By now, Steve was feeling good and they all realized that they really hadn't eaten anything in three days. Steve was starving, so they took a detour and went and had some great BBQ before leaving Nashville.

Once they were back on the plane, the agents explained the entire witness relocation process. How they could contact family and what they were allowed to say. There were bank accounts set up and money in them. Not a huge amount, but enough for them to take a few weeks to get oriented, buy the things they needed and get set up. It was explained that their cars would be sold at auction and then the money transferred to them. Same with their house and any money in bank accounts that they had. 401K's would be closed and the money laundered through them so that nothing was traceable.

They explained that it was as if the entire family had been killed and reborn.

From this time forward they were to use their new names and nothing else. Better to practice with each other than to slip up in public.

Clark laughed. "Jake, what do you think about moving to Georgia?"

He shrugged his shoulders. "Does that mean I will have to be a redneck?"

The agent laughed. "Have you guys ever been to Georgia? It's really nice there. It's not the redneck place of yesteryear."

Patricia shook her head no. "We both grew up in Louisiana. That's where we met and decided to live. We both have some family there. That made it nice."

As she said that, the horror of what Carlos might do terrified her. "What about our family. What if Carlos goes after our family?"

"Talk to Blake about that tomorrow. Hopefully they will get the guy tonight. Most likely we will have you get in touch with each and see if it is convenient for them to get out of town for a few days."

Clark shook his head. "This is never gonna end until this guy is dead. Even from jail he could arrange stuff."

The agent shook his head. "We almost never see the families of witnesses in danger. I'm sure it will be fine."

Clark laughed. "You don't know this guy like I do. He even threatened where I work." Clark sat up quickly. "Shit, I told Tyrone to go get your car and to lay low in case I need help. I have to call him and tell him what's going on."

"Nope, I'm afraid not. We'll send somebody to get him and let him know. You really can't reach out to anybody right now. You need to be completely off the grid for a few days. Let the trail go cold. Do you know where he lives?"

"Not really. Near the shop. He's in Heather's, I mean Patricia's car. It's older, just let him keep it. He's a really good kid though. You guys need to protect him."

He smiled. I'll make the call and get somebody over to the garage.

Clark looked at Patricia. "I hope he's okay. Such a nice kid."

Patricia looked at Clark. "Why is he in my car?"

He shook his head. "Because I told him to go to the house and get your car, the cash I keep in my sock drawer and go buy some guns on the street. At the time I didn't know what would happen in this deal. I thought I may have to shoot my way out of it. The FBI wasn't involved at that point."

She reached over and grabbed his hand. "These last few days must have been hell for you. Not knowing if Max, I mean Jake, and I were dead or alive. I can't imagine what you were going through."

He swallowed hard. "It was hell. I never thought I would be in a position to kill a man again, once I left the Army. This guy has made me do things I never wanted to do again. Taking a life was never what I wanted to do. Even when I was a sniper. The only thing that kept me sane, was knowing that if I didn't, those men would kill American soldiers. No different this week. If those men got control of that truck, I knew you and Max were dead. Hardest thing I have ever done."

Max came over and hugged his dad. "You mean Jake right?"

Clark laughed. "That's right Jake. Keep me straight." He hugged him tight. "I'm sorry you guys had to go through what you did. This is one evil man."

Just then the Agent came back over with a terrible look on his face. Clark looked up. "What?"

"I just got a call back from Blake. They sent a guy to the garage. The place was burned to the ground. So is your house. Apparently, Carlos is in a rage."

"What about Tyrone and Jack at the garage?"

"Tyrone is not there, neither is your car. They found an older man in the office area. Burned badly but they think he was probably dead before the fire. "I'm sorry."

"My whole family is in danger. This guy is a maniac, you get that right?"

"Yes I do, but we don't have the manpower to be in all these places."

"Take me back to New Orleans right now."

"No way. That's not happening. All that will do is get you killed."

"Get Blake on the phone."

Patricia stood next to him. "Baby you can't fight this guy. Your shoulder is torn up. You're not a cop! You have to let them handle it."

"Heather they will kill our family, your mom. My brother in Gulf shores. Our cousins. This guy won't stop. You don't know him like I do."

She looked at him. "I don't, he hit me in front of Max. He threatened to rape me every day. He told me how he would kill you in front of us, over and over. I do know him."

He hugged her again. I'm so sorry babe. I didn't mean that you didn't know how awful this guy was. I just know how angry he is and he told me several times that he would kill everybody I knew if I didn't do what I was supposed to. You know I have to end this with him."

"No you don't."

He looked at the agent again. "Back to New Orleans. If Carlos thinks I am in the picture he will focus on me and not my family. Turn around now."

The guy shook his head and called Blake. In a few minutes Blake was on the phone. "Clark, listen to me."

Steve cut him off. "Not so fast, and for now it's still Steve."

"No, no, no" is all he heard.

"Blake you know good and well that if I show up and become visible, Carlos will lose his mind trying to get at me. Otherwise, my whole family is in danger. You can't protect all those people. Hell, look at Jack's garage. It's gone now and he's dead because he just knew me. I'm sure he's tracking down my Dad right now. Heather's Mom. You need to get agents there right now."

"Steve, I know and we can get agents to each of those places. You're a civilian and if you go after him, he will kill you on site. There won't be any coming in to get you. This is too much man. Now go to your new home and settle in. Heal your shoulder and let us handle it. We'll get the guy. I promise."

"Blake, either tell this guy to turn around or I will get a car as soon as we land and go at this on my own. I'm sick of this guy running my life. By now, I bet he already has the drugs even though he set it up like tonight was the night. By tomorrow he'll disappear and you'll never catch him. Two months from now he will have another wife and kid in captivity and some guy driving a truck. This ends with me. I'm the bait damn it. Now let's catch the wolf and be done."

Steve handed the phone back to the agent and walked away.

The agent slowly put the phone back to his ear. "Yes sir. I know sir. I'll tell the pilot."

He hung up the phone. Made eye contact with Steve and turned to go talk to the pilot. In another minute, they could feel the plane bank left and begin to circle back around. Steve turned and looked at Heather.

Heather stood furious. "Why the hell does it have to be you? Why can't you just get our family all together for a week's paid trip to somewhere and let them finish this guy?"

Steve sat on the double chair and pulled her down beside him. Tears began to fill her eyes as she looked at him. "Why You?"

"Because there is nobody else. Carlos hates me with a passion and that will make him screw up enough to get caught."

"Yeah and it will get you killed in the process."

Steve looked down at the carpet, away from her. "I hope not."

Heather hit him in the arm. "You hope not! What the fuck is wrong with you? Why would you put your life up for grabs to stop this guy, knowing he will kill you on sight? That makes no sense. You're just gonna leave Max and me alone. Away from home and family, because we can never go back to New Orleans. You'll be dead and we'll be alone."

She turned away from Steve now an emotional wreck.

He reached out and touched her leg. "I can't live with another person I love being hurt by this guy. He will never stop. The minute I took control of that truck I knew it would be a fight to the death. His or mine. I'm sorry that you don't understand, but I will sacrifice my life for you and Max. I will kill the asshole if it's the last thing I do."

Steve stood and walked towards the pilot. "How long before we're in New Orleans?"

The guy turned around and looked at Steve. "One hour and forty-five minutes."

Steve sat down towards the front of the plane for a minute gathering his thoughts. He looked back at Heather to see Max hugging his mother while she cried. They had been through so much together because of this man. He knew right then, that he would do whatever it took to get Carlos in the open so that he or the FBI could kill him once and for all.

He sat back and closed his eyes. His head was killing him at this point. His shoulder hurt and he just wanted to be done with this whole thing. He needed to figure out how to get Carlos out in the open. He needed to find Tyrone and make sure he was okay. He needed to apologize to Heather and make her understand why he had to do this.

Just then he felt Heathers hand touch his leg and she sat down beside him. He opened his eyes and looked over at her. She was still crying but she laid her head on Steve's good shoulder and put her arms around him.

He reached over and put his arm around her. "I love you, babe."

"I know." She squeezed him a little bit tighter.

Max came up and stood in front of his dad. Steve looked up at him and pulled him into his lap. They rode that way for the next thirty minutes. Nobody saying anything. An understanding had passed between Steve and Heather. She knew he had to do it and why. He knew she understood and would not make things hard for him to go.

Heather finally sat up and looked at Steve. "How are you going to get this guy out in the open? If he just keeps sending his men to get you, eventually someone will."

Steve nodded. "I know. The best thing I got going for me, is he hates my guts right now and that makes him sloppy. Once you guys are safely gone and I don't have to worry about him getting to you, I will call him and tell him how much I enjoyed killing all his men."

She looked at him like he was crazy. "Don't try and be subtle or anything. Just piss him off right out of the gate."

He laughed. "He will tell me how he is going to hurt me and I will draw him out. He's not as smart as he thinks. I'll also have a team of FBI bad asses backing me up this time."

She smiled. "I hope they never leave your side. Those guys are tough. I like all of them."

Steve nodded. "Me too. Good guys."

Steve laid his head back and closed his eyes again. He needed sleep. He needed to quit hurting so bad. His shoulder was still bad, he had been punched in the face several times and almost drowned. So far this week had been pretty bad.

Sleep came and the last hour of the flight went fast. The agent on board the plane touched Steve's arm as they began to make the approach to New Orleans. Steve looked and nodded. He slowly woke up heather and she laid Max on the bench seat next to them.

Steve kissed her and held her face in his hands. "I wish I could think of a better way to do this. This guy will never stop chasing us and hurting the ones we love. I have to end it."

Heather nodded and understood. "Just get it done. Don't let this guy get the best of you. He'll kill you in a heartbeat if he gets the chance."

"I know he will. I won't let him."

The plane landed and Blake stood there waiting. Shaking his head. "You are one hard headed son-of-a-bitch. You know that?"

Steve climbed down the steps and shook his hand. "I know. I just couldn't leave you guys hanging. I know you need me."

Blake laughed. "Yeah, it's a miracle we got anything done before you came into our lives."

Steve laughed. "I know right."

Blake held out both hands wide in surrender. "Okay big man, what's the plan?"

"Give me your back up piece." And pointed at his ankle.

Blake shook his head. "Look man, I ain't no gun store. I can't even authorize you to carry a weapon. Especially one I give you."

Steve smiled. "It's not for me. It's for Heather. She's not going anywhere anymore without one. I don't care who you have watching her."

Blake stood there for a long minute and let out a loud sigh. "Come around to my trunk. I have a bag back there that I don't know about anything in there. If Heather has a gun when she gets to her final destination, I will swear I have no idea where it came from. You understand me?"

Steve nodded. "Loud and clear."

Steve walked around to the trunk and Blake opened a black bag and walked away. Steve looked in and saw a variety of guns. Everything from a small snub nose 38 to an Uzi. He wanted the whole bag for himself. Gingerly he pulled the 38 out for Heather. Checked the bullets and the weight. It was perfect and would fit easily in her purse.

He looked back in the bag and tugged on the handle of a Glock 23. He pulled it from the bag and dropped the clip out in his hand. Looking at the top round he saw a nice shiny brass hollow point. He flipped the clip over and saw brass all the way down. Eight rounds in the clip. He slowly slid the action back and saw one in the chamber. Steve slide the clip back in the gun until it clipped into place. He then pulled up his shirt and stuck the gun in his back waist band.

He closed the trunk and began walking back towards the plane. He nodded at Blake as he went by. "Thanks man. I'll only be a second or two."

Blake nodded back. "Hurry, I have twenty-five DEA agents and thirty FBI agents all waiting for Carlos to show us those drugs. We need to get you safe so I can go back to the fight."

"Good. I'll be right back."

Steve walked to the plane and boarded again. Heather was sitting there hanging onto Max. Not sure really what to do.

Steve came and sat beside her. "Where's your purse?"

She pointed to the back. "Why?"

Steve held up the pistol. "This is a 38 special. It's double action. That means you can pull the hammer back or just pull the trigger. You have six shots. It doesn't kick and it doesn't have a safety."

He looked at Max. "Buddy don't you ever touch this okay."

Max nodded his head. "Got it."

Steve walked to the back and put the gun in her purse.

Heather stood. "Please be careful. I don't know if I can take much more."

Steve put his arms around her. "I will be Patricia. You and Jake use your new names from now on. Nothing to tie you to this life from here forward. You understand? For the next few weeks don't call anybody, don't text, don't do anything. Your Facebook account will need to be deleted, twitter, everything. No matter what you see or hear on the news. Okay."

She looked hard at him. "Are you going to be gone for several weeks?"

"I don't know. I hope not. I hope this thing is over tonight. Maybe they will catch him and that will be the end of it. I don't know. But, I am going to have them do a press conference where I will tell them what happened and who did it to us. Hopefully that will draw him out in the open. Who knows."

"Jesus Steve, please think this through. If this guy gets one shot at you, you're dead. You know that?"

"I do. I am going to sleep tonight and see what happens with the drugs. Blake and I will get together tomorrow on all the other stuff and work out a plan. I'll be careful."

He kissed her hard and hugged her again tightly. Then bent down and hugged Max. Telling them both how much he loved them.

He turned, shook the FBI guys hand on the plane. "Watch after my family for me."

The guy gripped hard and assured him that he would. Steve let go and looked back at Heather and Max one more time. He smiled and waved as he stepped through the door. The door raised and the plane began to power up. Steve walked over to Blake's car and leaned against the door looking over at Blake.

Blake smiled. "Don't think for one second I don't see that piece in the back of your jeans pal."

Steve smiled. "Not trying to hide it my friend. If you didn't want me to have one, you wouldn't have left me back there alone with that bag of goodies. Lucky I didn't just take the hole bag. What is that anyway, your throw down weapon stash?"

"Damn right it is. If I catch Carlos tonight, he will be dead with a gun in his hand. Self-defense all the way."

"Nice!"

"You gonna tell me the plan or just keep me guessing."

Steve opened the door and got in. "Let's go!"

Blake shook his head and got in. "You're gonna tell me the plan or I swear I will take you in and book your ass for obstructing justice until the morning."

Steve laughed. "No you're not. You got bigger fish to fry tonight and I need some sleep."

"Yes I do. Let's get you to the safe house."

Steve put up his hand. "Dude no offense, but I don't think so. Who knows I'm back here?"

"Me, my guys, and the SAC. Of course the pilot changed the flight plan so there will be a handful on that end but they won't know why he turned around."

"Yeah, I don't trust anybody in New Orleans at this point but you, Tom and Ed. I think if it's okay with you, I'll check into somewhere low key with Clark's credit card and just lay low. Nobody knows where I am but me and you. Sound good?"

Blake nodded. "Yeah, I think that's a good plan. Let's go to the Sheraton downtown. Right in the tourist part, high rise structure, and lots of people. Nobody will notice or care who you are."

"Good plan. Look I need a Walmart or something. I have no clothes, tooth brush, razor or anything. Hell I've had the same underwear on for two days."

Blake looked at Steve with a puckered face. "TMI dude! I did not need to know that. Okay, there's a Walmart right down the road. Will get you set up and get you tucked in. Tomorrow, we'll get together and work out a plan. Hopefully we won't need to. I hope this asshole shows up tonight. If we don't get these drugs, it's gonna be a bad day for me at the bureau."

Steve shook his head. "I'm sorry man. I know your boss wanted those drugs, but I couldn't give up my family for it. You know what I mean?"

"Yeah man, I know. So does my boss, but that won't mean he doesn't have to chew my ass out for it in the morning."

"Will he fire you over it?"

"No, but in a no-win situation like things were, protocol is to cease the drugs. Better to lose one or two lives than to have millions of dollars' worth of deadly drugs hit our streets. You know how the media makes things look."

"Yeah, you tell him it ain't near as bad as it would be if I told the media the FBI sacrificed my family to cease those drugs."

"I know. Bottom line was that he wouldn't have done that. That's why he told me to do what I thought was best. It worked out. Heather and Max are safe."

"Patricia and Jake you mean."

They both laughed. "That's right. You did tell her no calls, no nothing for now, right?"

He nodded. "Yeah. Her and Jake can use a few days to heal and rest. Will they give her some kind of burner phone or something so that I can call her each day?"

Blake nodded. I'll make arrangements. Make sure she understands to just wait for you to call her."

Steve smiled. "I appreciate that Blake. You've been a good friend to me through all of this."

Blake smiled and patted him on the shoulder. "No problem man. You're one of the toughest guys I've ever met. What you did with that truck and fighting Carlos was bad ass. You got guts man. We'll get through this. We'll get you back to your wife and kid, I promise."

Steve closed his eyes and laid his head back. "I hope so, cause if I end up dead, heather is going to kill you."

"You mean Patricia?"

"Yeah, both of them. I die and you're a dead man."

Blake laughed. "Hey so if you die, how long should I wait before I ask her out? She's pretty hot! Kind of a badass too."

Steve sat up and looked at Blake. Blake busted out laughing.

Steve shook his head. "That ain't funny dude."

Blake grinning. "I know I couldn't help it. Really though, how long?"

Steve sat back and closed his eyes. "Go fuck yourself, that's how long."

The car got quiet as they headed to Walmart.

Blake looked over at Steve just as they pulled in. "I would at least wait a month."

CHAPTER 16

Catching the Drugs

After Blake got Steve in the hotel and quiet, he headed for his team. It was now close to one in the morning and all the teams were reporting in, that all was quiet. Blake got to the Irish Bayou Lagoon at One twenty in the morning. Tom and Ed were at two different marinas' just down the coastline. The agent for the DEA, was waiting on Blake at the Lagoon.

Agent Jeremy Farmer had been with the DEA for close to twenty years now and had been tracking Carlos for the last five. On multiple occasions, they had gotten close and had tracked the drugs through the border but managed to lose them every time. Carlos had been a very clever man when it came to smuggling drugs. By far, this was the closest they had ever come to catching the guy.

Blake radioed Jeremy as he approached. "Agent Farmer, what's your location?"

The agent quietly spoke. "I'm on Ridgeway Boulevard, near the small bridge that enters the Little Bayou area. A boat just pulled up about fifty yards out and is sitting there idling. Do not drive anywhere near here until I see what this guy is doing."

Blake killed the lights to his car as he pulled into the travel center. "Roger that. I'm at the travel center and staying put. Call if you see anything. We have a stealth chopper about a quarter of a mile out watching boat traffic. Let me know what you need."

"10/4." He said quietly.

Blake backed into a spot and shut the car off. It was quiet now and he could hear the sounds of the night. He pulled up his binoculars and began to search the water for anything. It was dark out on the water.

The radio cracked. Quietly the DEA agent spoke. "I have two black cargo vans approaching from my left on the service road next to highway ten. They have both stopped by the bridge."

Blake sat up. "That's Frontage Rd. Which way are the going?"

It was silent. "Standby."

Blake was dying. Could this be the brake they had been waiting on. Blake keyed the mic. "What do you see?"

At a whisper he heard. "Another boat just went past my location. Two men. One driving and one heavily armed. These are our guys. Wait for my signal."

Blake called Tom. Tom answered first ring in a whisper. "Boss, what's up, I can't really talk now. I have two boats approaching the marina. No lights, real quiet."

Blake knew instantly what was going on. Carlos was hitting multiple locations to see what happened. "Tom where are you?"

"South Shore marina. Gotta go."

The phone went dead. Each team had two men and certainly they could handle just about anything. Blake understood that this thing was about to blow up at a bunch of different locations. Carlos was smart. Blake got back on the coms. He set his radio to all teams.

"All teams listen up. Carlos is hitting multiple locations all at once. We have boats at two marinas' so far and I am sure there are more. They are heavily armed. Wait for them to unload the boats and then take them down. Don't play around with these guys. Shoot to kill."

Two other teams checked in with boats approaching. One at West End and another at North shore. That was at least four locations. No other areas were reporting traffic. Blake wondered how many they were missing. He got back on the coms. "All teams, if you have no boat traffic at this point head to the Irish Lagoon area. This is going down all around here."

The radio buzzed with chatter. Twenty teams began to report in and move. Five location now were reporting movement both in the water and on land. Blake reminded each to hold positions until the transfer of the drugs were in the vehicles and not in the boats. He knew once one of Carlos's teams got taken, they would all know. They would scatter like rats.

As back up, the FBI had called both the Coast Guard drug enforcement team and the Military. In New Orleans the Marines had an attack helicopter wing that was ready to rock. They all jumped at the chance for some nighttime live ammunition training. Both were on standby and Blake was ready to make the call. He wanted each of these boat guys to be captured as well.

Blake called and got the additional help coming. Two teams had reported men moving quickly from the boats to the vans.

As Blake sat quiet in his car coordinating, he looked up to see a New Orleans police cruiser turn into the parking lot. He slid down in his seat to keep from being seen. Blake and the SAC had intentionally left the NOPD out of this operation. Knowing the corruption level in the force, it would only take one to tip Carlos off.

The cruiser stopped about thirty feet away and sat there. Blake pulled his Glock from his side. Waiting for whatever came next. His radio was going crazy in his ear. All five locations now had drugs moving. Teams were racing in from more southern locations to back up and contain the drugs. The Coast Guard and Marines were minutes out. This was about to get ugly.

Blake sat up slightly and looked straight at a cop walking towards his car. The guy froze and pulled his gun. Blake swore. What the hell was this guy doing out here. Was this a random check or was this guy one of Carlos's men.

Blake eased the door open. "Easy now. FBI."

"Show me your hands!"

Blake could hear in his ear that the teams were now moving. He had to get across the road and intercept the two vans.

Blake stood up out of the car with his left hand up and his Glock in his right. "Look I said I am FBI. I am going to show you my badge. Relax!"

The cop yelled again. "I'm telling you, get both hands up where I can see them. Do it or I'll shoot."

Blake easily dropped the Glock on the front seat where it would be easy to get to if he needed it. He raised his other hand up in surrender. "Okay there up. Do you not see my vest and jacket both say FBI. I am here on a stake out."

The guy kept his gun trained on Blake. "Step out from behind the door. Close the door and put your hands on top of the car. Now!"

Blake started to get pissed. "Look officer, you are interfering with a federal investigation. I suggest you take that gun out of my face and let me hand you my credentials. Besides that, It's not like I'm breaking any laws sitting in a public parking area. I am not acting hostile towards you in any way."

The first shot hit Blake dead center of his chest. Blake's steel plate in the front of his armor took most of the impact but Blake stumbled back two steps. Grabbing his chest in natural reaction. As he gathered his thoughts he dove for the Glock. The second shot shattered the back window of his car. This guy was clearly trying to kill him and not just some scared cop at two in the morning on a traffic stop.

Blake dove into the car grabbing his Glock as he went across the front seat. He hit the passenger door and pulled the handle. He rolled out onto the ground firing back through the car to try and pause the guys third shot. It did. As Blake shot, the cop dove for cover between the two cars using the door as a shield. Blake scrambled to the back of the car.

Everything was quiet around the car. Blake's earpiece was going crazy with chatter from each team. He wanted desperately to call for backup but didn't want to give his position away. As he got to the back of the car, he looked under the car to see the guy's feet. He didn't see them.

Blake slowly peaked his head up to look through the windows. He still didn't see the guy. He was now crouched down duck walking to the corner so that he could look up the driver's side.

Just as he stuck his head around the corner a shot rang out and Blake felt the compression of air on his face as the bullet passed right by his left cheek. It missed him by centimeters. Blake stumbled back only to see this cop flying over the trunk of the car. His pistol was out in front and he was trying to get his aim for another shot. Blake rolled against the back bumper as the next shot hit the pavement where he had been lying.

The cop landed in a heap right next to Blake. Blake didn't hesitate and pushed hard against the car rolling the cop on the pavement. As he did he heard the clank of steel from the guy's gun hitting pavement. Blake spun his body as they rolled so that he could punch the guy hard in the face.

They rolled and Blake hit the guy hard in the back of the head. As he did, he heard the sound of teeth hitting the pavement. The guy screamed and started to push back against Blake. Blake looked over and saw his Glock lying on the pavement next to him. With his right hand he grabbed the guy's gun in his hand and reached for his own. With his left hand he grabbed the gun putting the muzzle to the guy's head.

He froze. "You better pull the trigger, cause Carlos will kill me if I let you go."

Blake looked into the guy's eyes six inches away. "Tell me where he is, and I will let you run away."

The guy laughed. "There's no running away from Carlos. Your boy Steve will soon find that out."

"Last chance."

"F….." The shot struck him in the side of the face.

Blake rolled away from the guy and began to get up just as Agent Farmer pulled up. Blake was dusting off his clothes as he approached.

"Agent Hardy, are you ok?"

Blake holster the Glock and bent down to pick up his radio. When he plugged the earpiece back in, it was chaos. Agent were calling for back up. Shots were being fired and drugs were being seized.

Blake looked up at Jeremy. "What about our guys?"

Jeremy turned and pointed as the two vans pulled out onto the road right in front of them. "Let's go. I was coming to get you. Tom is coming from the other direction to intercept. You good here or what?"

Blake looked back at the dead cop. "Yeah. One of Carlos's guys trying to prove a point. He lost."

He took off running. "Okay follow me."

Blake got into his car as Jeremy floored the surveillance van chasing the drugs. Blake and Jeremy hit the main road wide open. The two vans were about a quarter of a mile ahead and moving fast.

Blake hit his communicator. "Tom, are you there?"

Tom came back. "Go ahead."

"We just left the marina area. The two vans we are after are about a quarter of a mile ahead of us on highway ten. What's your location?"

"I am headed towards you, but I'm on the other side. I have to get over this damn cable in the median."

"There's a bridge coming up. I think you can get past it there. We're coming up on it fast."

The vans went under the bridge and Blake saw headlights weaving through the bridge supports as they approached. Tom got past the guy wire fence and stomped the gas to join the chase. Blake blew past him doing almost a hundred.

"I guess that's you under the bridge."

"Yep, I just saw the two vans. Looked like two guys in the first one. Couldn't see the second one's occupants."

"Catch up with us, and we'll take them down. Probably be a gun fight, so be ready."

"No problem."

They were out over the water now as Tom caught up to Blake and Jeremy. Blake was trying to decide if it would be better to take them on the bridge or wait for land. Clearly with the other teams being hit, the guys in the van would know the deal.

Blake decided on the water was better. He keyed his mic. "Okay guys, let's do this right now while we are still on the bridge. Less place for them to hide."

Jeremy was in front in the surveillance van, then Blake in his Malibu and Tom in a charger at the rear.

Jeremy keyed back. "Okay I am going to try and pass both vans to block the road. If I get on that side, I will lock it up and block both lanes. Don't shoot me!"

Blake came back. "If you get through, tell me when you do it and I will pit maneuver the van in the back. Tom, when this goes down you get stopped and start covering Jeremy and I."

Tom came back. "Roger that. I don't want my car wrecked in this. That would be two in one month."

"Okay here we go."

Jeremy began to pass the first van. The guy braked slightly, but Jeremy kept on going. Blake could see the second van swerve slightly. "Jeremy look out. I think…"

Shoots came from the second van as Blake spoke. When they did, Jeremy slammed his van into the second van and began to push it to the guard rail. Blake floored the Malibu approaching the first van fast. As he got close, he yanked the wheel hard. The nose of the Malibu hit and lifted the van up as it began to go sideways.

With the weight of the drugs inside, the van slid sideways and then flipped onto its side. Blake's momentum sent his car slamming into the concrete guard rail with a huge shower of sparks. Blake fought it back to try and gain control so that he could push all the way through to where Jeremy had ended up. There was now about a hundred feet between the vans. One on its side and the other against the guard rail.

As Blake broke away from the guard rail, he still was moving about fifty miles an hour. He could see the muzzle of the riffle sticking out the driver's window aiming directly at Jeremy. Blake pushed the peddle to the floor and hit the back end of the drug dealers van. His air bag exploded in his face.

Tom had slid to a stop and came out of his car in full attack mode. AR15 at the ready. He ran up to the first van and waited for sounds. He heard moaning but no real movement. He opened the back door to a cloud of white smoke. He stepped away quickly realizing that the cocaine inside the van had busted open during the roll over and the inside of the van, was now a huge cocaine covered mess.

He ran towards Blake's car. Now smoking and smelling like rubber burning. As he approached, Blake's door opened and Blake began to push out from behind the air bag.

Tom grabbed his arm. "You okay?"

Blake looked up and smiled at Tom with blood all over his teeth. "Did the guy shoot agent Farmer?" He pointed at the agent's van.

Tom looked that way. "You good?"

Blake nodded. "Yeah, go."

Tom raised his AR and started towards the van. As he passed the agents van, he could see blood splatter on the driver's window but didn't see Agent Farmer. He eased his way around the front of the Surveillance van watching the drug van. Blake was now out of his car standing beside it checking himself for damage. Tom whistled and pointed at the van on its side. Pointing at his own eyes and then pointing at the van. Blake nodded and pulled his Glock from the holster.

Over the mic Tom heard Blake call for backup and an ambulance. Tom could see a chopper coming towards them fast over the water. He eased himself next to the door of Farmers van. Jeremy was lying between the front seats holding his throat. He was hit and it was bad. He opened the door and looked down at Jeremy. He had one hand on his throat and the other was gripping his Glock laying on his chest.

Jeremy's eyes shifted to Tom and the Glock moved slightly. Tom put a hand up. "Easy. FBI. I got help on the way."

Tom heard the drug dealer's door squeak as it opened. He spun towards the van as bullets began to hit Farmers van all around him. He dove in the van on top of Jeremy scrambling across to the other side. From the right, he heard Blake returning fire but knew it would only last for a few seconds as Blake burned through a clip.

Tom hit the passenger side, but the door was jammed from the impact of Jeremy pinning the other van to the guard rail. Bullets were still flying all over the place as Tom moved towards the back. The side door to the van was partially open and Tom began to kick his way out. Luckily there was surveillance equipment all along the driver's side and preventing the bullets from passing straight through the vans thin metal side and hitting him. He hit the ground and turned towards Blake. Blake was out on his first clip and diving towards the back of his car frantically trying to get another clip from his belt.

Tom came around the side of the van with his AR up and ready. Tom flipped the selector to full auto as he rounded the corner. The burst of gun fire sounded like a stream of bullets all at once. Tom's aim started about a foot behind the door to the van and quickly consumed the door of the van. The guy dove and Tom followed him to the ground with a hailstorm of bullets. Thirty rounds in a matter of seconds. Tom ejected the clip and slid another into place.

Looking back at Blake for status, he saw he was crouched and reloaded. Blake pointed at the van on its side and then at himself. Tom understood. He keyed his mic. "Watch out for the cocaine. It's all over the place in there. I opened the back, neither guy was moving but I don't think they were dead. I'll clear the other van and then come to you."

Blake nodded. "Roger that. Be careful. I think there's another guy in there."

Tom looked towards the helicopter now a hundred yards away. "Blake, is this chopper ours coming at us or not. I don't see any lights."

Blake turned and looked for identifiers on the chopper. He pulled his radio off his belt and changed channels. "Approaching helicopter, identify yourself."

Nothing came back. Blake switched the radio to the military frequency. "Tango, Tango Charlie, are you near highway ten on the north end of the bridge."

Blake turned back towards Tom. Yelling! "Tom take cover. We got company."

The military channel came back. "This is Tango, Tango Charlie. We are not near the end of the bridge. Do we need to be?"

Blake crouched behind the concrete guard rail. "Yes, you do and in a fucking hurry. We've got unfriendly's in the sky in an unidentified chopper approaching the scene, a quarter of a mile in on the bridge heading north from New Orleans. We might have a minute before they're on us."

"Roger that. I'm a mile out following a boat that just left that scene. You want me to abandon that and come back?"

Blake looked back at the chopper. "Yes, how long?"

"I'm in an apache gun ship. Not long."

"Make it quick soldier. I think we're about to be in a world of shit."

"Roger that. Take cover and we'll deal with the unfriendly skies."

Blake switched back to coms. "Tom, I got an apache coming in hot, but we may have to deal with this guy ourselves for a minute. What do you have in that van?"

Tom looked down at the dead guy at the door. Pulled his Glock from his leg holster and eased closer to the door of the van. "You inside the van. You want to give up or get dead like your buddy here?"

Two shots rang out from inside the van. One barely missing Tom's head. "Shit!" Tom let out as he crouched down and began duck walking back away from the door. One more shot went through the wall of the van about two feet above his head. Tom was getting pissed.

Blake came back over the com. "We got about thirty seconds here before we are in serious trouble. End that guy or get under the van."

Tom reached down to his belt and pulled a grenade of his belt. "Roger that. I'll end him right now. Take cover."

Tom eased back up to the door and pulled the pin. He quickly stood and tossed it into the van. In a dead run he took off for Blake. As he ran away from the van, he could hear the guy scream inside something in Spanish. The van exploded in a fire ball throwing Tom to the ground next to Blake.

Blake took cover as parts and pieces of the van began to rain down on both of them. Blake grabbed Tom by the gear and pulled him behind his car to hide from the chopper approaching.

ROAD RAGE

They could hear the gunfire begin as they huddled between the car and the concrete wall. Chunks of car and concrete began to shower around them from the bullets hitting. A guy stepped out of the back of the van on its side as the chopper flew over banking hard to one side. Blake raised his Glock and dropped the guy where he stood.

Tom got himself together and got his AR up and ready for the next pass. They knew where they were now and wouldn't be shooting wild this time. Tom took aim at the windshield of the chopper and started firing. The chopper shifted course slightly and began to pull up. Taking away its line of sight to fire at Blake and him.

The chopper banked again as it went over them and began to turn to give the guy in the door a good shooting angle.

That's when they heard the first missile come over them. The hellfire missile hit the gunner sitting in the open door and the chopper burst into flames in midair. The wreckage fell to the water below and disappeared.

Blake's radio chirped. "Agent Hardy, this is Tango, Tango, Charlie. Are you two huddled against the concrete guard rail behind that car?"

Blake smiled at Tom. "Yes sir we are. You're a life saver my friend."

"Anything we can do to help sir."

"Roger that. We appreciate it. How about watching our back here for a minute while we secure the scene?"

"Will do. I don't see anything else on my radar, so the skies are clear. But we'll check the surrounding area for any other predators."

"Thanks man. Come find me when this is done and I'll buy you as much beer as you want to drink."

He laughed in the radio. "Yes Sir, we'll do that. Tango out."

The chopper swung in low and the guy saluted Blake and Tom. Then pulled up and headed back towards land.

Tom and Blake got to their feet and headed towards the van on its side. Tom took the back and Blake went to the front to look through the window. Tom slowly opened the door and looked inside. He could see the guy still in the front seat but not moving. The van was filled with cocaine. Millions of dollars' worth.

Tom hit his communicator. "One guy in the front seat. Can't tell what his condition is. Be careful."

Blake eased around the front and looked through the window. The guy was still in the seat but bleeding bad from a head injury. He wasn't seat belted in and the windshield was busted. He had most likely hit the windshield on impact. Blake kicked the glass hard breaking it more. With a hard push by his boot the front windshield hit the ground. Blake reached in and grabbed the guys arm. Pulling him from the van. As he did the guy began to moan. Blake quickly cuffed him and searched for weapons. He was clean. No wallet, no identification at all. Tom came through the van and produced a cell phone he had found amongst the drugs and weapons.

Blake smiled. "Bet Carlos has been calling that phone."

Tom opened the phone. "Yep. Four missed calls in the last ten minutes."

He handed the phone to Blake as it began to ring again. Blake smiled at Tom. "Watch this. Hello who is this?"

The guy on the other end of the line was dead silent. "Carlos, is that you?"

An angered low voice answered. "Who am I talking to?"

Blake smiled and put the phone on speaker. "Why this is the FBI. This is the guy that just shot your helicopter out of the sky and seized all your drugs. What do you think about that Carlos?"

Carlos screamed into the phone and hung up.

Blake looked at Tom. "Awe. I don't think Carlos likes me."

Tom laughed and looked up at the wreckage. "Shit the DEA guy."

Blake and Tom took off running towards the surveillance van. There was no sound as they approached. Tom went through the side door and Blake came around to the driver's side. Jeremy was laying there no longer holding his neck. He had blead out during the fight.

Blake checked for a pulse but found nothing. The windshield had two bullet holes in it from the drug van guy. He had managed two shots before Blake hit the back end of the van.

Blake slammed the van door spinning away. "Shit! Shit! Shit!

Tom stepped back out of the van as an ambulance approached the scene along with two other FBI cars.

All together that night they had seized almost three tons of cocaine and another one and half tons of heroin. All sealed in waterproof packages.

The FBI determined that it wasn't Carlos's plan to dump the truck into the water, but his intent was to seal it so well that drug sniffing dogs wouldn't be able to detect it if the truck was stopped. This was apparently a standard practice. Carlos knew the drugs could withstand the water and that's why he opted to run the truck off the bridge. It was a good plan and if Steve hadn't heard them talking about it, it would have worked.

Blake wrapped up the operation at nearly five am that morning. The phone hadn't rung again and the one guy injured in the drug van was not likely to recover from the head injury. The ER doctor told Blake that if he lived, he probably wouldn't remember anything for some time. Blake knew that as soon as Carlos heard they had a survivor he would have someone kill him.

None of the other men that night collecting drugs for Carlos survived. Every one of them went down fighting. Between the FBI and the DEA, they had lost three in the fight. Jeremy Farmer was pronounced dead at the scene from one gunshot wound to the neck. Glen Patrick with the FBI was hit in the leg in his femoral artery and bled out on the way to the hospital. Dale Swanson with the FBI took a gunshot to the head taking down the first guys that began unloading.

Three men had been lost during the takedown but almost all of the drugs Carlos had tried to bring in were seized. One van was able to escape during the night. In total. Sixteen of Carlos's men had been killed and one was in critical condition.

It was a hard night, but it was a success. Blake called Steve and woke him up at six. "Hey man, whatcha ya doing?"

Steve winced from pain as he sat up. "Sleeping. What are you doing? You okay?"

"Yeah I'm good. We got his drugs thanks to you. Man, you hit it right on the head."

"What about Carlos?"

"Na! he sure is pissed though. I pulled a Steve and answered one of the drug guys phone, told him we got his drugs, killed all his men and blew up one of his helicopters."

Steve laughed. "Holy shit dude. He will want to kill you as much as me now."

"No, no chance of that. He hates you way more than me. Besides I was smart enough not to tell him my name."

"Yeah, that's real funny. But with guys on the NOPD and FBI like he has, he already knows it was you. Better watch your back."

"I will brother. Listen I haven't been to bed in like three days. I'm gonna sleep for about six hours and then I'll bring you some food. Don't leave that room for anything, okay. You need to recover anyway and now that we have the drugs, we can rethink things."

"This guy is going to kill everybody he can get his hands on that knows me. You do understand that right. He won't stop. We don't have much time."

"I know. We have good agents; guys I know, going to all your family's houses right now. They'll relocate them for now to safe places until we get Carlos. We just need to flush him out."

"I don't like it Blake. This guy needs to focus on me, not anybody else. We need to set up the press conference now. Show the drugs and me and I'll say I'm right here in New Orleans. I'll look right at the camera and say I'm not scared of you Carlos. That guy will go out of his mind trying to find me."

"You're right about that, but, I need a few hours of sleep dude. Just stay put and I will come get you."

"Alright. That's fair. Get some sleep. Have the press conference set up for like noon. That will get you five hours and a shower."

"Gee thanks. You're a real friend."

"Hey, good job tonight. We got my family back and the drugs off the streets. That's a good day."

"We lost three guys tonight. Good guys."

"Was it Tom or Ed?"

"No. A DEA guy that was with me and two other guys from the FBI. What a waste of life this guy Carlos is. I want him as bad as you do. That's five FBI guys so far and one DEA guy. This son-of-bitch needs to go down hard."

"I'm sorry Blake. Get some sleep and let's get on with it." Steve hung up and laid back down on the bed.

So much pain. So much loss. Carlos needed to pay for all that he had done. He wouldn't rest until Carlos was the one suffering.

He wanted to kill this guy with his bare hands. He wanted to feel his neck brake in his grip. He wanted to watch his face as he cut off every one of his fingers with a pair of rusty old tin snips. He wanted Carlos to scream in pain like his son did.

CHAPTER 17

The Bait

At noon, Blake knocked on the hotel room door. Steve jumped up, pulling the Glock from his waste and aiming at the door. "Who is it?"

Blake smiled outside the door. "It's Carlos dummy and I'm all by myself. Go ahead and shoot."

Steve laughed as he opened the door. "You know that's a name that can get shots fired right through the door."

"Whatever. Nobody even knows you're in New Orleans. Much less where you are. Are you ready to end this?"

Steve stuck his weapon in the back of his pants. "I'm ready to get Carlos alone in a warehouse down in the ninth ward and beat him to a bloody pulp. What about you?"

"Will see what happens. Carlos ain't going to jail, I can tell you that. Let's make sure you don't either okay."

Steve stopped and looked at Blake. "Seriously, there's not a jury in this country that would convict me of killing that guy. I could shoot him in the face in Time Square and never go to jail for it."

Blake shook his head. "Okay Donald Trump. Let's not get crazy."

Steve put the do not disturb sign on the doorknob and stuck a small piece of paper in the top of the door. Blake looked at him in confusion. "What are you doing?"

"When I come back, I want to know if someone's been in this room. I'm not taking any chances."

Blake held up his hands. "It's been a rough week hasn't it?"

They started walking down the hall. "You can say that again. I thought my military days and covert opps were behind me."

Blake smiled at Steve. "Is that what you did in the Army?"

Steve nodded. "I was a sniper in Iraq and Afghanistan. A lot of sneaking around waiting on guy to walk out of a house. What about you? You in the military?"

"Yep. I was in the first War when we hit Bagdad. Air Force Intel. I did three tours over there watching those guys sneak around house to house. Targeting was my thing."

"What about Tom and Ed?"

Blake laughed. "Are you kidding? Third Special forces, straight out of Bragg. Those guys live for this shit."

Steve smiled. "Good. Then that needs to be the team when we go get Carlos."

Blake was shaking his head no. "The team needs to be the FBI and you need to go home to your wife and child. This is something that happened to you Steve. You don't have to be part of the solution. We'll get this guy, because of you and what you've done. That's all you need to do."

Steve patted Blake on the back. "I know, but this guy hurt my family! With or without the FBI, I'll get this asshole. I'll hurt him, just like he did my son. I'll make sure he never does this again. So, quit trying to get rid of me. I'm not going anywhere. Now look dude, I'm not stupid either. Doing this with you is a better deal for me, but I'm doing it either way. I'm not spending the rest of my life looking over my shoulder."

Blake threw his hands up. "No, I'm sure you won't, because Carlos is going to kill you at first sight. He won't take the chance of missing out on that again. Hell, I'm sure by now there is a price on your head of at least a million dollars. Maybe more."

Steve stopped. "Seriously? You think it's that much?"

"Yeah it's that much. You fucked this guy's operation up bad. You got a whole truck load of drugs taken by the DEA. You've killed six or seven of his guys. Carlos is done in New Orleans. Maybe for good. When the cartel finds out that all these drugs are gone, Carlos will have a contract out on him too."

Steve shook his head now. "That would suck."

"What would?"

"If the cartel got to him before me. I'd be pissed."

Blake looked at Steve like he was crazy. "What is wrong with you? You understand that the cartel will be after you too, right?"

Steve looked at the floor. "Oh, that's bad. I was thinking I could kill Carlos and collect the bounty, but we better kill all of them too."

Blake laughed.

The elevator doors opened, and Blake and Steve instinctively stepped to the sides out of firing range. They both laughed at the caution they both took. They got on the elevator and headed for the lobby.

Blake turned to face Steve. "Look, I know you want this guy and I get that. He put your family through hell. But you don't have to risk your life over this. Why don't we do this press conference, set the trap and get you the hell out of here."

Get you to some city far from here and live your life. I can't take you on a mission to get Carlos. You're a civilian. The bureau will have my job over something like that. My career would be gone."

"Blake, I'm already in the middle of this thing and have been for days. I didn't want any of this, but it is what it is. Let's just finish it and I'll go home."

Blake stared at Steve. "What part of I can't take you, do you not understand? I will lose my job, you will go to jail for killing this guy, because killing him in cold blood is murder you know. It doesn't matter what he did, it's murder if you kill this guy. Revenge isn't a get out of jail free card for you. You do understand that right?"

Steve shook his head. "Yes! I get what you're saying, but I'm the bait for this guy. He hates me beyond anything else. He'll stop at nothing to get to me. You have to put me out there in plain sight and lure this guy in. It's the easiest way to make sure we get him. Go to the director and tell him that I'm willing to sign whatever to protect the FBI. We have to get Carlos. My family will never be safe unless we do."

Blake took in a deep breath and stared up at the ceiling. "Why did I choose this profession? I could have been a doctor. A lawyer, hell a bus driver would be better. Your wife will kill me when Carlos kills you. You know that right?"

Steve laughed. "Yeah, I do. She's a tough cookie, way more than I thought."

"I know. You piss her off and she may kill us both."

The elevator hit the ground floor and both men peered out checking for potential threats. They moved slowly and headed for the street. Blake's car was parked just out the front doors. Blake motioned for Steve to wait and he went to the car first. He looked around and motioned for Steve to move. Steve did quickly and they pulled away as soon as he was in the car.

Blake had arranged a meeting with the director to discuss the entire case. He wanted to rehearse the press conference with Steve and talk about the plan moving forward. The director wanted to help Steve understand that he would soon be done with this investigation. Steve had other plans.

They walked into Alan Carson's office forty-five minutes later. The director stood and shook both men's hands. "Hell of a job last night agent. I'm really sorry we lost two of our guys and one of the DEA's. I need a full report on what happened as soon as you can."

Blake nodded. "I will have it to you as soon as I can Sir."

The director turned his gaze to Steve. "So, Blake tells me you want to put yourself out there as bait."

Steve started to speak.

"I'm not done. That's a ridiculous idea and we're not doing it that way. You have been kidnapped, shot, beaten and through hell these last few days. So has your family. Agent Hardy will escort you to a plane waiting at the airfield. You will get on that plane and immediately leave New Orleans forever. I promised your wife and child that you would not be involved in chasing Carlos down and I don't think I want her mad at me."

Steve started to open his mouth.

The director put his hand up silencing the thought. "Are we clear on what you're doing Agent Hardy?"

Blake stood. "Yes sir, I am perfectly clear on what I'm to do and couldn't agree more."

Steve stood. "Can I say one thing?"

The director sighed. "What is it?"

"This guy will never give up. I will spend the rest of my life worrying and looking over my shoulder. Let's do the press conference and draw him out. I want this guy gone and his whole team with him. Without me you'll never get him. He'll fade into the woodwork just like before and start up somewhere else. Then, some other kid and Mom will suffer just like mine did. I need to end this right now."

Blake looked at Steve and then at the director.

The director sighed and didn't say anything for a long minute.

"You know I'm right. I'll sign whatever you want relieving the FBI of all liability for my life. Because honestly, with Carlos still out there I have no life sir and you know it."

He held up his hands in surrender. "Okay, we do the press conference with you right out front. You say this is your home and you're not going anywhere. Taunt him as you speak. Laugh and put your hands on top of the drugs and tell the world that you took this drug dealer down and destroyed his operation."

Steve was smiling.

"But listen to me now. As soon as the press conference is over you are gone from here. Blake you will take your team and lead him straight to the airport. I don't want to ever see you back in New Orleans. Do I make myself clear? Agent Hardy will keep in touch and tell you as we take Carlos down so that you can live your life without worry."

Steve stuck out his hand and the two men shook. "Thanks for letting me help. I would love to be the one to put a bullet in this guy's brain but Agent Hardy has made it clear that revenge is not a get out of jail free card for me."

The director smiled and looked at Blake. "No it is not. This is a bad guy Steve. He's killed my men too and I want him gone just as bad as you do. We want him gone just as bad as you do. Now go do the press deal and get out of here before he catches you. I am not explaining to your wife why you're dead after we saved you twice. Now get out of my office before I change my mind."

Blake and Steve went down to the room that the press conference was to be held in. There were six FBI agents standing guard. Two outside the room and the other four inside protecting the table full drugs on display. There was a podium behind the drugs and several press guys beginning to set up. Steve paused as he saw the press crew guys.

Blake looked at Steve and then at the press crew. "No worries. Our regular guys only in this press conference. Nobody in here we don't already know."

Each of the guys stopped and looked at Steve as they walked by. Blake talked over where Steve would stand and who would talk first. The director would run down the facts and then introduce Blake. Blake would do ten minutes of questions and then introduce Steve. Steve was to give the show to entice Carlos and then answer questions. Blake had given the reporters several questions they wanted asked. Was he planning on staying in New Orleans? Was he working with the FBI to get Carlos? And, was he glad this was over?

Steve nodded knowing this would put Carlos in an outrage. He still worried about who else Carlos may have on the inside of the FBI. Was one of these press guys a long-term Carlos man with a gun inside his camera? In here Steve had no idea who might be a bad guy. At least on the street he knew it was everyone.

At three, the conference started. The director got up and talked facts about the drugs and how Carlos operated. He talked for several minutes on each of the men that had been killed during the operation and how much they meant to the team. He then took several minutes politicking on how he and the entire New Orleans branch of the FBI were tough on drugs and the people that broke the law.

Once Blake was introduced the ciaos began. He talked about the many men of Carlos crew that had been killed in the take down and roughly eluded to the men that had been killed trying to seize the truck back along the way. The reporters were rapid firing questions.

As they did Steve began to get nervous. He had never been on TV or had this kind of attention. He could feel the sweat beading up on his forehead under the lights in the room. He began to rehearse what he would say. How many questions he would have to take before Blake cut it off. They seemed to have talked about everything but that. Steve began to look around the room and realized the room was now full of people. He began to squint against the lights to try and focus on every face to see who he might recognize in the crowd. There were so many faces. His heart was pounding. His breath had gotten deeper and more haggard. Maybe this wasn't a good idea.

Just then he felt Blake grab his arm. "Steve. Steve, are you good?"

Steve looked at Blake. "Maybe this wasn't a good plan."

Blake laughed. "No shit Sherlock, but too late now. Get up there and do your best. Remember, you want to piss Carlos off. Say your deal and then I will pull the plug. You good?"

Steve took a deep breath and wiped the sweat from his forehead. "I'm good. I'm ready to get the hell out of here."

Steve stepped up and looked into the crowd. "Good after noon. My name is Steve Lawson and I am responsible for these drugs being in here today instead of on our streets." The room broke out in applause and Steve waited for it to die down.

"The man that was trying to get these drugs here, Carlos, is not very happy with me. You see he kidnapped my wife and child and forced me to go to Mexico and drive a truck load of drugs back to New Orleans. He told me that if I did that he would let my family go and me to if I cooperated."

By now Steve was feeling stronger and he felt the anger inside him. "What he didn't count on was me knowing that was a lie. So, I took his truck full of drugs and killed several of his drug dealing friends in the process. I forced him to keep my family alive by telling him I would trade the truck for their lives."

Steve paused looking hard into the camera's. "Carlos, you were a fool. I was never going to give you these drugs because I knew you would never let my family go."

Steve smiled as he reached down and picked up a kilo of cocaine. "Look Carlos, I got your drugs and I got my wife and kid back. I guess you're not as smart as you think you are after all, are you?"

Blake stepped up to the podium next to Steve. "Ok that's it folks."

Steve pushed Blake to the side. Pointing at the camera. "Carlos I'm right hear in New Orleans. I'll be damned if I am leaving my home because of some idiot drug dealer that thinks he runs this town."

Blake was now physically grabbing both of Steve's arms forcing him off the stand. "That's it folks."

Steve continued as the reporters started to shout questions. "I'm right here Carlos and so is my family. Right under your nose. You better be looking over your shoulder pal. I'm coming for you!"

Blake shoved Steve through the side door into a back hallway. "What the fuck Steve? Have you lost your mind? We said entice the guy not start an all-out war."

Steve paced back and forth. "I want this guy dead."

"I get that man but the director is going to put you on a plane to nowhere in about five minutes after that and you're done. You start a war on the streets of New Orleans and he will bring you up on charges!"

Steve stopped pacing, now starring at Blake. "Can he do that? I didn't start this shit, Carlos did. How the hell can he bring me up on charges? What charges? Self-defense!"

"He can do whatever he wants man. He's the director dumb ass. I told you to stay cool during this thing."

The door slammed open and Steve jumped. The director walked into the room. His face was red with anger, his fist clinched by his side.

Starring at Blake while pointing at Steve. "Get this asshole out of this town right now. I want him on that jet in the next thirty minutes or your career is over."

Steve took a step toward the director. "Sir I….."

The director snapped his head toward Steve. "Not another word. I swear to God, if you say a word, I will have you arrested for obstructing justice, ensuing a riot and anything else I can come up with. If one more of my agents dies because of what you just did I will add involuntary manslaughter to the charges. Are we clear?"

Steve stepped back. "Yes sir. I'm sorry."

He turned and started walking out of the room. "On the plane in thirty minutes."

The door slammed and Blake looked at Steve. "Ok, I guess that was clear enough. Let's go to the hotel and get your stuff. You're out of here."

Steve looked at the floor. "This sucks. I want this guy caught. I'll spend the rest of my life worried that I will get home and Heather and Max will be dead and Carlos will be waiting on me."

"I'll get this guy, I swear."

"You better."

They left the building in a convoy of SUV's. Ed and Tom were in the first SUV and Blake and Steve followed. Two more of Blake's team fell in behind. Everyone was expecting

Carlos's men to hit them. Steve's Glock rested on his leg in his right hand. His knee bouncing the gun up and down as they drove.

Blake looked over and watched him for a minute. "If you bounce that gun to hard with your finger on the trigger like that you will shoot a hole in my dash."

Steve looked down at the gun and realized his finger was on the trigger. "Jesus man. I'm sorry. I know better than that. I'm nervous as hell. I know he's watching us."

"Probably so, but you're in an armored vehicle with a team in front and back. We also have NOPD ahead clearing the route. We'll be fine. Soon you'll be on a jet starting a new life Clark."

He shook his head. "Clark, I don't look like a Clark."

He laughed. "I know, you'll get used to it. Time will pass and Clark will seem like it has always been your name."

"Maybe."

"Listen, I know you want this guy and so do I. I lost one of my best men in that hospital. Me, Tom Ed and Vince have been together for fifteen years. Carlos ain't walking away from this. He picked the wrong guy when he picked you and you picked me so he's fucked."

Steve laughed. "You got to end this guy. No trial, no jail. If I can't be there to do it, I want you to and tell him it's for me and my family."

Blake held out his hand and they shook.

"I promise, I'll make him wish he was never born."

They turned off the main road heading to the airport. The first SUV made the turn as a NOPD cruiser pulled to a stop coming from the airport. As Blake made the turn the cop driving gave a slight wave. It struck Blake as kind of strange but not alarming.

He made the turn but as soon as he straightened out he watched the cruiser in the side mirror. The driver window went down and the guy threw something out on the ground. As he did he began to move away from the stop sign. Blake spun in his seat to look at the third SUV. As it made the turn the front end exploded and the SUV was engulfed in flames.

Blake grabbed the radio. "Shit! Unit three..."

Nothing came back. Nothing but static. Blake floored it and started gaining on the first SUV. He tried the radio again.

"Unit one"

Static.

Steve looked out the window just as the RPG hit the first SUV. It hit the back end and flipped the SUV like it was nothing. Blake slammed on the brakes to keep from hitting the wreckage. He threw the truck into reverse and started back down the street towards the other burning SUV. He could see his two men climbing out staggering from the impact.

He slid to a stop. "Get in now!"

Bullets began to strike the front of the truck. Three men had come over the ridge of the road off to the right. All of them with fully automatic machine guns. All of them firing. Blake hit the unlock button just as the two guys got to the SUV. Matt on the driver's side got in and slammed the door.

Pete Gorman on the driver's side got the door open just as the first round struck his arm just above the elbow. The second hit was just below the knee. Pete fell as he tried to get in. Matt was already reaching for the guy as he was hit again. He was dead weight at that point and Matt couldn't hang on as Blake began to reverse. Steve turned and tried to grab the guy from the front seat as he went down.

Bullets were pinging all over the truck. Pete fell to the ground. It was too late. The SUV slammed backwards into the rear of the third SUV putting it between the gunman and them.

Blake grabbed his radio again. "Unit One, Tom, are you guys ok."

Static again. "Fuck they're jamming our radios."

Matt yelled from the back. "We got to get the hell out of here Blake. If they have another RPG we're fucked."

Blake started backing up again keeping the burning SUV between the gunman and him. As he backed up he could see Tom and ED running around the first SUV. Pulling weapons up to the ready position.

Blake stopped again. "Fuck, Ed and Tom are stranded. Matt are you good back there. What do you have for weapons?"

"My Glock and two clips. Both our AR's were in the back of the SUV."

Steve held his up. "I have mine and one full clip."

Blake shook his head. "No way. You stay low and just be my eyes. You don't roll down that window for shit. Matt I'm gonna floor it. If I can get these guys with the truck great if not shoot what you can."

"Roger that. Let's roll!"

Blake floored it as he came out from behind the burning SUV. The three guys had been joined by two others now and all five were firing at Ed and Tom until they heard the SUV engine roar to life. Two of the men immediately turned and bullets began to bounce off the windshield.

Blake sunk down and aimed the big SUV straight at the guys. Within seconds the SUV had covered the ground between the men and the SUV. ED and Tom didn't let up and one of the men dropped as their bullets found purpose. The other four began to scatter as Blake hit the first one. He bounced across the hood and then off the windshield. As we went through them the other had stepped back enough to be missed. Matt was ready and as they went by his open window he let loose.

Steve saw the guy's head explode as he went down. Bullets began striking the back of the SUV from the remaining two men that were now running for the ridge. ED and Tom let up as Blake was moving at full throttle towards them. Matt continued to fire out the window as Blake drove.

Blake slammed on the brakes and slid sideways right up to ED and Tom. "Hey guys, need a lift? I was just in the neighborhood."

They both took turns diving through the open window. No time to open the door.

Steve was steady looking back towards the ridge of the road. He saw the tip of the RPG swing around and aim straight at them. "Go!"

Blake hit the gas as the RPG flew past the back window within inches hitting the first SUV. The explosion busted all the windows on the right side. Glass flew everywhere cutting like tiny razors. Steve had turned away as it went off, so he got most of it in the back of the head. Blake got hit on the side of the face. ED, Tom and Matt were just tossed around like rag dolls as the SUV did a 180 from the impact of the blast.

Blake bleeding and stunned, floored it again. "Will somebody please shoot that asshole."

Ed was the first to raise up putting the muzzle of his AR on the window seal. Four shots later and the guy was down. Blake was going back down the road towards the stop sign and first burning SUV. Pete was still laying there not moving. The fifth shooter never came back over the ridge. Blake put the left side of the SUV between Pete and the ridge. Matt and Tom climbed out the right side and got Pete in the truck. He was still alive but shot up pretty bad.

CHAPTER 18

Change of Plans

After getting Pete to the closest hospital, the guys headed back to the FBI headquarters. The director had been briefed and wanted a full report.

As they walked in to the director's office he looked at Steve and shook his head. "Dammit man, you're like a bad dream that just won't end. You know that kind that you wake up screaming get calmed down and go back to sleep and it starts again."

Steve nodded. "Yeah, I do, mine has a name too. Carlos."

The director sighed and patted Steve on the back. "I'm sorry man. I know this last week has been hell for you. I can't imagine what it was like to know that animal had your wife and kid. I would want to kill him too. Hell, I want to kill him myself. Another agent today shot up, barely hanging on."

Blake looked at me then at the director. "How is Pete doing? Have you talked to the hospital since we dropped him off?"

"Yeah about ten minutes ago. He's stable but shot in the arm and both legs. He's bad but he'll live. Probably the end of his career with the FBI though. Good agent, what a waste. I hate this fucking guy Carlos. How in the hell does this guy have this much pull in this town? And an RPG's? What the fuck?"

Blake shook his head. "This guy is a problem for sure. And the NOPD is infected bad. He has guys on the payroll there and here. We can't fly Steve out of here right now. They were on the road going to the airport. I think they were trying to take Steve alive by hitting the car in front and back but, if we had gotten to the plane, I am sure one of those RPG's would have been launched at it. We would have never had a chance."

The director sat down in his chair and ran his fingers through his hair. "Okay, so what's the plan?"

Steve smiled. "Put me on the payroll, give me a badge and let's go kill this mother fucker and everybody he knows."

The director laughed. "I am sure you would like that, but it ain't happening. I'm not explaining to your wife and my boss in DC, how we saved the only guy to have ever seen this guy Carlos, much less the only one to survive his kidnapping, only to let you get killed. Can't do it my friend. I can set you up in a nice holding cell though to guarantee your safety for the next forty-eight hours while we get this scum bag."

Steve was already shaking his head. "No way that's happening. I'm not sitting in some cell helpless. I'll walk right out the front door of this place and take my chances."

Blake put his hand on Steve's shoulder. "Sir, I think we can hide him somewhere without Carlos knowing. It just has to be completely off the books. I don't know who to trust anymore besides the people in this room and those two guys standing outside that door. Even in here there's no guarantee that somebody won't come in, in the middle of the night and put a bullet in him."

"Okay, you sure about hiding him?"

"Yeah, we'll dress him up like a woman and walk right out the front doors."

Steve looked at Blake. "What!"

Everybody started to laugh.

"I'm kidding. We'll call out the SWAT team and dress him in full gear with a helmet on. He'll look like twelve other guys going to do the job. Plus we can get him in full body armor to help save his life in case we get into something like today again. That SUV took a hell of a beating."

He started shaking his head. "Okay that sounds good. But you tell no one but your team. Nobody else knows a damn thing about this. No NOPD involvement either."

Blake tapped the arm of his chair. "Sir I have another plan that might get us some info on Carlos."

The director spread his arms wide. "Please enlighten me."

Let's find an agent Steve's Hight and build and set up a decoy. Roll him back out in SUV's just like before, but this time, we'll be ready with our own team of guys. We've got to get somebody on this guy's team that knows where to find Carlos. We need somebody alive that we can get information from."

"I agree. Stop killing everybody you come in contact with."

"Use me as bait. I mean I still want the body armor and all but let them see me leave. I was a sniper in the Army. I'm no stranger to bullets flying around. I certainly did okay out there on the road by myself."

The director sat up and leaned on his desk. "Steve, I appreciate your willingness to do that and I know how bad you want this guy, but I can't. That guy gets you, he will torture you to death. It won't be quick. The FBI doesn't take those kinds of chances with civilians. Sorry."

Blake nodded. "I agree with him. You can't be in the middle of this. I need to get you somewhere safe and let you stay that way. Don't you want to get back to Heather and Max?"

"Yes, of course, but I want this done. I want to be there when it happens, or I want to do it with my own hands. I know you get that. Every one of you guys has been affected by this maniac. He has filled this city full of drugs for decades I'm sure. He's kidnapped no telling how many men and ruined their lives. How many has he killed?"

"Thirty-five."

Steve looked at the director. "What?"

"Thirty-five people, not counting the agents, that we know of. He's a serial killer and a drug dealer. He plays this game that he does, right under the FBI's nose and I have had enough, just like you Mr. Lawson. But you will not be involved in his take down. You're a civilian and I won't let you get hurt any more than you already have been. Hell, you're not even healed from the wound in your shoulder. These men are trained. They are well equipped. And, they are just as pissed off by this guy as you are. So, go get SWATed up and go hide somewhere. I promise when this guy gets the gas chamber, I will personally make sure you have a front row seat."

"Carlos will never see the inside of a jail. Hell, I'm sure he's in Mexico already. Probably has been for days now.

You'll never get this guy and I'll be looking over my shoulder forever. Am I under arrest of any kind?"

"What?"

"Am I in custody? Under arrest? Anything like that?"

"No, you are free to do whatever you want. But if you're smart, you'll stick with this man right here. Otherwise, you walk out that door on your own. You walk out that door and you're not my problem anymore. Understand?"

"Yeah, I understand. But this is my city. I've lived here my whole life. I got friends too. I got people that know where drug dealers live. I'll get the truth on the street."

Steve turned and walked out of his office. Blake turned and looked at the director. "Sir, you can't let him leave. You know what will happen."

"Of course I do, dammit! He's not a prisoner. I can't make him do anything. Fuck!"

"Well what do you want me to do?"

"Go with him."

"And do what?"

"I don't know Blake. Keep him from getting killed."

The director sighed. "Take him with you. Put his ass in full gear at all times. Find Carlos and end it. I don't want to know any details about anything after this. Do what you have to do."

Blake took one step towards the door and stopped looking back at the director. "Is my career in jeopardy here if this shit goes bad?"

"Yes! Now go with that idiot and make sure this shit doesn't go bad. Get it done. I'll feed you any information I can."

Blake ran out of his office looking at Ed and Tom. "Let's go hunting fellas."

Both men jumped to their feet as Blake called after Steve. Steve stopped in the hallway ready to put up a fight.

Blake was shaking his head when he got to Steve. "You're one crazy son-of-a bitch you know that?"

Steve smiled. "Yeah, but why do you say so?"

"Because the director just gave me the green light to go with you and do what we have to do to end this."

Steve smiled. "Now that's what I'm talking about. I need an AR15."

"I don't think so, but you can have the Glock back when we get to the truck. I also can put you in the latest body armor. After that my friend, it's arrogance and inspiration. Try to not get me killed."

"I'll do my best. So, it's the four of us?"

"That's the team. Do you really know people on the street that can get us info?"

Steve smiled. "Yeah, I know somebody that does. My man Tyrone. I need a cell phone."

They got suited up and Steve lost the shoulder harness. His shoulder hurt from the surgery but he could move it. If he had to fight, it would be a problem, but shooting would be fine. He was right handed so everything he did that was important was covered. They left the armory and went to the cafeteria. None of them had eaten in a day.

During the meal, Steve reached out to Tyrone who had been lying low for several days. He answered on the fourth ring. "Who dis?"

Steve laughed at the sound of his voice. "It's your daddy."

A loud. "Man, I thought you was dead. Where you been fool?"

"Everywhere Tyrone. You okay?"

"Yeah I seen them boys comin to the garage. I couldn't get there in time to save Mr. Jack. The next thing I know, the whole place was up in flames and them two mother fuckers ran off. Got in black BMW. I couldn't get the plate though."

That's alright. I know the car. Did you go to the house and get Heather's car and what I told you?"

"Yeah man I did. You know they burnt your house to the ground, right?"

"Yeah I heard. Look Tyrone I don't want to get you in this thing, but I need some info that maybe you can get."

"I already know what you gonna ask and I don't know nothin about these dudes man. The drug business in this town is bad news. I stay the hell away."

"I know you do. But I need to get to people that know where this guy is. Where can I find some of the Mexican dealers?"

"I don't know man, but there's a bunch of money at this club called Carnival Latino. Down on St Charles. You know wher I'm talkin about?"

"Yeah I know the place."

"I hooked up with this Latino chic and she took me down there one time. Couldn't stand that place man. Bunch rich mother fuckers, you know what I mean? They'll know who Carlos is. You get some of them guys in the back. They sit way in the back at few tables. They there all the time."

"Alright man. Keep laying low. I'll call when this thing is done."

"Hey man. Steve you watch yo back messin with these dudes. They don't play."

"I hear ya. I appreciate it. I'll talk to ya soon."

Steve handed the phone back. "Carnival Latino downtown, St. Charles. The guys in the back know the drug deal."

Blake smiled. "Okay, think we should just walk in and ask?"

Steve smiled. "Funny man aren't ya! I think we send somebody in there to see who's sitting at the back tables. Wait on them to leave and bring the rain of terror down on them known as SWAT. Get them in a room with just me and you and treat them like Carlos did my wife and kid. They'll talk."

Blake shook his head. "No SWAT. It's just us."

Steve nodded. "Okay fine. We wait on the guys and get them alone. We take them one by one until somebody talks. If they don't talk, so what, another piece of shit off our streets."

"We're not gonna start torturing guys and leaving dead bodies lying around town."

"Oh yeah! Seems like to me I've been hanging around you guys for a couple of days and the body count is pretty high. I don't really see a problem. You think for one second one of these guys won't kill you in a heartbeat?"

Ed spoke up. "Hell no they wouldn't. I got no problem ending some of these drug dealing ass-holes. Let's do this."

Tom stood. "I'm in."

Steve laughed and stood. "I like these guys."

Blake shook his head. "I hate all you people. If I get through this alive, I swear I am moving to Bocca and retiring."

He got up and threw his half-eaten sandwich in the trash. Downed the coke he was drinking and crushed the can. Each of the men slapped him on the back as they headed out.

They went to the motor pool and Blake signed out an SUV with bullet proof glass. They each put on helmets and sunglasses. Blake and Ed were up front, and Steve and Tom were in the back behind tinted glass.

The decoy driving Blake's crown vic with a Steve look alike pulled out first. They're instructions were to drive to a hotel downtown. Get out and Walk inside. Blake had positioned the SUV so that he could watch the Crown vic for a good 3 blocks before he pulled out. Two cars pulled out and fell in behind the decoy.

Blake eased out and began to follow. He hung way back since he knew the route and final destination. At one point they cut across a few alleys and positioned themselves to watch the decoy drive by. One of the two cars were still following. Blake fell back in behind and watched. The Decoy pulled into the garage of the hotel and parked. The follower stopped on the street and parked. Blake in turn, pulled over and parked.

Ed pulled out a small pair of binoculars. "Two men. Latino. Both looking hard at the hotel."

Blake looked in the rear view. "Want to grab em?"

"What?"

Blake put the SUV in gear. "I'm gonna haul ass down there slide up beside them and you guys jump out guns blazing. Lock them down and get them out of their car into this one. We'll take them to someplace quiet and see what they know."

Tom slapped Steve on the leg. "In the back! You're back up on this and don't need to even get out. Ed and I will handle these guys."

Tom was climbing over him before he could even move. Blake was hard on the gas now flying down the street towards the parked car.

Blake was also barking out orders. "Steve, you stay low and stay calm. When they get the guys in the car, you check them for cell phones, knives or any other weapons. Don't be crazy. We want information. That goes for you guys too. Threaten but don't shoot. These guys are followers not heavy artillery."

Blake slide to a stop next to the guys. Both flinching fearing they were about to be hit by an out of control driver. Ed and Tom were out so fast with AR's up and ready.

Windows were busted and men were grabbed so fast they never even reached for weapons. The AR's were slung around to their backs and the men were out and on the ground. Zip ties were secured and the men were locked down. Thirty seconds tops and these two guys were in the SUV and we were moving. The car that they were in was still running. It was poetry in motion.

Blake was on his cell to the decoy's. Job well done. "Stay put for a little bit and head back to headquarters."

The men began to protest. "What the hell are you doing? Why are you kidnapping us?"

Tom had jumped in beside the guy and elbowed him hard in the face. You could hear the guys nose crack on impact. Blood covered the front of his shirt. He screamed in pain and then passed out.

Tom looked over at the other guy. "You want to save yourself some pain and tell me where Carlos is?"

The guy smiled. "I don't know where he is. He doesn't tell anybody where he is. He tells you where to be and when. You're a dead man though, I can tell you that. You can tell your friend Steve that he and his whole family will be dead soon too. He can't hide forever."

Steve leaned up and started taking cell phones and weapons out of their pockets. "You tell Carlos, Steve will meet him any time he wants."

The guy tried to turn to see Steve's face. Steve sat back as he did. Steve opened the guys phone and strolled through the numbers. Carlos's name was the first number in recent calls. Four other numbers appeared and had been called within the last ten minutes.

Steve sat back up and held the phone in front of the guys face. "Who are these other numbers?"

The guy didn't speak. Steve grabbed a handful of hair and snatched the guys head backward as far as it would go. "Where is Carlos? If you catch Steve what are your instructions?"

The guy that had been hit in the face began to wake up. He started speaking in Spanish to the other man. Tom turned and put a gun to the guys forehead. "English Mother Fucker!"

He then looked at me sitting behind him. "You might want to slide over a little."

We were flying through the city. Blake was headed out towards the 9th ward to the empty warehouses where Steve first met Carlos.

The guy spoke again, and the first word came out in Spanish. Tom Hit the guy on the bridge of his nose with the barrel of the Glock 23. "What did I tell You?"

His eyes were watering from the pain. Steve leaned up again. "One of you better start talking, or it will be bad for both of you. Carlos will put a bullet in your head and be done. We will start with kneecaps and work our way up. However, you want it to be."

The guy on the left spoke first. "Our orders were to get the guy Steve and call Carlos when we did. That's it."

"Where were you supposed to take him?"

"I don't know man. I told you we just drive."

ROAD RAGE

Blake was out of town now and in some fairly deserted parts. We stopped and got the guys out and down on their knees.

Blake came around to Steve. "Okay, your move. These guys are low level. They don't know anything. I'm not killing them."

Steve looked at the two and then back at Blake. "You think Carlos would give a shit if it were you and Tom on your knees right now out here in the dirt? He wouldn't. He would put a bullet in your head and walk away."

"I'm not a cold blooded killer Steve. That's not happening here."

Steve sighed deep. "I agree, but these guys can't go back on the street. If we turn them loose, they will run straight to Carlos or whoever and we'll be fighting them tomorrow. They gotta go away till this is done. We need them to call Carlos and tell him that they have me. If he's here that will bring him out."

Blake nodded. "We need somebody on this team that speaks Spanish. No matter where this leads us someone has to be able to translate."

"Who can you trust?"

Blake went to Ed. "Who do you know that speaks perfect Spanish and would like to completely jeopardize their career by joining us? We need somebody on the team that knows and speaks Spanish."

Ed thought for a second. "Tom, where is Alex Rodriquez these days?"

CHAPTER 19

Moving Forward

Alex was working an undercover assignment in Baton Rouge and had been for the last six months. The FBI had infiltrated part of a cartel moving drugs through Texas into Louisiana. As it turned out Carlos was not the only drug dealer in town.

After a few minutes on the phone a plan began to shape up that we would play the two drug lords against each other.

Alex would tell the guy a cousin in New Orleans had trouble with Carlos. The story would be that Alex wanted to kill Carlos and had to leave immediately so the cover wouldn't be blown.

Emanuel Castiel was a drug dealer that had grown up on the streets and moved to Baton Rouge when he was sixteen. He was tough, he was smart, and he was connected to the Columbians. This made him automatically hate Carlos and he was his rival.

As Alex told Emanuel about leaving, the guy wanted to help. He offered two men and weapons. Alex had to decline and think quick. "I want to do this myself boss. I want to cut his throat for hurting my cousin."

Emanuel shook his head. "What did your cousin do?"

"Got pinched with some drugs making a run across the border. Cost Carlos some money."

Emanuel stared at Alex. "I thought Carlos only used Mules to move his drugs. Was your cousin a mule?"

Alex panicked inside. "I don't think so. Not sure."

"The word is, that the guy uses people to move the drugs and kills them and their families. If your cousin was moving drugs he's dead already."

"He just called me from jail. Needs bail and my help with Carlos. I'll deal with it and be back next week."

Emanuel grabbed Alex's arm. "I've been to this guys house for a party a while back. It's a fortress on lake Pontchartrain. You won't get to him. It's suicide for you and your cousin."

"Boss I gotta go. Tell me where this guy lives."

"North Shore. Go over the bridge and take a left. But you can't get to the guys house in a car. Boat only. I'm telling you this guy is bad news. As much as I would love for him to be dead and take his territory, you ain't doing it by yourself. Take two men and plenty of ammo. He is protected by a small army Alex. I'm telling you this guy is brutal and will have no problem killing you and your cousin."

Alex paused and put a hand out to shake hands. Emanuel picked up an Uzi and put it in Alex's hand. Came in, and hugged Alex. "Take care of yourself my friend. Don't get dead!"

Alex for second felt bad about being an FBI agent. This guy really cared. "I'll be careful, and I'll call if I need backup. My cousin is my only family. I need to do this. If I'm successful you gain New Orleans as a territory. If I'm not you need a new runner."

Emanuel shook his head. "You are the best runner I've ever had Alex, be careful."

Alex left and ten minutes later called Blake. After telling Blake where Carlos lived and the details of the mansion, Blake knew they would need to draw him out to be able to get him in the open. Trying to fight him in his home would be a disaster.

Alex set the rendezvous for two hours and hung up. Blake told the others that Alex was in and new where Carlos lived. Cheers came from Steve and the guys, but Blake shook them off.

"Not so easy. Alex said the guy has a fortress on the North Shore. The only way to the house is by boat. No sneaking up on him there."

Tom punched the seat in front of him. "I'm tired of this asshole always having the advantage."

Blake laughed and looked at Steve. "So, here's the plan. We're gonna drop you off downtown and when Carlos grabs you just tell us where he takes you. We'll swing by later and pick you up. What ya think?"

Steve laughed. "Yeah we did that already. I got shot and almost drowned. I think we better do something different this time. Can we get a chopper and fly over this guys house to see what's up? Maybe we can see a way in."

"Yeah probably. We have two hours before Alex is here."

Blake went over to the two guys now cuffed, gagged and subdued. "Either of you been to Carlos's house on the North shore?"

Both looked up quickly with surprise in their eyes. Blake smiled. "I think that's a yes."

Blake turned to the team. "Let's roll. We can drop these guys off with some friends for safe keeping and get in a chopper for a little sightseeing trip.

They got to the helicopter and took off. The pilot knew the area and knew the types of houses there. All were millions of dollars and all of them had security 24/7. He flew high, so they wouldn't be noticed. The FBI chopper had serious surveillance video equipment and was recording the whole time.

As they flew over, the place was busy with activity. There were multiple boats at the dock and a Limo was moving towards the boat from the house.

Steve laughed. "Who has a Hummer limo for a shuttle from the house to the boat? I hate this guy more and more."

Blake nodded at Steve. "We'll get this guy don't worry. If we figure out for sure he's there, will call in the Calvary. We may be off the books but we ain't off the reservation yet. We got friends."

Steve smiled and then got serious. "Blake, I want Carlos for myself. This guy put my family through hell. When this shit goes down in the end, I want just me and him. If he starts killing me, jump in, otherwise let it go. I want to see the life leave his body. However, that ends up being."

"Yeah yeah. We'll see what happens at the end. I prefer you not even be there to tell you the truth. I promised your wife I would keep you safe."

"That was a bad promise my friend."

They got back to the heli-pad and the pilot pulled an SD card from the console. "Here's what we recorded. Good luck!"

Blake patted the guy on the shoulder and thanked him for the ride. We all went into the FBI office to a video room. The camera view was much closer up than what they saw from the copter. You could see body guards on the boats with weapons. We could see luggage being loaded, but no Carlos.

Steve leaned over Blake's shoulder. "He's there and you know it. Look at all those guys with guns."

Blake nodded in agreement. "I think so, but he's leaving right now, and this was forty-five minutes ago."

"Where can he go from Lake Pontchartrain?"

Blake laughed. "Anywhere! He can go all the way to Mexico in that boat."

The director walked in the room. "Fellas. What are we looking at, porn?"

Blake laughed again. "No sir. This is what we believe to be Carlos getting on his yacht heading to Mexico."

The director leaned in close. "What? Are you kidding me? Where is this and how long ago?"

"This is the North shore of Pontchartrain about an hour ago maybe. Forty-five minutes."

Carson snatched his cell phone from its holder on his belt. "Get me coordinates on that house immediately."

Blake pulled up a map and plotted the house. The longitude and latitude appeared on the screen.

Carson had dialed a number and was already talking when they answered. "I need satellite surveillance on 30 degrees North and 90 degrees west. Lake Pontchartrain. I need any boats leaving from that location in the last hour. This is a top priority most wanted list. Retask everything we have. Call me back as soon as you find that boat."

He patted Blake on the back. "Good work right there. How the hell did you guys find out where he lived?"

"Alex Rodriquez is under cover and the guy told Alex where Carlos threw a party one time. We went looking and sure enough there he was. We didn't get footage of Carlos, but bodyguards everywhere, heavily armed and all getting on that boat. We think he's bugging out."

"You guys need to get over to that house. Take SWAT and see what you find. I'll have the coast guard and military catch that yacht. We'll get him, now go. Get back in that chopper and land in his front yard."

The director looked at Steve. "Go! I still know nothing about you being there or anything that has to do with you. You get yourself killed the story will be that we were there trying to save you. You kill somebody the story is, Blake, Tom or Ed did the shooting. Got it?"

Steve smiled. "Yes sir. Loud and clear."

The helicopter pilot was still in the waiting area drinking a cup of coffee. He saw the group come back in with more weapons, helmets and shields.

He stood. "I guess this trips not's for sightseeing is it?"

Blake smiled. "Nope, this time we come in hot and put it down in the front yard."

He smiled. "Let me get some weapons then."

They were air borne in minutes and as they flew, they searched the lake for big boats like they had seen at the dock. They saw nothing as they flew. If Carlos was headed for Mexico he was passed the bridges by now and in the gulf. He would be moving fast to get into international waters as quick as possible. If he was headed somewhere else on the lake they would have to search until they found him.

They flew over Carlos's house first to have a look. Not much to see. The boats were gone. The Hummer limo was parked at the dock and there was no one to see walking around. He was clearly gone at this point.

They circled the house and landed in the front yard. Everyone got out on high alert. They searched but the place was abandoned. The door to the house was standing open. Tom moved through the doorway checking high and low. Blake was next.

"You know we don't have a search warrant right."

Tom nodded and kept walking. Looking left, right and up. The place was empty.

They came back outside and stood on the front porch. Looking out over this beautiful property realizing they were too late.

Steve reached into his pocket and pulled out a cell. "Let's just call him and ask him to join us. This is one of the phones I took off his goon's downtown today."

Blake shrugged. "What have we got to lose?"

Steve opened the phone. Hit the recent call log and touched Carlos's name. The phone began to ring. Steve put it on speaker.

Two rings and Carlos answered. "Do you have him?"

Blake pointed at Steve and motioned to go ahead. "Hey Carlos, it's your old friend Steve. How's things going?"

"Ahh Steve, I am sorry we are not together right now. I would like to show you how it could be going. But I am sure we will be together soon enough. Soon I will have your wife and child back and then we will talk."

Steve looked at Blake in a panic. Blake pointed at Tom and motioned for him to go make the call and check on Heather and Max.

"Carlos, do you know where I am right now?"

"No, but if you tell me I will come pick you up so we can talk."

"I am standing on your front porch at your place on Lake Pontchartrain. We just missed you. In fact, we saw you getting on your yacht. I think when I kill you, I will keep that for myself. I always wanted one of those."

"I don't know what you are talking about. I don't have a place on Lake Pontchartrain. So, let me ask you something. What happen to my men I sent to pick you up today?"

"Oh, those two nice guys that were outside on the street in front of my hotel? Yeah, they won't be coming back. We had a nice talk with them and they both said they didn't want to work for you anymore. They told us where you lived and how to get here. Nice place too. Great view of the lake."

"You know what I am going to do when I find you?"

"I'm right here in your front yard you piece of shit. Come get me!"

"I am going to cut out your tongue first so you can't talk anymore. Then I am going to rape and torture your wife in front of you and your boy. How's his fingers by the way?"

Tom walked back over and gave the thumbs up that Heather and Max were fine.

Steve gritted his teeth thinking about Max and what he went through. "He's fine and when I get my hands on you Carlos, I swear it will be the longest day of your life. I will make you hurt like nothing you've ever seen. For my wife and my kid."

"Let me ask you something Steve. Do you think your wife will like Atlanta?"

Steve pulled the phone up close to his mouth. "You mother fucker come get me! You come deal with me. Just you and me. I'm gonna rip your fucking head off when I get my hands on you. Do you understand me?"

"You think you can hide from me Steve, but you can't. I have people everywhere."

Steve hung up the phone and turned to Blake. "You get my wife and kid on the phone right now. I want them back here with me right now. The FBI is corrupted by this guy. He knows where they are Blake."

Tom was back on the phone. Blake was holding Steve back trying to give Tom the space he needed to make the call.

"What the hell Blake. How does this mother fucker know they're in Atlanta? You said those guys were safe. You said they would be safe."

"They're safe. I don't know how he knows they went to Atlanta, but I know the agents they were with personally. They're on the right side of this."

Tom came over and handed Steve the phone. "Hello."

Heather answered. "Babe are you okay. Tell me what's going on?"

"Where is Max?"

"He's here right beside me."

"Listen, you can't trust anybody. I am going to arrange for you to get enough cash for you and Max to disappear. You get a car and a gun and take off. No agents, no FBI provided car, no nothing. You need to disappear for two weeks. I don't even want to know where you go. You pay cash for everything. No speeding, no big cities. You disappear into thin air and stay that way."

"Please Steve you're scaring me to death. What's happened?"

"He knows where you are."

"Oh Jesus!"

"Are the two agents still with you that Blake assigned?

"No, they were called off when we landed in Atlanta. Its two new guys. They said they would handle our case here. They brought us to a house somewhere in Atlanta and got us food. Are you sure they're bad?"

"Hold on. Blake, did you call off the guys the left with Heather?

"No. They were supposed to stay with her until I gave them the all clear."

"Okay listen to me. Carlos was just here but he left. I don't know where he is now. You have got to get away from these guys clean. Do you have the credit card Blake gave you?"

"Yes. How the hell am I supposed to get away from these guys?"

"Don't panic but you need to move. Look for weakness in their routine. Does one of them sleep while the other stands guard? Do they both leave the house at any time together? Look for the hole and take it. You have the credit card. Use it as little as possible. I will arrange for you to get cash somehow. Did they give you a burner phone?"

"Yes, but where we are, the cell service is terrible."

"Okay, keep this number. It's Tom's. Get out of there, get a new phone and call me when you're safely away from those guys. Do you still have the 38 I gave you?"

"No. The agent took it when we got here. No car either. I'll have to go on foot."

"Okay the main thing is to lose these guys. Are they both there now?"

"No just one."

"Can you knock him out?"

"What?"

"I'm serious. Knock the guy out take his gun, his cash and haul ass. Take his car if he has one. If it's Carlos's guy, there will be two phones. If you take his car just go to somewhere public and ditch it. Rent a car if you have to with the credit card. For right now the key is to stay mobile and make changes fast. I will arrange the money and set it up with Western Union. That way you can go to any Kroger or Walmart and get the cash. Don't keep any electronics at all."

"Okay let me figure this out and I will call you when we're clear."

"Blake will call some agents in Atlanta that he can trust. He will send them to where you are. Do you have an address?"

She gave him the address. Blake was making the call to a friend in the bureau he knew in Atlanta. The world had just crashed down on Steve and he was helpless.

Steve took in a deep breath. "Heather I love you. Tell Max I love him too. I'm sorry."

Heather was silent for a moment. "I love you too babe. We'll get through this. You do what you have to and I will too. I'm tired of this guy. I want you to kill him for me."

"I will!"

"Good, go get to it and I'll call you at this number later."

Steve sat down on the ground and put his hands over his face.

Blake came over a few minutes later. "My buddy and a few SWAT guys are going to the house now. They'll be there in ten minutes. Guys I know and trust."

Steve stood and shoved Blake back hard. "How the hell is this guy so fucking connected inside the Bureau? Do they go over how much it cost to buy an agent with you in school or do you just decide that for yourself?"

Steve turned and started walking towards the helicopter. Tom leaned over and picked up his phone from the ground. The four FBI men stood there watching Steve walk away.

Blake shook his head. "Boy this is a fucking mess. If they get his wife and kid, it's over. Carlos will kill her and that little boy."

Tom sighed. "No, it will be worse than death. They will torture her and the kid and force Steve to give himself up and he'll try and save them."

Blake's phone rang. It was the director. "This just got worse. Carlos chartered a plane out of the South Shore. New Orleans airport that left for Mexico thirty minutes ago."

"You don't know the half of it. Somebody called off my two guys protecting the wife and little boy when they got to Atlanta. Carlos knows their location. We decided to call Carlos with one of the phones we took off the guys this morning. This just got really ugly."

"Did you call the Atlanta office to see who?"

"I called a buddy and told him to get a couple of guys and go to the house. Hopefully we can get to them before Carlos does. Where is the flight going to in Mexico?"

"A little town on the coast called Tampico."

"We got anybody there we know?"

"Not that I know of, but I'll make some calls. You guys better get back here so we can manage Steve. If he goes ballistic, we'll have to lock him down until this is over."

"Yeah that'll never fly. He looks like somebody just took everything from him. We gotta end this boss, or this guy will absolutely end up getting himself killed trying to get Carlos."

"I know. I'm going to take this all the way up the chain. We need major help getting this guy locked down. I'll get with our CIA friends and whoever we can trust on the Mexican side. See you guys shortly. Bring Steve up here to me when you get back."

"What's the plan?"

"Back him all the way. Take this all the way! Carlos needs to be ended. Steve and his family need to be shown that we do have agents that are good and right in the world."

"See you soon."

CHAPTER 20

Restoring Hope

They walked into the SAC's office and director Carson was putting on his gear.

Blake looked at the director. "What are you doing sir?"

The director stuck out his hand to Steve. "You need to know that the FBI is behind you 100%. We'll get your wife and kid to safety and we'll get Carlos together. The plane is waiting. I got intel from the CIA that Carlos has a villa on the coast down there. We got satellite footage of him arriving in a limo five minutes ago."

Steve smiled. "That's good news, anything on my wife and kid?"

The director smiled. Well, I can tell you this, she is not at the house they took her to. I got one agent in custody that denies everything to do with Carlos but was found unconscientious at the scene, gun and cell phone missing and his car. The other agent that was there is missing."

Blake looked at Steve. "I guess in your family you don't play around."

Steve looked at Tom. "Anything on your cell yet?"

Tom pulled out his cell and looked at the screen. "Nothing yet but she'll call. She's smart. She'll get to safety and then call."

Carson patted Steve on the back. She's smart. She'll call, now let's go to Mexico and catch a drug dealer."

Steve smiled. "I don't know about any catch. Kill maybe."

Carson smiled back. "That works for me."

Alex walked into the room and greeted the guys. Steve turned to see a five foot tall Latino women in tight black jeans, black shirt and leather jacket. Tom and Ed walked over and gave her hugs.

Tom held on to her just a few seconds longer and then stepped back. "Damn I forgot how good you looked girl."

Alex smiled. "Shut up Tom. You had your chance."

She came over and stuck her hand out to Steve.

Steve took it and laughed. "I got to be honest, I thought you were a guy. They didn't tell me."

Alex smiled. "They like doing that to people, I think. Throws them off guard when I walk in. I'm sorry to hear about everything that's happen to you."

"It's been crazy. But you gave us the info that may change everything. We know where he is."

Alex turned to Blake and the director. "You got him?"

The director smiled. "We tracked him on a charter, I was able to use resources to find out that he has a villa on the coast down there. We got imagery of him there. We're headed there now. Want to tag along?"

Blake interrupted the exchange. "Okay, you know the Mexican government is telling him when we cross into their air space right. Carlos knew when we went down and put GPS locators on the truck. We cleared our flight with the Federalizes. They told Carlos."

"That's why we aren't landing."

Blake looked puzzled. "Are we bombing his house, cause I'm good with that?"

Carson smiled. "So, Steve in your military service did you parachute?"

Steve smiled. "I jumped a few times. Not in the service but after. I can handle it."

"Good, we'll be punching out of the back of a C130 at fifteen thousand feet just off the coast where Carlos lives. Welcome to black opps gentleman. This was my specialty in the military. We go in quiet and we don't leave witnesses. There will be a fishing boat half a mile offshore waiting to pick us up. We get in quick and quiet. Let's head down to the armory to get some quiet weapons and the rest of the gear we need. We go wheels up in an hour. Meantime I have a satellite watching the house and the CIA on the ground. Let's end this Mother Fucker."

He turned to Steve. "That okay with you?"

Steve smiled. "Oh yeah. But let's get something clear. I end Carlos."

"Alex you good with jumping out of a plane?"

Alex smiled. "Hell yeah I am!"

Steve blocked the doorway. "I'm not kidding, I end Carlos unless it's just an all-out gun fight. I owe that guy the beating of his life and I intend on delivering it for my wife and kid."

Carson nodded. "Okay!" and headed out of the office. Blake stuck out his hand flat towards Steve. Steve slapped it and smiled. "Hell yeah!"

They got silenced M5's, wet suits and black out gear. As they were gearing up, four more guys walked into the room.

Carson shook hands with each and pointed at the gear. "Get what you need."

The lead guy of the four came over to Steve. Stuck out his hand. "Mark Stewart, SBT team 22 at your service."

Steve shook his hand. "What is SBT-22?"

"Seal boat team sir. This is my team. Bill, Jeff and Tyler."

"Navy Seals?"

"Yes sir. Out of Mississippi. We got the call from the director a few hours ago. Grabbed our gear and headed over. He said you guys had a little problem and needed a little help. The fishing boat off the coast will be our guys."

Steve let go of his hand and shook hands with the others. "I thought you guys were all seal team six or something like that."

"Those guys are whimps. We hang off the side of boats and shoot while we fish for dinner."

Steve laughed. "Hey, glad to have you along for the ride. I'm sure this guy will have a small army around him."

"Not when we get done with him."

The director told us what he did to your wife and kid. Sorry man, that must have been hell. Sounds like you handled yourself pretty well. He said you were a sniper in Iraq."

"Yeah that's been a while, but you never forget the training."

"Carson stuck his head back in the doorway, you ladies gonna chat for the rest of the day or kill bad guys?"

They all headed for the joint base to get on the plane. Steve was now looking like a member of a seal team down to the silenced m5 and night vision head gear. He was ready to give some payback to Carlos.

On the plane they blacked out their faces and talked about the plan. They had satellite photos of Carlos's house, the grounds and the guards. The director slid a picture across the table to Steve of Carlos. Steve could feel the anger in him as he saw the face of the man who had torn his family apart.

The director watched Steve tense up and clinch his jaws so tight he thought he may break his own teeth. "That's him, right?"

Steve looked up from the picture. "That's him."

Steve picked up the picture and walked to every man on the team. "This is Carlos. I want him for myself. If you have no choice take him out, but if you can leave him for me. I want to kill this son-of-a-bitch with my bare hands. I want to hear him scream just like I heard my son scream as he cut off his fingers. He's mine!"

Everyone in the group understood and nodded yes. They all felt the pain in Steve's eyes. They all understood his anger.

The plane fell silent after that. It was twenty minutes until the drop and everyone on the team sat silent searching their own souls knowing they would kill tonight. Steve too. He understood that killing a man was wrong, but this man was a monster. This man had killed many. This man had tried to kill him and his family. He would kill him and his family if he got the chance. Steve was going to make sure he never got that chance even if it meant his own life. This night, he would make sure that his wife and child would never have to look over their shoulder at who was behind them.

The buzzer sounded, and the rear door of the plane began to open. The wind rushed in taking Steve's breath for a second. Steve could feel his heart rate quicken. The adrenalin pumping through his veins.

Mark came over and picked up Steve's M5. "I'll jump with yours, so you don't have to worry. Just focus on the jump and where you land. Remember ten feet above the ground pull down hard on the toggles to flair the chute. Knees bent and role on the beach. That's the target landing. The beach just below his house. We'll gather there and make entry from the lower side."

Steve nodded. Blake came over and grabbed his shoulder. "You remember everything on the rig?"

Steve nodded. "Yeah I'm good."

Blake pointed at the D ring. "Look if something goes wrong, aim for about thirty feet off the shore. Land in the water vs the sand. It won't hurt near as much. Pull hard on this D ring and it will cut your chute away. We don't want you breaking an ankle on the landing."

"I'm good. It's only been ten years since I jumped. I got this."

Blake turned and headed towards the ramp. The green light came on and a buzzer sounded. Everyone stood. Mark waved his arm in a circular motion. Steve checked his gear and walked towards the ramp. Tom came up beside him and gave him the thumbs up. Steve nodded and returned the gesture. They ran off the end of the ramp together.

Steve tumbled several times as he fell. Steve felt an arm come across him and then Tom came around in front. He grabbed Steve's hands and they flattened out into a free fall. Tom pointed at Steve's altimeter and held his hand up make a fist and then a five. Steve remembered, pull the cord at 5000 feet. They plunged downward in the night sky. Several of the other guys also flew up next them and soon they had a five-way circle.

At about six thousand feet all but Tom peeled away. Tom flashed the five signal and flew off. Steve reached back and pulled the cord. The violent snatch of the parachute yanked hard on Steve's shoulder and he felt the pain of the recent surgery. Soon he was hanging in the harness and the hundred mile an hour free fall had slowed dramatically.

Steve got his bearings and below could see the beach and the house on the hill. He could see the others below him slowly flying back and forth. They each began to land on the beach. Steve's chute was larger and flew at a much slower speed. He circled a few times to get used to how it flew. He began to fly hundred foot turns up and down the beach as his altitude dropped.

His last turn brought him down close to where the men had landed. Thirty feet. Now twenty and then ten. Steve pulled down on the toggles and felt the chute slow as he dropped those final feet. His boots hit harder than he thought, and he tumbled to the ground. Ending up face first in the sand. He immediately felt hands grab him and pull him to his feet. Steve spit sand and wiped sand from is face.

Blake patted him on the back. "Not bad for a civilian."

Steve spit one more time. "I ain't dead yet."

Mark walked up and handed Steve the M5. "Time to go to work. You good?"

Steve shook off the rest of the sand. "I'm ready. Let's get this guy.

They started to climb the rocks from the shore to the house. The shore side of the estate was the only area that was not protected by a ten-foot fence. Everything was quiet now since it was close to 3am. Intel reports were that there were two guards on the grounds.

They slowly and silently climbed the hill. The seals were first and got to the top in under a minute. They disappeared over the top guns ready.

Steve was last up with the sore shoulder. He topped the hill and there were two bodies lying there. Both shot in the head and Steve never heard a sound.

The group gathered at the top. The seals had taken both guards out as they rounded the corner of the house. Neither man had a clue what hit them.

The house was still dark. The seals had taken the keys and radios from the guards. The plan was to enter the back of the house through what looked to be the kitchen. Take the house room by room. That plan went to shit as soon as they opened the back door. They had disabled the alarm, but another guard walked into the kitchen just as the team came through the door.

Gun shots rang out as the guard fired at Mark and his team. They took him down immediately, but shouts came from upstairs and we could hear running above us. Blake motioned for Steve to hang back with Alex and let the team take on whatever was coming. Guards came from everywhere. The Seal team went left and the FBI team went right.

Steve checked his M5 and started for the steps. Alex tapped his shoulder and pointed to the yard. Just then he saw Carlos run across the back yard. Gun shots were steady upstairs and clearly both teams were in a standoff. Carlos must have had some way to get out of the house without using the stairs. Steve and Alex took off after him.

Carlos ran into the garage and two seconds later a Porsche 911 roared out of one of the bays.

As they came into the garage Steve looked at the key board and saw a Ferrari key. He smiled, grabbed it and hit the unlock button. A red Ferrari Spider beeped, and the lights flashed.

Steve handed Alex his M5. "I'll drive and you shoot."

Alex smiled. "You got it!"

They flew out of the garage just as the team was coming out of the house. Steve pointed at the headlights going down the driveway as he hammered the gas. The Ferrari took off. Steve could see the team running toward the garage as he went through the gate a few hundred yards behind Carlos.

Carlos slid onto the main road in the Porsche and hit the gas hard. The 911 grabbed the road and was gone. He was doing a hundred in seconds. Steve downshifted as he came through the gate and drifted the Ferrari hard through the turn. The power the car had was unbelievable and Steve was loving it. He was doing over a hundred in seconds and could see that he was catching up with Carlos.

The road was curvy and Alex couldn't get a great shot. She took several but nothing looked like it was paying off. They had to get closer. Steve pushed the car but both cars handled the curves in the road well. They were now about fifty feet back from Carlos. As they went around the curve of the mountain, Alex could see the headlights of two more cars behind them. As she told Steve he nodded as he bumped the back end of the Porsche.

Carlos swerved and gravel flew up as the back tires of the 911 slid off the road. Carlos got control and hit the gas pulling away from the Ferrari. Alex fired a burst and the back window of the 911 shattered.

Steve saw the muzzle flash just as a hole and a bullet came through the front window of the Ferrari. Steve instinctively let off the gas and looked at Alex. "That was close."

She nodded. "Well, we know he's armed. You need to push this guy right off this mountain."

"Can you radio the guys and find out how far behind us they are? I get this guy stopped I want some back up."

Alex radioed Blake. "Come on guys, catch up."

Blake came back right away. "We're in Range Rovers, not sports cars. Can you slow Carlos down?"

"We're trying but he's shooting back."

Alex leaned out the window and sprayed the side of the 911 with bullets. Carlos jerked hard and skipped off the guard rail slightly. More bullets flew back from Carlos but luckily this time none came close.

Steve yelled at Alex over the wind. "Aim for the back end. The engine is right there. You hit something good and he'll lose power."

Alex was hanging out of the car as they went through a set of tight curves. The back end of the Porsche was whipping back and forth so fast she couldn't get a clean shot.

Just then they came around a corner and into a town. The streets were empty at three thirty am but there were cars and business's everywhere. Carlos went the first block and took a hard right. Steve was right on him. A hard left at the next stop sign and Carlos was on the gas. Steve again was right on him. The Porsche was good but no match for the speed of the Ferrari.

Alex leaned out again and tore the back of the Porsche up with bullets. Instantly smoke began to come from the Porsche. Carlos made the next turn and Steve hit the back end of the Porsche. Steve yanked the wheel in reaction and hit the curb shredding the front tire of the Ferrari.

The hit sent the Porsche spinning and Carlos recovered. Going back the way they had been. Alex was on the radio immediately.

"Blake he is headed back your way"

Steve backed the Ferrari up and hit the gas. He could feel the torn rubber of the front tire slamming into the fender well as it came apart. The steering had gone from tight and responsive to loose and sloppy. But they were moving and still chasing.

Alex changed mags on the M5 and stayed ready. They saw Carlos take the next turn but lost him after that. The Ferrari was not moving as fast as it did, now on nothing but rim. Steve could see a slight smoke in the air from the Porsche and could smell burning oil. He knew the Porsche wouldn't last long.

Blake came over their earpieces. "We got him. He just ran from the Porsche into this theater on the square. We're going in. What's your location?"

Just then they pulled around the corner and saw the teams exiting the Range Rovers. Steve pulled up beside them. "Hey guys, what ya say we catch a movie. I think it's called Kill Carlos."

Alex handed Steve back his M5. "I'm down with that."

The glass by the front door was shattered. The team went in slow and cautious. Blake had several of the guys cover the perimeter of the building exits.

There were four theaters on the main floor and stairs going upstairs to projector rooms. Those doors were locked so he had to be on this floor. They split into two groups and began the search.

All of a sudden, the radio went crazy. It was Tyler from the seal team. "Back right corner. He just came out the back door. We fired on him and he went back in. The door is locked from out here. He's in the back right corner of the building."

The entire team inside came running to the center and headed to the back corner.

Just as they were about to open the door Carlos came through and started firing. Three shots hit wild and his gun locked open. He was empty. He turned and ran back into the theater.

Blake hit his radio. Don't let him get out. Lock the exits down hard.

Director Carson opened the door. The theater was dark, and we could hear Carlos slamming against the rear door.

Carson screamed out. "Carlos give it up. You're surrounded and there is no way out."

Carson turned back to us. "Lights! Find the lights."

Blake found the switches behind a curtain and turned the lights on. Carlos was standing down in front of the screen.

He stretched his arms out wide. "Take me to jail FBI man. You got no authority down here. You got to turn me over to the locals."

Steve pushed past the seals and the FBI guys. "No authorities Carlos. Just you and me from here on."

Carlos laughed out loud. "No, not today. You take me to jail. Not fair with all your buddies anyway. Take me to jail."

Blake stepped up. "You sure you want to do this. We can take this guy right now back to the beach and in hours he will be behind bars forever.

Steve handed Blake his M5. "Have your boys go down and make sure he's not armed. Just me and him first. If he beats me, he goes to jail. If not, this ends here.

CHAPTER 21

Fight to the End

Ed and Tom went down and frisked him. Checked his shoes. Pockets and belt line. He was clean.

Tom turned Carlos around and hit him hard right in the face. It knocked Carlos flat on his back. Tom leaned over and spit on the guys face. "That's for Vince and every other guy on the force you hurt."

Tom and Ed walked back up to Steve. "End this mother fucker."

Carlos stood. Blood was coming from both nostrils. Tom had hit him hard. Carlos wobbled slightly but got his feet steady. He looked at Steve. "What do I get if I beat you?"

Steve turned and looked at the group. "You get to go to jail. You can try your luck there. I'm sure some of your men will be there to keep you company."

Carlos charged Steve and hit him mid-section. Steve took the hit folded his legs under him and flipped Carlos hard against the floor.

Steve jumped up and took the bullet proof vest off. "You better hope you got something more than that."

Carlos smiled. "How's that shoulder feeling. No way that's healed enough yet to not hurt."

Steve swung his arm around holding the shoulder. "It's good enough for this. Good thing I'm right-handed."

Carlos took a few steps forward. When he did Steve took a giant step and hit Carlos again square in the nose. This time everyone in the room heard the bones break. Carlos went down on one knee grabbing his face.

Steve came around with his right foot and kicked Carlos hard on the side of his head. Carlos went down hard.

Steve stood over him screaming. "Fight you son-of-a-bitch. Fight me or I swear I will get a gun and put one in the back of your head right now."

Carlos arched up and the back of his head connected with Steve's face. It was a blow hard enough for Steve to stumble back a few steps.

Carlos was on his feet and swinging. His first punch hit Steve square in the left shoulder. Steve screamed with pain and grabbed the shoulder.

Carlos wiped blood away from his mouth and nose. "You ain't so tough after all, are you?"

Steve came in like he was going to hit Carlos in the face again. Carlos ducted and Steve connected hard with a knee to his chest. You could hear the wind leave Carlos. While he was still bent Steve slammed his right fist hard to the back of Carlos's neck.

Carlos went down again. Steve landed center of his back with both knees. He grabbed Carlos's head and began to slam him into the concrete floor. Carlos threw his weight to one side and rolled away from Steve.

Carson yelled out. "Get him Steve."

Steve, like a crab, scrambled to get back on top of Carlos. The two men fought and rolled along the ground. Both punching and gouging at each other's face.

Tom began to move forward. Blake put his hand on his chest. "Don't you dare. Steve needs to do this."

Tom screamed. "Kill this mother fucker Steve."

Steve looked over at Tom briefly and back up at Carlos. He was on top and hitting Steve in his bad shoulder. Steve could feel the skin tearing. He had to end this.

In a quick motion Steve took his thumb and jabbed it hard into Carlos's eye. He felt his eyeball bust as he put harder pressure on it. Carlos screamed and grabbed his face.

Steve stood and kneed Carlos hard in the face. Carlos flew backwards landing on his back. His legs twisted up below him. Steve jumped up in the air landing with his full weight on Carlos's ankle. Steve felt the bones break as he landed.

Carlos screamed again as Steve came around behind him. Again, he kneed him hard in the back of the head. Carlos went forward in a heap.

Blake yelled. "Finish him!"

Steve walked over to Tom and pulled his knife off his vest. Tom didn't move other than the corners of his mouth turning up in a smile.

Steve smiled back. "Need to borrow this for a minute."

Carlos was trying to pick himself up when Steve walked back over. "I give up."

Carlos was putting his hands up in surrender. Steve grabbed one hand, flipped the knife open and cut Carlos's pinky finger off with one snatch of the knife.

Carlos screamed and grabbed his hand.

"Now you know how my son felt."

Steve took the knife and stuck it all the way to the hilt into Carlo's left shoulder. "Now you know how I felt when you shot me."

Carlos had gone from a scream to murmurs now. Steve wrapped his arm around his neck and with a hard snatch broke it solidly.

Carlos's arms dropped to his sides and his body fell to the floor.

Steve looked up at the guys. Nobody moved. Steve slowly fell to his knees beside Carlos and just stared at the man.

Blake went over and took the knife from Steve's hand. He handed that to Tom and began to help Steve up. "Come on man. We need to get the hell out of here before the Mexican police show up."

Carson got the other side and they picked Steve straight up. They started up the aisle as Alex walked over to Carlos. She raised her M5 and put three rounds through his head.

The guys all stopped and looked at her. She looked and shrugged. "What? I don't want this fucker to come back no matter what. Now let's get the hell out of here."

She grabbed Steve's gear off the front row and headed up the aisle.

The guys parted to let her pass. They looked at each other and laughed.

They got back in the Range Rovers, leaving the Porsche and Ferrari behind. They made their way back down the mountain and back to Carlos's Villa. Steve had recovered from the fight and was ready to find Heather now.

He wanted this to be done now and back to his family.

They went through the villa again gathering any information they could on the drug cartels and drug trade the Carlos had been involved with. They collected cell phones off each guy they had killed earlier.

Mark made the call to the boat and it came up to within a hundred yards of the beach. The team made the swim and they were headed back to America.

Steve sat on the bow for most of the ride. After a few hours Blake went up and sat down beside him. "Whatcha thinking about up here?"

Steve smiled still starring out into the night. "You think this is over or just one layer gone."

Blake now starred into the darkness too. "I think it's over for you. It will never be over for me. Carlos is gone but three will step into his territory and try and get control. The drug business never ends."

Steve shook his head. "I don't know how you do it man. So much death and destruction all the time."

Blake put his hand on Steve's shoulder. "I do it to protect people just like you. People that get affected by these people need someone to fight for them. Not everyone can do what you did over the last week. Most can't fight back like your family did."

Steve turned looking back at Tom. "Tom has my wife called you?"

Tom pulled his phone from his pocket. Opened it and looked. "No"

Steve hung his head. "Great. I have no idea where she is now. After all this if they got to her, I don't know what I would do."

Blake patted him on the back. "She's fine. You told her to disappear. She did. She'll call soon and we will take you to her."

"I need two weeks with her and Max on a beach somewhere not in Mexico."

Blake laughed. "I'll see what I can do.

Steve turned back to the ocean and began to pray. He prayed for his wife and kid and he prayed for forgiveness for the lives he had taken. It had been the fight of his life since the day Carlos took him captive.

Heather had walked up behind the one FBI guy still in the house with a frying pan in her hand. She asked him if he wanted a grill cheese sandwich and he said yes. As soon as he turned back around, she had hit him in the head with the frying pan.

The guy went down hard. Heather leaned over him and took his gun and phone. There was only one phone. She turned his head to make sure he was breathing fine and told him to dream about grill cheese. She took the keys and yelled for Max.

They left the little house in a hurry. She took Max to a bus station and got on the next bus to leave. They were headed to Charlotte North Carolina.

She threw the phone in the trash as they boarded the bus. She never made time to stop and get a burner phone. She really didn't want anyone to know where they were.

They got to Charlotte late that afternoon. She took a cab and found a little hotel. Her and Max got a room with cash and stayed the night. The next day she would rent a car with the credit card, fill it with gas and buy a phone.

She could leave immediately and drive onto another city in another state. She had decided to wait to call Tom until she knew her and Max were safe.

She made it to Bowling Green Kentucky when she decided to make the call. It had been almost twenty-fours since she last talked to Steve. She had no idea what had happened to Steve, Carlos or the FBI guy she knocked out.

CHAPTER 22

Reunited

Heather charged the phone and pulled out the number she had written down for Tom. It was eight in the morning.

The guys had gotten back to the FBI headquarters at six that morning. Most of them had been up for about two days now and were ready to just lay down on the floor and close their eyes. Steve had slept for an hour on the boat, but couldn't really rest not knowing if Heather and Max were safe.

They all had put the gear away and got showers when Tom's phone rang. They all looked and stood when it did.

Tom pulled it from his pocket and saw the number was blocked. "Hello."

"Tom its Heather. Is Steve okay?"

Tom smiled and handed the phone to Steve. "It's for you pal."

Steve grabbed the phone. "Heather?"

"Hi baby, are you okay."

"Oh my God it's good to hear your voice. Are you and Max safe?"

"Yeah we got out of there and took off. I took a bus and then rented a car. I don't want to tell you where we are now."

Steve smiled and just sat down on the floor where he was. Tears filled his eyes. "Babe it's over. Carlos is dead. His whole crew is dead."

"Oh my God that's so good to hear. Can I come home?"

Steve looked at Blake. "Can she come home?"

Blake looked at Carson. "She better not. We still need to put you guys in the witness relocation program. Carlos may have hits out on you still. Once the word is out that he is dead and his drug ring is gone it will be fine, but."

Steve stood. "But, what?"

Blake shook his head. "You guys can never live in New Orleans again. Who knows what the cartel will do over this, left over guys from Carlos's group seeking revenge. You just can't live here anymore."

Heather was talking as Steve put the phone back to his ear. "What is he saying?"

"He is saying that we can't be in New Orleans ever again. Somebody may want revenge. The cartel may look for us here. I don't know."

"So what am I supposed to do now?"

Blake took the phone from Steve. "Heather, I want you to stay wherever you are today and tonight. Just lay low. Use the card as you need it but pay cash if you can for things. We could still have a few traders in the mix here. We will put Steve on the plane tomorrow and come get you. In the meantime, we will figure out new identities and a location for you guys. Any place you like a lot?"

"Yeah New Orleans!" The phone hung up.

Blake shook his head. "She's mad."

Steve shook his head. "You guys suck. All our family is here. Our friends. My job. I have to just walk away from that even though Carlos is dead?"

Director Carson came over. "Steve we can't make you do anything. But this guy has people everywhere. Hell, you know he has guys in both the NOPD and the FBI here. Do you really want to risk that with your family after all you guys have been through?"

Steve pulled out a chair and sat down. "No, I guess not."

"Okay then, let us get you guys somewhere safe that no one knows you. You become the Smith's or the Jones's and start over."

"Can we go anywhere?"

"Anywhere you want. Just tell me and I will have the witsec folks set it up. Hell, for what you did helping us take down Carlos, I think I can get you the reward money we had been offering."

Steve turned and looked up. "Really, how much is that?"

Carson smiled. "Two Hundred and fifty thousand dollars my friend."

Steve laughed. "Let's go back to Carlos's Villa. I bet I can get a few million from that place. Hell, if I gotta relocate and start over I want to do it in style."

Blake smiled and patted Steve on the back. "You know we seized all that money when we took the drugs right."

Steve looked at Blake. "No, I don't know. Y'all want to turn your backs for an hour and let me in the evidence room. I'll only take what I can carry."

Carson laughed. "Now Steve, you know we can't take you in there. They have cameras everywhere. How would I explain that?"

"I don't care how you explain it. I'll be gone with a new identity."

Blake laughed. You know I don't even think we've counted that yet. Who knows how much money there is in evidence? Maybe they'll miss a bag. You never know."

"Yeah well, my fee for taking down a major drug ring in the city is a lot. I can't help you guys out like this all the time. I got stuff to do you know."

Blake laughed. "Let's go get you a room somewhere. We all need some sleep. Tomorrow we'll go get Heather and figure out the future."

The seal team guys all came over and shook hands. Alex hugged him and told him to say hello to Heather and Max for her.

When they left it was just the director, Blake, Tom and Ed.

Tom cam over first. "Steve my brother, it has been a pleasure working and fighting with you. You keep my number. Wherever you end up, if you ever need me for anything, you just call. Huge respect for what you did here. Huge respect."

He hugged Steve hard and patted him on the back. "I'll see you tomorrow on the plane. Till the end my friend."

Tom headed out and Ed came over. "Just what he said man. You are one tough dude. Your family too. I'll see you tomorrow. Get some rest."

Blake looked at Carson and Carson Nodded. "I'll be outside when you're ready Steve."

Director Carson walked over and stuck out his hand. Steve took it and they shook. Carson didn't let go of his hand. "I underestimated you Steve. You absolutely proved yourself with me and this whole crew. You put your family through hell to take this guy down, and you did it. We have been trying to get this guy for years and you did it. The city and the FBI owe you a huge debt."

"Sir, I was just doing what I had to do to protect my family. You would have done the same. All of you guys would have done the same thing. You have a great team here. Really good guys."

"I do. Blake and his crew are my best. We will get to the bottom of the other agents involved with Carlos before this is over. That I can promise you."

"That's the problem with a guy like Carlos. What he can't buy with money he threatens with family's lives. It's not a good situation."

Carson shook one more time and let his hand go. "You're right. Money is a powerful tool. So is fear. It can take an ordinary man like you and turn him into a killer."

Steve looked up expecting the director to begin talking about him killing Carlos.

Carson looked at Steve and understood the look. He put both hands up. "I didn't mean what happen in Mexico. You have nothing to worry about. Carlos was killed by Alex don't you remember. The shots to the head. It was a clean kill."

Steve shook his head. "Man, for a second there I thought I was in trouble."

"No, not at all. You were one of the team and we couldn't have done it without you. Tomorrow when you guys head to your final destination, you make sure you take all the bags on the plane, you hear me?"

Steve looked into the director's eyes. "I hear you, but I don't really have any bags."

"Just take all the bags on the plane when you get off. Now get out of here before you fall over."

Steve shook his hand again and headed out with Blake. They went back downtown and got a room for Steve. As they got to the room Blake handed Steve a pistol and a cell phone.

Steve looked puzzled as he took them. "It's over man. Why do I still need this?"

"Because it ain't over until you are long gone from here and the news is out that Carlos is dead. Until then don't go anywhere, don't answer the door and don't be stupid. He still has people looking for you."

"That means there are people still looking for Heather."

"That's true, but she is in the middle of nowhere and there are like three people on the planet that knows where. She's just fine. You on the other hand are in downtown New Orleans with a price still on your head. You need anything, there are three numbers programed in that phone. Mine, Tom's and Ed's. Call one of us and we'll come."

"All I want to do now is sleep."

"Me too. I'm tired of you keeping me up for days at a time."

Steve laughed and shook his hand. "So about seven tonight who should I call to come have some dinner with me?"

"Call Tom. The rest of us will be having a live press conference announcing that Carlos's whole organization has been taken down. The largest drug dealer in the history of New Orleans."

"Nice."

"Yeah, you should watch because during that we will announce that unfortunately Carlos's men killed the Lawson family before we could get to them. Your funerals will be next week by the way."

"Really. I should maybe call my parents and in-laws before that happens don't you think."

"They will be contacted today in person. Keep the allusion going in case there is someone watching for you guys. You need to wait a while before you make contact. We'll let them know the deal."

"So, I'm dying today. Cool, I knew I would be late for my own funeral."

Blake laughed. Call Tom around six. He'll get some food and bring it to you. Otherwise stay put. Anybody else comes to the door, it ain't good."

"Great. I'm sure I'll sleep well knowing that."

"You'll be fine. Tomorrow will get you back together with Heather and Max. You think about a place to live yet?"

Steve smiled. "Yeah, maybe somewhere in Florida on the gulf side. We always liked it there. I think Heather would like that."

"I'll let them know."

Steve slept hard for the next few hours. The news conference came on when the six o'clock news started. It was a braking story. Director Carson and Blake both stood strong at the podium and described the nightmare that Carlos was. They talked about the millions of dollars in drugs he moved through the city. When they got done talking about him, they gave the credit for the take down to the Lawson family and the heroic effort by the father to save his wife and son. When Blake announced that the family had been killed during the fight and take down of Carlos, Steve felt himself get a bit chocked up. His life as Steve Lawson had ended. His life in New Orleans was over. The friends that he had and the people he knew now thought him to dead at the hands of a wicked drug dealer. It was sad and he wished it could be different somehow.

In his heart he knew there was no other way.

The next morning Tom came to get Steve. He had already heard from Heather and gave him the number she had. Tom went out on the balcony to give Steve time to call her.

Steve called her immediately. She answered on the first ring. "Steve is that you?"

"Yeah baby. I sound pretty good for a dead guy right."

She laughed. "I saw the news conference. It kind of freaked me out. My mom must be hysterical."

"No, they sent agents over to tell them the deal. They know. Blake said we have to wait a while before we try and see them. You know, let the dust settle some. I'm sure we can call though."

"So we can't stay in New Orleans can we?"

Steve sighed. "No. I guess there are still people that may be looking for revenge or loyal to Carlos. Just too much to risk."

"So where are we going?"

"I told them the gulf side of Florida to start. You always liked it there."

"Yeah I can do that. I like Florida."

"Oh hey and another thing, they are giving us a two hundred and fifty thousand dollar reward for leading them to the capture of Carlos. That will help with starting over for a while."

Heather was quiet for a moment. "You gonna tell me what really happened to Carlos?"

Steve paused. "He was shot by an agent during a shootout in Mexico."

Heather laughed. "Uh huh. You gonna tell me the real story?"

"I broke that son-of-a-bitch's neck. Right after I cut off his little finger. That's what happen to him."

The phone was silent for a moment and Heather whispered. "Good."

Tom came in and motioned that they needed to go. Steve said goodbye after talking to Max for a minute. They were coming to get them and begin a new life.

Three hours later they landed at a small airport in Kentucky just outside of Bowling Green.

The pilot didn't even shut off the engines. Heather and Max got onboard, and they were off again.

The next stop was a small town in Florida called Cedar Key. The witsec guy came aboard and handed them new identities once again. Steve was now Tim and Heather was Rebecca. Max was now Charlie. Together they were the Scott's and they had moved from Birmingham Alabama. They had a six year old Honda minivan and had rented a house down by the ocean.

Max stomped his feet when he saw his passport. "Seriously, Charlie! Can't you guys come up with any cool names ever?"

He stomped away and got in the van. Heather hugged Blake and thanked him for keeping his promise to keep her husband alive.

Steve shook each of their hands again and thanked them for being with him throughout it all. He vowed to keep in touch and offered them a place to stay whenever they wanted. Heather got in the van and Steve hugged Blake before he turned away.

Blake yelled as he turned. "Wait."

Steve stopped and turned back. "What man, I got a new life to start."

Blake stepped back in the plane and came out with a black duffle bag. "The director said to take all the bags on the plane. I think you forgot one."

Steve starred at the bag and took it from Blake. It was heavy and he looked puzzled. "What is it?"

Blake smiled and got on the plane. "Take care my friend. You guys have a nice life."

The door shut and the engine started to wine as it started.

Steve stepped away in a hurry and went to the passenger door to Heather. She opened the door. "What was that about?"

"I don't know Mrs. Scott. Why don't you look in the bag and tell me what's inside?"

Steve went around and got in the driver's side.

Heather tilted the bag towards him and saw bundled stacks of hundred-dollar bills.

Steve smiled and cranked the car. "I guess running out to find a job won't be such a big deal now will it."

Heather sipped the bag and put it in the back seat next to Max. "I guess it won't Mr. Scott. I guess it won't!"

They drove away as the FBI jet took off behind them. Blake looked out the window as the minivan drove down and nondescript road in a nondescript town. With a family inside that was anything but nondescript.

The End

POST SCRIPT

In the following several months, there were six FBI agents arrested and convicted for having taken bribes from Carlos and the cartel. The NOPD was far worse with fifteen of its officers charged with collusion, murder and obstruction of justice.

Blake was promoted for his involvement and made special agent in charge of drug related crimes.

Max, aka Charlie never went by that name. Instead he decided the middle name they gave him was better. He liked Jeff much better.

They all lived happily ever after in Cedar key.

Tyrone ironically moved to Cedar Key the next year and opened his own garage. His friend Tim and he still fight over who is going to work on Honda's when they come in.

Six months later Alex took down the entire drug ring she had infiltrated in Baton Rouge. She felt bad for the guy since he had thrown her a party for killing Carlos.

www.ingramcontent.com/pod-product-compliance
Lightning Source LLC
LaVergne TN
LVHW021757060526
838201LV00058B/3136